a, lifetime in 30 days

T0282102

OTHER TITLES BY A.C. ARTHUR

a lifetime in 30 days

A NOVEL

A.C. ARTHUR

 Montlake

Published by Montlake, Seattle

www.apub.com

Amazon, the Amazon logo, and Montlake are trademarks of Amazon.com, Inc., or its affiliates.

ISBN-13: 9781662524905 (paperback)
ISBN-13: 9781662524912 (digital)

Cover design by Mumtaz Mustafa
Cover image: © Nicole Matthews / Arcangel

Printed in the United States of America

To Asia and Amaya. You inspire me every day.
Love, Mama

celebrate child,

take all the time you need.

   —from "Black Folk Don't Have Birthdays"

   By Steven Willis

Chapter 1

July 31

"So, this is what a dead body looks like," Savannah Carlson murmured, her voice low amid the loud thumping of her heart.

My husband's *dead body,* she corrected in her mind. The man—or rather, the body—lying perfectly still on the metal table a couple of feet in front of her was her husband.

"Caleb." She forced herself to say his name.

Forced her eyes to remain open and her knees not to wobble. All those things were hard to do because, really, she just wanted to run up out of there.

She shouldn't be the one making the identification. But that was her own fault. Caleb had sickle cell anemia and, at Vanna's insistence, had worn a MedicAlert bracelet; that was how the medical examiner had gotten her name and phone number. Since receiving that call, she'd been chastising herself yet again for what she deemed the biggest mistake of her life—marrying Caleb Carlson. Well, no, an even bigger mistake had been not divorcing his trifling ass immediately after putting him out five years ago.

Forget blaming her failure to divorce him on the alcohol—that decision rested solely on the heart that refused to learn its lesson. Love didn't come easily, and if it did, then Vanna must've missed the boat that was supposed to take her to it, because damn . . . having her heart broken so completely twice in her thirty-nine years of life was some majorly bad mojo.

Although, if anybody asked her, she'd vehemently deny that for those first three years after she sent Caleb on his way, she'd held out hope that her taking a stand would shock him into acting right. She certainly hadn't been able to love the red flags out of him, and she'd definitely tried in the twenty years she'd known him—had prayed and tried, wished, hoped, and waited. But that change never came. And when she'd finally started to realize that it never would, the process of letting him and all the dreams she'd had for their marriage go had begun.

Once she'd taken her vows, Vanna hadn't thought she would ever walk away from them, so the letting-go part of their separation had taken a lot longer than she would've imagined.

"Are you okay, ma'am?"

She jumped at the voice and kept her gaze focused on Caleb's swollen and ashen face. She knew damn well he wasn't the one talking.

Caleb's and all the other dead bodies that were probably in this building were freaking her out. But she couldn't let the uneasiness get the best of her, so she put a hand to her chest and took a deep breath. "Y-yes," she stammered when she lifted her gaze and saw the medical examiner who'd escorted her into the room standing on the other side of the table.

He looked like he might've been younger than she was, maybe in his early thirties. There wasn't a speck of gray in his low-cut black hair, but a box of Bigen hair color could always be the culprit for that.

"Would you like me to go out and get the woman who accompanied you?" Mr. ME Guy asked.

"No" was her hurried reply. The last person she wanted with her right now was Granny. Or Frito, Granny's moody French bulldog, whom she never traveled without.

Vanna cleared her throat. The ME wanted her to confirm that this was Caleb so they could get on with whatever the next steps were. Vanna wasn't too sure what that involved, because while she worked as an office manager in a law firm now and had been in the legal field for over a decade, her expertise regarding the handling of dead bodies stretched toward the medical malpractice realm, not homicide or anything else criminal.

She could do this. She nodded in agreement with herself. She could look at him one more time, just to be sure. But her throat had already started to tighten, her rapid heartbeats giving the tears she'd sworn on the ride over that she wouldn't shed permission to at least form in her eyes.

"I'm okay," she told the ME, more so trying to convince herself, and continued to stare down at the man she'd once loved.

From the time she'd received the call to the moment she'd sent a text to let her boss know she would be in late—and even when her car hadn't started and she'd had to call Granny for a ride—Vanna hadn't felt sad, glad, or even angry over the news that Caleb might be dead. But the second she'd walked through the doors of this building, an uneasiness settled over her. Yet she'd marched into this room, fake bravado in action, and stepped up to this table like what, or rather who, lay on it didn't faze her.

But it did. Her breath hitched, and she suddenly clapped her hand over her mouth. Those tears threatened to fall, and her knees said to hell with the previous warnings—they began to shake.

This was indeed the once-handsome face she'd loved to stare at. One of his eyes was blackened and even puffier than his other features. They'd found him in the Potomac River, in an area of National Harbor where the Maryland state line met Washington, DC. So she presumed that was why he appeared to be bloated.

She shook her head, a motion that seemed to trigger the rest of her body to begin quaking as well. This wasn't the Caleb she knew. And yet it was definitely Caleb. She had no idea how or from where she summoned the strength, but she took a step forward and then another, until she was standing right next to the table. The hand clamped to the strap of the purse on her shoulder moved, shook, and lightly touched the sheet where it rested just beneath his chin.

"Caleb," she whispered again.

Then, as if a partition had been dropped down on her emotions, she sucked in a breath and squared her shoulders. "This . . . ," she said, and swallowed deeply. "This is Caleb."

Pulling her hand from the sheet, she took a step back. Her gaze lifted and she repeated, "This is Caleb Carlson."

"Well, you've done your part, right? You made the ID like they asked?" Granny said as Vanna sat quietly in the back seat of her grandmother's twenty-year-old Buick.

Frito danced around in the front passenger seat, as if the ridiculous dog needed to remind her that that was his spot. Never—not in the last seven or eight years since Granny had bought that fawn-colored pooch home from some breeder she claimed to have met in the parking lot at Target—had Granny allowed anyone in that front passenger seat other than that dog.

Mabeline Jackson, with her roller-set, fluffy gray curls and lean caramel-brown face, turned to give Vanna a quick but serious glare. She'd raised Vanna, had taken her in to live with her when Vanna was just seven years old and Diane, Mabeline's only child, had left *her* only child at a bus station. She knew Vanna better than anyone in this world—loved her better than the whole world did too.

"Yes, ma'am," Vanna replied, but she continued to stare out the window as Granny broke the speed limit without remorse.

"Then they'll send the body to a funeral home and his mother can bury him."

Vanna's head jerked back in Granny's direction. "His mother?"

"Yeah. That triflin' hussy that birthed him and defended him at every turn."

In addition to not liking Caleb, Granny couldn't stand his mother, Gail Carlson-Ledwig. Vanna didn't like Gail too much either—for pretty much the same reasons Granny had—but she had tried to respect the woman for Caleb's sake.

"Yeah, I guess she'll want to bury him." She sighed. "And since they didn't call her first, I guess I'll have to tell her." Damn, she had hoped after she'd put Caleb out of her house and her life that she'd never have to see or speak to his mother again.

"Mothers shouldn't have to bury their kids," Granny said, and for the first time since she'd picked Vanna up that morning, there was just a hint of sadness in her tone. It probably wasn't so much for Caleb or Gail, but more for the sentiment.

Frito barked vehemently as they passed a man walking his rottweiler down the street. This little dog had a complex. He really thought he was bigger and stronger than his compact twenty-five-pound body was.

"I still have a policy on him," Vanna stated as an afterthought.

"What? Why?" Granny asked. "You don't owe that man squat. Why would you continue to pay premiums on a policy for him?"

She shrugged. "We bought the policies at the same time. The auto pay was set to my account, and I wasn't trying to die first and have you struggling to pay for my burial. 'Cause you know if he wasn't paying the mortgage, car payment, or utilities, he definitely wasn't going to pay life insurance premiums."

And truth be told, she hadn't really thought about those policies until now. It was a debit she saw on her monthly account statements, but that was it. At the time of their separation, the only other bills they had jointly were the car insurance and the cable bills, which he had actually canceled during those first few weeks when he was pissed at her for saying it was over.

"He wasn't paying those bills because you were too busy doing it for him," Granny said, then held up a hand to halt Vanna's words. "Don't sass me. I know what was what between you two, and you know it."

Vanna did know it, because for all the things she sometimes held back from her best friends, Jamaica and Ronni, she told Granny everything. Always had.

"Anyway," Vanna continued, but without the response she'd previously planned to say, "I'm sure his mother has a policy on him too. So I'll just cash mine out and go on about my business."

"Hmmpf" was Granny's only response.

Frito apparently had more to say, as his yapping once again filled the air. Vanna was used to his gravelly dog talk, but she really wasn't in the mood for it with the morning she was having.

"I know, I know!" Granny shouted at the dog. "We'll get back home in time."

"Did you have something planned for today, Granny?" Vanna asked, ignoring the fact that her grandmother acted like that dog had really spoken English to her just now. "I could've gotten a rideshare to bring me down here."

"Sam is buying me lunch today," Granny said, and made a turn that felt like they were on two wheels instead of four.

Vanna gripped the door handle to keep from sliding across the back seat.

"And you know I'm never too busy for you." Granny continued talking as if horns weren't blaring at her and one driver hadn't rolled down their window to curse at her. "I already told him I want a sub from Jersey Mike's, so he can put the order in and have it delivered to the building by the time we get back. I'm gettin' the Italian today."

The ME's office hadn't opened until ten that morning, and they'd been in there for about half an hour. By the time Granny dropped her off at the rental-car place Vanna had given her the address to when they were sitting in the waiting room, she could easily make it back to the senior building she and Sam lived in, located about fifteen minutes from Vanna's house in Upper Marlboro.

"You don't need all that lunch meat. The salt is going to give you a horrible headache; then you'll be whining the rest of the day," Vanna said.

She reached for her purse and dug around inside to pull out her phone and check her emails. Her notifications were on, so she would've gotten a buzz with a new email or text message, but she needed to do something that felt halfway normal today. Because this impromptu trip to the morgue, with her speeding grandmother and this loud yapping dog, wasn't it.

Oh, how wrong the card she pulled from the box of affirmations and motivations on her dresser had been. At least once a day she plucked one out to give herself a mental boost, and they always worked. Today's card had read: *All journeys need a first step.*

If staring at her husband's dead body without puking up the two cups of coffee and strawberries she'd had for breakfast was the first step, she was fairly certain she didn't want to be on this journey. Just let her off the train right now before the wreck ensued.

Okay, that was probably the exact type of thought those cards were supposed to combat. Especially since the anxiety she'd sought counseling for years ago—but refused any type of medication to help balance—had been on full blast since the phone call informing her that her husband was dead.

"Already took my pressure pills," Granny continued without knowing about the secondary conversation Vanna was having in her head. "So I'll be just fine. I'm getting the regular-size sandwich too. Gonna eat half for lunch and save the rest for my dinner."

"You could've gotten the mini and then had something a little healthier for dinner," Vanna said before navigating to her personal inbox on her phone.

She was infinitely more invested in those messages than the ones in her work inbox.

Great! The bowling party she'd booked for next Saturday was confirmed. She'd ordered cupcakes too, and was waiting for the baker she'd been using for the last year and a half to respond to the design ideas she'd proposed. After all the business she'd been sending the girl's way, Vanna didn't want to hear a word about the intricate designs for the two dozen cupcakes she'd ordered for every week of this month. Each design would represent something special in her life's journey, so she wanted them to be perfect. She'd come a long way and was ready to face what was ahead, but she needed to mark this milestone even if nobody else cared to share it with her. And by *nobody*, she meant the mother who'd never wanted her for anything more than a check.

All her life, with every curveball that was thrown her way and every obstacle she had to overcome, Vanna kept her head held high and did whatever was necessary not to break under pressure. Not to falter beneath the dark cloud she swore was stalking her. She did whatever it took to save herself and to live up to those high-ass standards of a Black woman. And she did it without putting her hands on someone else's child or burning shit down, the way she probably should have.

Now, that in no way compared to what her ancestors had gone through during those years of being enslaved, but she could certainly relate to Steven Willis's poem about why Black people should honor their birthdays.

So this year, as she embarked on what she considered the next phase of her life, she wanted to celebrate. There were thirty more days until she turned forty—freakin' forty and still fly, to be correct. That was what she was calling this monthlong celebration: Vanna's FFSF Celebration. She'd already made the flyers and sent them out to everyone invited to the first of the events planned for the month. Dinner and clubbin' were scheduled for Friday night, which was two days away, and she still needed to find shoes to go with her outfit.

"Savannah!"

Vanna's head snapped up to see her grandmother peering back at her. They were stopped at a red light. "What? Oh, sorry, I was reading an email."

"I said, you betta not tell me you still in love with him."

"In love with who?" Vanna asked, wondering if she'd missed another part of this conversation.

Granny sucked her teeth. "You know damn well with who. Caleb!"

"Oh." Vanna frowned. "No, I'm not—or I mean, I wasn't still in love with him." She sighed now that Granny had brought the current source of Vanna's distress back to the forefront. "But I never wished death on him. I just wanted him to finally get his life together."

Granny pursed her thin lips before she turned back around to put her hands on the steering wheel. "He needed to want that for himself. Just like he needed to keep a job and pay some bills. Always talkin' 'bout he had some kind of get-rich scheme. His head wasn't never on straight, not since day one."

Granny had told Vanna that the night before the three of them had gone down to the courthouse, and again ten minutes after the ceremony, when Vanna had to rush to the bathroom because she'd been holding her pee so long.

The light changed, and Granny turned her attention back to the road. "Did they say how he died?"

"Drowned. At least, that's what they said," Vanna replied, and wondered for the second time since she'd received the call why the police hadn't been the ones to notify her.

She wasn't 100 percent sure that they should have, because again, she worked in medical malpractice and personal injury cases. The extent of her criminal-law knowledge had been obtained from her favorite police procedural shows, *Criminal Minds* and *Law and Order*—the original, not those other convoluted spin-offs. She was fairly certain she'd seen episodes where the detectives knocked on somebody's door and told them their loved one had been killed. Was there a different procedure if the person drowned?

"Hmm. Well, I guess that was painful enough to teach him a lesson."

"Granny!" Vanna shouldn't have been surprised. Her grandmother did not bite her tongue for anybody. Vanna had inherited that candor

9

but had also developed a modicum of act-right throughout her years of working in the legal field.

Granny was a retired cafeteria worker from the DC Public School system who had taken on the job of trying to guide her only granddaughter through a rewarding life. That wasn't an easy feat, but Vanna was grateful for her attempts.

"What? Don't act like you thought I was gonna be in this car shedding tears for the likes of Caleb Carlson, because you know better," Granny said. "I taught you better. At least most of the time you act like I did."

Vanna rolled her eyes at that response and looked back at the city whizzing by through the window. It was no secret that Granny created her own speed limit, which was evidenced by the mountain of speeding tickets Vanna was always paying for her.

And as she turned her attention once again to her emails, tuning out the new conversation Frito and Granny had begun, Vanna knew she would be writing even more checks to keep her grandmother's driving privileges. Although she wasn't totally sure if that was a good idea.

Chapter 2

Immediately after receiving the call from the ME's office that morning, Vanna had sent a text to let everyone at her job know she was going to be late. Herbert Cahill Hampton Sr., as expected, had been the first to respond to the message. As the senior partner at Hampton Associates, he liked to keep his nose and his unnecessary comments in everything except the right thing at the firm. HC Jr. had more important matters to tend to at that time of morning: making sure he woke up in the right bed—meaning the one beside his wife of twenty-two years—being the top one. Sanni, the paralegal, and Neshawn, the secretary, couldn't care less when Vanna came in, mostly because they were usually late themselves.

While Vanna was in the car on her way to the rental-car lot, she called HC Sr. to tell him that her husband had been found dead, she was having car trouble, and, subsequently, she would not be coming in today. Surprisingly, he hadn't given her a smart retort. His curt "Okay, keep me posted" signaled he was in the middle of dealing with an insurance company that had offered an insufficient amount to settle one of their cases. That always put him in a bad mood. Vanna didn't have the mental capacity or enough give-a-damn to inquire about it at the time, so she hadn't. After that, she'd called AAA to arrange for her vehicle to be picked up from the house and taken to her mechanic.

Now it was a little past one in the afternoon when she pulled up in front of the row house on Bryant Street.

She'd been to this house many times in the twenty years since she'd known Caleb. Had stood on this front porch, her body trembling with rage over something that someone in Caleb's rude-ass family had said. Had sat in the backyard during summer cookouts and at the dining room table for Thanksgiving and whoever's birthday was being celebrated, or dinners . . . She knew the scent of coffee and cigarettes that would greet her the moment the red door was opened, just as she anticipated the scowl that would be on Gail's face the second she noticed it was her.

That's why she needed a few extra minutes to get her head right. She pulled down her visor and looked into the mirror.

Who was this woman staring back at her?

She was a smart and driven thirty-nine-year-old with fabulous cheekbones; flawless walnut-brown skin, thanks to an expensive skincare regimen; a soft, full hourglass figure; and straight white teeth, which Granny's good city-employee dental insurance had financed. She was a fighter, a survivor, generally a morning person, and a lover of the color pink. She was not built to break.

Not even when the world steadily threw punches at her. Because that's exactly what this morning had been: a sucker punch to the gut that would've knocked the wind right out of her had she not been so used to taking her licks and keeping it movin'. That's what she was supposed to do—or at least, that's what she'd been taught.

Granny had never faltered. Not when her daughter showed her ass and proved she wasn't made to be a parent, and not when the courts had given her grief about getting guardianship because Diane had shown up crying a river of tears about missing her child. The report from the police officer who'd found seven-year-old Vanna sitting alone in the bus station where Diane had left her had, fortunately, sealed the deal. But Granny never bristled about having to start all over raising a child, not that Vanna ever heard.

Her grandmother had continued to work and moved into a bigger house, since she'd been living in an apartment during those early years when Vanna had lived with her mother. And Granny proceeded to do whatever she had to do to make sure Vanna had everything she needed, including working a part-time job during the last three years Vanna was in high school to pay for all the things that came with a child graduating from school and applying to colleges.

The woman she was today was completely thanks to Granny and the handful of friends her grandmother had who'd been like aunties to her. Each of them had taught her how to hold her head up high, to be the best she could be, and to never take any crap from anyone. She'd failed dismally at that last part in all the years she'd put up with Caleb's nonsense.

But now wasn't the time to take that trip down memory lane. Too many flashes from her past had been attempting to take control of her thoughts today. She couldn't allow them in, not right now. There would be a time and place for the breakdown she knew was coming, but it definitely wouldn't be here at her mother-in-law's house.

A few more minutes passed before she finally stepped out of the SUV she would now be paying for, in addition to her car payment, for who knew how long. Her heels clunked over the sidewalk as she made her way up to the front steps. She took them one at a time, in no particular hurry, and yet trying to get through this as quickly as she possibly could.

In the time since she'd walked out of that room at the ME's office, she'd gathered her thoughts and emotions, putting them in that same trash can in the corner of her mind where she'd stored all the other memories of Caleb and what they had together. She'd told herself it was okay to shed a few tears for the death of a man, a son, a friend to many. Then she'd resigned herself to taking care of business.

This was the last thing on her agenda for today. Then she was going home to fix herself a drink—an alcoholic beverage, to be clear. Not because she needed it to calm any grief or sorrow threatening to surface, but because she wanted it. Badly.

A.C. Arthur

The turquoise gel nail polish her nail tech, Gemini, had applied almost two weeks ago to the day had just started to peel back from the nail of her pointer finger. She frowned a bit when she noticed it as she pressed the doorbell. Thankfully, she had an appointment tomorrow after work for a mani-pedi.

Not twenty seconds later, the door opened and Gail's forehead furrowed as she glared at Vanna. "What are you doing at my house?"

"Hello, to you too, Gail." Vanna had long ago dropped the *Ms.* she'd been taught to put in front of any name of elder women she came in contact with, when the woman had continually disrespected her. "May I come in?"

"No," Gail snapped. "You're not welcome in my home. Just like you told my son he was no longer welcome in the house that has his name on the deed."

"His name was never on the deed," Vanna replied, even though she'd told this woman all this before.

Gail pursed her lips. The woman would be three inches shorter than Vanna's five-foot-eight-inch stature if Vanna weren't lifted an additional three and a half inches thanks to the chunky heel of her sandals. Gail had the same complexion as her son's—when he'd been alive—a rich cocoa brown. Her hair was a sandy-brown, gold-highlight mix of sisterlocks that were always maintained and styled. Today's style was an updo that almost made her look younger. The wrinkles at her eyes and around her mouth, which could've easily come from her being a bitter tyrant, prevented that from happening.

"Selfish ho," Gail spat.

"Again," Vanna said on a huff, "may I come in?"

Gail looked her up and down. "Again, no."

"Fine," Vanna said. "I'll tell you right here. Caleb is dead. I just came from the medical examiner's office, and I have identified his body." She reached into the front pocket of her pants, where she'd slipped the card the receptionist from the ME's office had given her and extended it to Gail. "You can call the number on this card and arrange for where you want the body transported."

Then, relieved to have gotten that over with, Vanna turned and was about to walk away when Gail's scream halted her.

By the time she turned back around, Gail was screaming again. She gripped that card in her hand, held on to the door with the other, and let her head fall back. The noise was as jolting as the sight of her completely losing it in the doorway. Vanna wanted to fast-walk to the SUV parked at the curb and get out of there, but she couldn't.

With a groan, she stepped closer to Gail and reached out to put a hand on her shoulder. "C'mon inside. You need to sit down."

Which was what the annoying woman should've done when Vanna had originally asked if she could come in. But noooo, Gail loved to make a scene. Still, Vanna was able to push her former mother-in-law back into the house. She had to step into the vestibule to do that, but Gail was too busy screaming to protest.

"What did you do? What did you do to him?" Gail wailed, and Vanna rolled her eyes.

"I didn't do anything to him," she replied. "I hadn't seen Caleb in months. And even that was by chance when I went to the Cheesecake Factory after church one Sunday."

Caleb had been sitting at a table with a woman, on a date or whatever. Vanna had intended to go on about her business, until he'd come over to her table to speak. The exchange had been brutally cordial, since she was with Jamaica and Ronni, either of whom would've quickly put him in his place if he said something out of the way to Vanna. But he hadn't. If she recalled, he'd actually been really nice that day. Overly nice. The way he always was when he wanted to apologize and get back in Vanna's good graces. She'd sent him back to his table and his date with the kindest smile she could muster.

"Then what happened to him?" Gail raged. "What happened?"

"I don't know," Vanna said, shaking her head. "I mean, I guess he drowned. All the ME said was that his body was pulled out of the water. Over at National Harbor."

Right, Caleb had drowned. Maybe that's why there'd been no police call to notify her. He'd somehow fallen into the water and drowned.

"I told them at the ME's office that you could make all the decisions regarding transporting the body, as Caleb and I have been separated for some time," Vanna said. And she'd been happy to relinquish those duties.

Gail was shaking her head now. She leaned forward, her hands resting on her knees. "My baby! My baby!" she screamed.

"I'm sorry for your loss," Vanna said, and took a step back toward the door.

"My baby! My baby!" Gail screamed again.

But she didn't look up at Vanna. Hadn't accused her of doing something to Caleb again either. So Vanna left her there.

She walked away, stepped outside, and closed the door behind her. Just as she'd done five years ago when she put Caleb out of her house.

It was later that night, while Vanna was soaking in a tub filled with lavender-scented bubbles—which she prayed would promote sleep once she was finished—that the breakdown she'd been pushing aside all day broke free.

Caleb was dead.

Her trifling, lying-ass ex-husband—well, not officially *ex*, a fact that honestly had been haunting her in the last couple of months—was dead.

She leaned her head back against the ergonomic bath pillow and closed her eyes. So many memories, so many plans. More disappointments, more anger, more heartache. Had she failed? Was she destined to be alone? Abandoned by those she'd desperately wanted to love her back?

One deep inhale, a shaky-ass exhale. Repeat. Refocus. Breathe. Emotions volleyed for first place, slapping against her psyche like a hurricane rolling in from the sea. Confusion, relief, annoyance, and, yes, sorrow—she tried hard not to tremble. Tried not to travel further down the path she knew all too well.

Her chest heaved, and her fingers fluttered on the lips of the tub where her arms rested. Beneath the bubbles, her legs twitched, water sloshing with the motion. Her breaths came quicker, the scent of lavender wafting up until her nostrils stung. She knew exactly what this was, and hated that he'd brought her to this place once again.

Forcing her legs to still took an extreme bout of concentration. Then came the breathing, different from the pants that had her clenching her teeth just moments ago. Deeper inhales; slow, concentrated exhales. Good thoughts, positive words. This would pass; she just needed to help it along. Anxiety was a sneaky bitch.

It was also a liar and a thief, but she was going to be okay.

Several moments—and several deeper, slower breaths later—she let those last words continue to play in her mind until they grew louder than the thoughts, the memories, the questions. She was going to be okay.

When she finally opened her eyes again, her lids felt heavy, and tears that had accumulated beneath them streamed down. She swallowed and stared up at the ceiling. Caleb was gone.

He was a huge part of her past—the biggest part of her adult life so far. He was a mistake. Every second since that first night they'd kissed when they were sophomores in college had been a mistake. One she continued to make for fifteen years, until she'd found the nerve to stop the madness. At one point, she thought maybe they just weren't compatible; that had been the stage right after *What the Hell Am I Doing Wrong?*, about three years into their marriage. During the course of their relationship, she'd believed that prayer and hard work would help put the pieces that so blatantly didn't fit into the puzzle of her life together. She'd forgiven, excused, faked, and ignored every warning sign that had flashed like neon lights in her face before finally admitting the truth: Caleb had never been good enough for her.

And in the five years she'd been single—in every sense of the word except for legally—she'd been certain of that fact. She deserved more from a man—any man, whether he be simply a lover or if she ever took the plunge and got married again. She deserved and would demand more. Or she would be alone.

Like she was now.

Chapter 3

August 2

"I'm not gonna make it tonight," Jamaica said.

"What?" Vanna screeched, then caught herself and rubbed her free hand over her forehead. "What do you mean you can't make it?" she asked. "It's the first night of the first FFSF weekend."

She stood then and walked around her desk so she could close the door to her office.

"I'm mad that you even gave it that silly-ass name," Jamaica said with a chuckle. "You know you can just call it your *birthday celebration, part one*, or something like that."

"I can also call it FFSF, because it's *my* birthday celebration," Vanna replied, and made her way back to her chair. "Just like when you planned *your* fortieth-birthday trip and called it Jamaica Turns Forty in Jamaica."

"That's because that was cute and you know it." Jamaica laughed again. "And we had a ball!"

"Yes, we did," Vanna said, releasing the deep breath she'd taken. She didn't want to go off on Jamaica, especially while she was in the office. "And I didn't say a word about what you named your celebration. I just went along with every single thing you had planned. Even that part where all of us had to buy the same purple bathing suit to wear on the yacht that we had to help you pay for."

"Well, y'all were gonna be on there, drinking and eating too, so it made sense that everybody pitch in."

Vanna propped her elbows on her desk and frowned. "Whatever, girl. That was last year. This is my fortieth celebration, and you know I've taken my time to plan out each weekend this month so we can get in the maximum amount of party time."

"I still think one weeklong trip would've been a better idea," Jamaica added.

"That's because you work for the government and have a bunch of paid vacation time, plus sick time and all those other holidays y'all get."

"Now, you know we don't get holidays at the jail. We're open seven days a week, twenty-four hours a day. As a matter of fact, I'm supposed to be working right now, but I took a break to come outside and call you when I could've just sent a text."

"You really would've sent a text to cancel on me tonight? Damn, J, that's foul." Vanna didn't want to sound like she was whining, but like she'd just said—damn! This was the kickoff to the festivities. She, Jamaica, and Ronni were supposed to hit Glitz, an upscale nightclub, tonight. They were doing dinner, drinks, and dancing, just the three of them because Vanna wanted the kickoff to be with those she was closest to.

She was also hoping this would be the night she found a viable candidate to end the three-month-long sexual drought she'd been experiencing. Not by choice, but by lack of suitable contenders.

"Look, I'm off this weekend, and Davon has been complaining about us not spending time together. So I figured I'd hang with him tonight, then meet up with you tomorrow for . . . What's happening again tomorrow? I don't have that long-ass schedule you emailed in front of me."

Vanna rolled her eyes. "The schedule's not that long," Vanna said. "And you and Davon have been a couple for four years—plus, y'all live in the same house. How much more 'spending time together' can y'all do?"

"Don't do that," Jamaica replied. "When you were sittin' in that house waiting for Caleb to decide when he would come home, you didn't hear me complaining."

"Um, yes, ma'am, you sure did complain. And called me all types of ridiculous for letting him walk all over me. So now I'm returning the favor—the only reason Davon is tossing out that 'not spending enough time together' nonsense is because you told him about FFSF, which I told you not to tell him about."

"You can't tell me to lie to my man, Vanna. You know that's not right."

Drumming her newly painted Pink-ing of You nails on the desk, Vanna replied, "I didn't say 'lie,' I said don't tell. There's a difference."

"Oh, you mean like how Caleb used to not tell you he was taking the mortgage money out of y'all's account to go to Atlantic City for the weekend?"

Vanna sat back in her chair. "Wow. That was low, J. The man is dead."

"That's right. Okay, my bad. But you know what I'm trying to say."

"I do," Vanna said, then sighed. "Fine. But you better be at my house bright and early tomorrow for our spa day. I don't want to miss a minute of my massage or that delicious mud bath because you're running late. Spend the night with Davon and give him all the goodies you plan to give before ten o'clock tomorrow morning."

Jamaica laughed. "Hush up, girl. I'll be there."

They talked another few minutes about some mess going on at Jamaica's job—because there was always drama going on at the jail. Whether it was with inmates or the COs, that place was like a big ol' soap opera.

It was just after two, and Vanna was planning to leave at four instead of five like she normally did. She hadn't taken a lunch today, so it wouldn't throw off her time sheet. As she'd stated to Jamaica, she didn't have a huge bank of PTO time to use however she pleased. HC Sr. and Jr. were firm on their policy of fourteen days per year, per employee, to be used for vacation, sick, mental health, or I'm-just-sick-of-this-place days. It was an awful policy, one that, unfortunately, Vanna knew a lot of small law firms employed. Sanni and Neshawn complained about it all the time, since they both had children and often had to use their PTO for their kids being sick or out of school as well. She could relate to their complaints—not the part about having children, but the fact that there were only fourteen days for every possible scenario someone might need to miss work was asinine. But her job as office manager was to enforce the policy. Which usually meant the three of them ended up taking a few unpaid days throughout the year—Sanni and Neshawn more than her, since children hadn't been part of God's plan for Vanna.

Caleb had been sterile, something she didn't learn until after they were married. And now that she was turning forty in four weeks, having a baby was only one slot from the bottom on Vanna's long bucket list.

Her cell rang before she could push it aside and get back to the invoices she was reviewing to be paid. For a second, she started not to answer it, but noticed the DC area code and wondered if it was something about Granny. Vanna was listed as Granny's contact person on everything, and one of her greatest fears was that something would happen to her grandmother and she might miss the call about it.

So she answered. "Hello?"

"Savannah Carlson?"

"Who is this?"

"This is Maggie from the DC Medical Examiner's office. I'm just calling to see if you've decided on a funeral home and when they'll be coming to pick up your husband's body."

"What?" Frowning, she grabbed a pen and scribbled the woman's name on her desk blotter. "I told you when I was there the other day that Gail Carlson-Ledwig was authorized to handle all those arrangements."

"We haven't heard from anyone by that name. And nobody has come by to pick up the body. The autopsy was completed yesterday. So we'll only be able to hold the body for another seven days before it'll be shipped off to a funeral home of our choice and either cremated or buried in an unmarked grave."

"Wait. What? An autopsy? I thought he drowned."

"The police ordered an autopsy," Maggie replied.

"Oh." That made sense. Or at least, she figured it did. Vanna didn't know what to think. Between Jamaica's cancellation and now this, a headache was creeping up.

"Well, I guess I'll call his mother and remind her," she said, thinking it was odd that Gail hadn't taken care of this already. The way that woman doted on Caleb like he was her man instead of child, Vanna thought she would've gone down to the ME's office the second she got herself together the other day.

Obviously not.

"Okay. I'll have to call you back," she said.

"That's fine. Just keep in mind the time frame I just gave you."

"I will," Vanna said as she continued writing the information onto the blotter. Once she got this woman off the phone, she'd get her notepad and transfer the information there.

But before she could do that, and just as she disconnected the call and set the phone down on her desk, there was a knock at the door.

"Come in," she said.

The door opened and Neshawn poked her head inside. "Hey, um, this woman is here to see you. She said it's personal and that you will definitely want to see her."

"What woman?"

Neshawn's eyes widened, and then she stepped farther into the office to whisper, "She said she's your mother-in law."

Damn. This day just wasn't getting any better.

Gail wore a floral-print wrap dress and nude-colored flat sandals. She walked slowly into Vanna's office after Vanna had given Neshawn permission to let Gail in. As she came closer to the desk, Vanna could see that her eyes were puffy and red, her fingers gripping the edge of the clutch she carried.

"Have a seat," Vanna said as she hurried to get up and walked over to the door to close it.

Once she returned to sit behind her desk, she asked, "How are you doing?"

It looked like the woman wasn't doing well, and that was understandable. Her only son had died. If there was nothing else in this world that Vanna could say by way of compliment to this woman, the fact that she loved her son was obvious and genuine. Gail also had a daughter, Cher, who was older than Caleb by seven years, but Cher lived in Atlanta with her husband.

"I'm . . . I'm . . . trying to understand all of this," Gail replied. "I've been walking around my house, hearing him call out to me. But then I go to his room and he's not there. I fix dinner for him like I always did, but he doesn't come home to eat it."

Caleb had missed plenty of dinners when he'd been living with Vanna, but she didn't mention that. "I'm so sorry you have to go through this," she said instead. And she was. Just as she'd told Granny, she'd never wished death on Caleb, and she certainly didn't wish this type of hurt on Gail. She could not like either of them very much but still not want any harm to come their way. If nothing else, and even for people who didn't deserve it, Vanna had compassion.

"I don't know what I'm gonna do without him," Gail said, then released a heavy sigh.

"Have you called Cher? Is she coming up here to help you with the arrangements?" Considering the phone call she'd just received, Vanna wasn't going to let this meeting end without discussing it.

Gail's eyes widened a bit; then she pressed her thin lips together. Her shoulders rose and settled with the next deep breath she took, and Vanna waited for her to respond.

"I've been waiting for you to call and let me know when we needed to go to the funeral home to make the arrangements," Gail replied.

That wasn't the answer Vanna was hoping for.

"Why are you waiting for me? I told you the other day that you could go down to the ME's office and tell them what you wanted to be done with him. I have nothing to do with it," she said. Even though she had planned to attend the funeral. Had already told Jamaica and Ronni she would need them to go with her. If Granny didn't mention it—which she hadn't so far—she wouldn't ask her to attend because she wasn't certain her grandmother wouldn't tip the coffin over and fall out laughing when Caleb's body rolled across the floor.

"What do you mean you have nothing to do with it? You're still his wife," Gail said. "You two never divorced, so you're *still* his wife. It's your responsibility to bury him."

Vanna blinked and took a moment to figure out how best to say *Are you out of your ever-loving mind?* Honestly, that didn't sound too bad, and it's really what she wanted to ask—but what she actually said was, "You're right, we weren't legally divorced. But you know that we haven't been together in five years." She let her hands fall to her lap as she sat back in her chair. "As his mother, I think you're the best person to make his final arrangements. Don't you?"

Gail flattened the purse on her lap. She folded her hands over it. Then she cleared her throat. "You're right. I'm his mother. I should do it."

One of the many things about Gail that had added to Vanna's annoyance for the woman was her ability to go from deceptively nice to outright-bitch mode in the blink of an eye.

"Okay," Vanna said, relieved. "Well, Maggie from the ME's office just called me. She said you have seven days to let them know what funeral home will come and pick him up."

"Merck Greenwood," Gail said. "You know our family always uses the Greenwoods."

"Right. Well, just call them and get the ball rolling," she said. Then all this could get off her plate.

"I'll need the policies before I go down to the funeral home," Gail said.

Now Vanna frowned. "Excuse me?"

Gail tilted her head, her face morphing from heartbroken to confused. "The life insurance policies, Vanna. You have to have policies to show the undertaker you've got money to bury him." She grabbed her purse again and sat forward in the chair. "When Caleb came back home to live with me and told me you'd tossed him out into the streets, I asked him if he'd looked out for himself when he was with you."

Here she was—this was the Gail Vanna knew best. The smart-mouthed, vindictive woman who'd chased away two husbands, her oldest child, and the used-car salesman who'd given her a car to show his affection a few years ago.

"I wanted to make sure he had his own bank accounts, insurance protection—you know, all of that," Gail continued. "And he told me the two of you had separated all your money and the accounts and that he'd gotten his own auto and life insurance policies. Had a deal with one of those companies, I think."

"Well, there you go," Vanna said. "He had his own policy. You should find that and take it to the funeral home with you."

Gail shook her head. "That policy lapsed a few months back. I saw the notice when it came to the house and said something to him about it. But he told me not to worry because you kept one of the life insurance policies you had on him when you were actually trying to act like his wife."

Vanna was certain what the woman meant to say was when Vanna had been taking care of her grown child instead of his mother continuing to do it. That headache she'd felt coming on a few minutes ago was now an insistent throbbing at her temples. She reached up, pressed two fingers to the spot, and rubbed. "I'm not gonna argue with you, Gail. It never did me any good anyway."

"And it's the respectful thing to do," Gail said. "I would think you'd been taught that, but then again, your mother was always more worried about finding her next drink than teaching her daughter manners."

"You can go now," Vanna said, and dropped her hand back to her lap. "If you don't have any insurance to cover the funeral expenses, I'll take care of it. Alone. I'll send you the information, and you can share it with your family."

Gail's eyes narrowed. "I want to be there to give my opinion on what's planned."

"Then you should've paid the premiums on his insurance policy," Vanna shot back. "But since you didn't, and it seems that this responsibility falls in my lap just like every other thing concerning your son has for the past twenty years, I'll handle it by myself. Now, you can leave. I'll call you when the arrangements are made."

Why couldn't this have fallen on someone else's shoulders? Why was it, and every damn thing else, Vanna's job to handle? A better question, one that she'd paid $175—or actually, a thirty-five-dollar co-pay—to the therapist she'd seen for two years prior to her thirtieth birthday, was, Why did she feel compelled to do all the things? To take care of *all* the issues? To make it—whatever *it* was in any given scenario—all better?

The resoundingly clear answer to that final question had been because she'd always wanted someone to do that for her. And yes, Granny had stepped in where her mother had slacked off. She'd taken care of Vanna and given her everything she possibly could to make her life appear as normal as possible, but there would always be the one thing that wasn't normal. The one thing that Vanna had been unable to—despite all the therapy and advice on how to do it—reconcile with. Disappointment. Disillusionment. Rejection.

Okay, that was three things, but they were all valid bullet points beneath the topic of emotional validation she'd seen her therapist scribble on a notepad long ago. The three things she felt most when she thought about her mother.

Diane, the alcoholic who'd had a baby by a man she'd met in a grocery store. A man who'd emphatically told her he would not claim or take care of any child she gave birth to and proceeded to threaten her life if she ever told his wife or anyone else about what they'd done together. She'd never been cut out to be a mother. Not when her one and only priority was getting as drunk as she possibly could, on as many days of the year as she could manage without being incarcerated or dropping dead. She'd never cared about or for Vanna and had no problem admitting that. So why did Vanna, after all these years, still crave her love?

Vanna was smart enough to know that it was a sentiment she would never receive from Diane, and surprisingly, she didn't hate her mother for that fact. Diane was who she was. Still, there was no ignoring the part of her that felt robbed every single day because of it. The part that always wanted to prove she could be there for others. That she was capable of loving and supporting the people in her life who expected and needed those things from her.

Like Caleb.

The first day she'd met him, she'd known she would give him her heart. He was so attractive, dressed in black jeans and a hoodie, black Tims, and that gold-and-white bandanna tied around his head. She'd met him at a step show that was held on campus. For two hours she'd watched six fraternities present their best step teams, and she'd been enamored. There was something about these intelligent Black men who not only looked good but were also getting their education and leading the way in several community-based programs. They were all enigmatic and driven, and she'd itched to learn more about them and what they did. Her roommate at the time had pledged to be in a sorority, but Vanna had dismissed the conversation wherein she was asked to do the same. Groups weren't her thing—too many people, too many opinions, too many judgments over who she was and what she'd come from. Still, that night, she'd felt a connection. Later, when the winners were crowned—Caleb's squad, of course—she realized that what, or rather who, she'd been so drawn to was him.

"Come sit over here and keep me company."

That's what he'd said to her, and she'd felt like her insides had immediately turned to slush. He had a great voice—not too deep, but just smooth enough, like LL Cool J in that *I Need Love* video. She'd had no choice but to fall, especially when Caleb's pursuit of her was nothing less than a man on a mission. A week after meeting, they were inseparable. Whenever they weren't in class, she wasn't working her part-time job at the bookstore, and he wasn't doing whatever frat stuff he needed to do, they were together. She spent more time in his room at the frat house than she did her own dorm. He wasn't her first boyfriend, or sex partner, but he was her first love. Her only love for so long that she didn't know how or if she'd ever have those feelings again.

And he'd broken her heart.

For the second time in her life, the person she'd needed to love and pour into her the most, hadn't. And that reality almost crushed her.

Not that anyone on the outside looking in would've noticed. No, Vanna was a pro at dressing and playing the part. So, while her closest friends knew that putting Caleb out had been a hard-fought decision and that he'd hurt her, they'd never had to come to her house to pick her up from a pity party. She didn't do those, nor did she look back once she walked away—not publicly, anyway.

"I don't want to lose you, Van," he'd said the Saturday morning she'd sat at their kitchen table and told him he had to go.

"You've already lost me, Caleb." She kept her hands around the mug still full of the heavily creamed and sugared coffee she preferred. "Truth be told, I've had one foot out of the door of this marriage for the last six years, since you spent a week in Vegas partying and gambling with Steve for his bachelor party."

"That's my boy, Van. And he was getting married; what was I supposed to do?"

"You were supposed to stay home with your wife, who'd just had emergency gall bladder surgery," she replied. "You were supposed to use your paycheck to pay your car payment and our car insurance. You were supposed to be a husband, not one of Steve's boys."

"That's not fair," he countered. "You had Granny, and your girls were here. You act like I left you alone."

"No," she told him, and looked up from her mug. "I'm acting like you left me, which you did. And now, after even more years of stunts like that, of your disregard and disrespect of me and this marriage, I'm finally saying I've had enough."

He pushed back from the table and stood. "So you're the only one who gets a say in this? I don't have any thoughts or opinions to put on the table? How is that right?"

"How was any of this ever right?" she asked. "How has the way you've treated me and our marriage for all these years ever been right?"

"Don't act like I've never made you happy. Don't sit there and play the victim, 'cause we both know you love doing that. Or the martyr—yeah, that's the one." Now he scowled. "Poor Vanna, she's gotta be the smart one and the responsible one because her mother was a drunk. Let's give Vanna all her flowers because she didn't fall apart just because she was abandoned and abused. All praise to Vanna for keeping a good credit score, for buying a house before she was thirty years old, for getting a promotion at work, for just breathing. Damn, Vanna! How you gon' just bail on us like this?"

He ranted for forty-five minutes after that, but Vanna had tuned him out after the remark about her drunk mother. He was trash. He was wrapped in a well-dressed, well-groomed, and fine-as-hell package—one she'd mostly paid for—but she was ready to throw that package away. To get on with her life without the heartache lying in bed beside her every night.

He broke parts of her she'd never revealed to anyone else, and now she had to be the one to make sure he had a respectable homegoing service, when what she really should've coordinated was the pine box he would be put in and tossed into an unmarked grave.

"We have Thursday morning available," the woman on the other end of the phone—Ramona—said.

Vanna had lost track of how long she'd been on hold with the funeral home trying to take care of what she could over the phone. "To pick him up?" she asked. "Is that as soon as you can get him?"

"Oh, no, Mrs. Carlson, I mean for the funeral," Ramona said. "I apologize, I should've started at the beginning. So we can pick Mr. Carlson up tomorrow morning at eight. I'll call the ME's office as soon as I hang up with you. Then, because you mentioned you wanted to take care of everything here, I went ahead and searched for our next available time, and it's Thursday morning at ten. If you'd like to do a viewing—"

"No," Vanna replied. "No viewing. We'll just do the funeral and burial."

"That's fine. You can come in on Wednesday afternoon and give your approval of him before the service. But first, we'll need you to come in tomorrow or Monday morning so we can handle all the paperwork."

"Monday," she said. Tomorrow was her spa day, and she wasn't going to miss her pampering to go and pick out a casket for Caleb.

When the dates and times were confirmed and she'd put them in the calendar on her phone, Vanna disconnected the call and yanked open the side-bottom drawer of her desk. She pulled her purse out and decided that 3:47 p.m. was going to be her check-out time today. Since she'd been on her desk phone for the call to the funeral home, she took her cell off the charger she kept at her desk and was about to put it in her purse when she saw that she had a text. It must've come through while she was talking all things cremation and burial options with Ramona.

Ronni: Can't make it tonight. Jonah's got diarrhea.

Great. That was just great. Not that three-year-old Jonah, with his adorably chubby cheeks, being sick was a good thing.

No, it was just great that now she would be hittin' the club by herself tonight because she needed this night out, this release, as desperately as she needed her next breath.

Chapter 4

Glitz had a nice vibe.

That is, once she'd gotten through the annoyingly long line and the ultrabright lighting in the main dancing area. After indicating to a host—who had close-shaved hair, creamy-hued skin, and a face that was beat to the heavens—that she was there for dinner and drinks, she was led through that loud and crowded space up a winding staircase into what felt like a totally different world.

Here, gorgeous portraits of Black women sporting lush Afros, stunning weaves, and glorious braids were painted larger than life along the walls. Vanna could appreciate the nod to the importance of Black women and their beloved hairstyles. Personally, she kept her natural 4A hair texture protected by wearing weaves and wigs. Hence tonight's shoulder-length, loose-wave look.

The ceiling and cement floors on this upper level were black. Sections of rich mahogany leather couches created half a dozen cozy seating areas along the walls, while glossed wood-top tables with low-back mahogany chairs occupied the center space.

She settled at a table for two at the back of the room so she could people-watch while she ate. Her meal selections were a small but scrumptious charcuterie board, loaded fresh-cut fries, and a cheesesteak egg roll that had received rave reviews online. They were all immensely enjoyable. She snapped pictures of everything and sent them to the group-text thread she shared with Ronni and Jamaica.

Ronni: That looks delish. You're mean.

Jamaica: Davon has me in here cooking spaghetti

Vanna's reply was a line of laughing emojis. Then she quickly determined they needed all the details from tonight since they both had decided to bail on her. Immediately after the server had taken her dessert order and removed the dinner plates, she stood from her seat and positioned herself in front of what she called the Angela Davis–vibe wall. It was right next to her table, so she didn't need to get up and walk around the room to find the perfect backdrop. She adjusted her phone and snapped seven or eight full-body and close-up selfies. After returning to her seat, she reviewed each photo, deciding which ones were delete-worthy and which ones were shout-to-the-mountaintops glamorous. She put two—a full-body and a close-up—into the next text and typed:

Vanna: Outfit #1

The elegant black three-piece ensemble—shorts, cropped top, and jacket—was equal parts cute and eye-catching. She was certain from the looks she'd received from the skinny girls as she'd stood outside in the line that they didn't approve of her size 20 body filling out the midthigh high shorts, or the way her generous breasts lifted and all but spilled over the blessedly fitted crop top, but Vanna didn't give a damn. She loved every inch of her curves and knew she looked good. It was a signature Freakin' Forty and Still Fine outfit, and she had six more she planned to rock this month. They weren't all sequins like this one, but they were likewise as show-stopping.

Ronni: Dayyuuuumm! You snatchin' all the wigs tonight, huh?

Jamaica: You wasn't lyin' about takin' somebody's son home tonight. I see you, Van!

Vanna was grinning down at the phone when the server returned with her dessert, a lovely slice of black forest cake that she prayed was as tasty as it was pretty.

"And the drink is from the gentleman in the gray over there," the server said. She wore large hoop earrings and had her blonde braids pulled into a high bun on top of her head. "Don't worry, I picked it up straight from the bartender and brought it to you, so it's safe."

"Uh, okay," Vanna replied. "Tell him I said thank you."

"Will do," the server replied with a wink.

Aside from the quick glance in his direction when the server had set the drink down, Vanna hadn't given the guy a good look. Nor did she plan to. Buying her a drink was cool, but it was also a little young, to her way of thinking. She was of the age and stage of a man knowing what he wanted and stepping up to get it. Not sitting across the room, sending a server with a free drink to break the ice for him. That didn't mean she wasn't going to happily sip this drink, though.

It was another mojito, so he must've told the server to bring her the same drink she previously had. That was smart instead of risking a drink she might not like at all. She was two sips in and had just put the first bite of her cake into her mouth when she heard his raspy voice.

"Can I join you?"

Chewing slowly and praying there were minimal crumbs on her peach-glossed lips, she raised her gaze to him.

Come through, height, was her first thought. At five nine, Vanna loved a man who was taller than she was. Dressed in gray khakis and a darker-gray button-front shirt, this guy was definitely tall—over six feet, she was sure. He had a decent, solid build, not muscular but not sloppy either.

"You need another drink to consider letting me sit with you?" he asked, and she swallowed her food.

She was just about to say *Hell no, and you can take this one with you* since he wanted to get smart, but then he held up a hand and grinned.

"I'm just kidding," he said. "You got a brotha all nervous and shit."

He had a nice smile. The kind that was wide and full and reached his eyes, so you knew his laughter would be boisterous and genuine.

She brought her napkin up to dab at her lips, then offered him a smile in return as she set it back onto the table. "You can have a seat."

When he was settled across from her, she got a better look at his face—handsome, in a mature Big Daddy Kane type of way. Old-school hip-hop was her jam, so she'd had several baes from that era and usually measured the looks of every guy she met against that prototype.

"I'm Tyson," he said, and extended a hand across the table to her. She accepted it for a shake and replied, "I'm Vanna."

Back in college, whenever she and Jamaica would hit the clubs, they each had a play name they would give the guys they weren't interested in. Vanna's had been Nicole, and Jamaica's had been Ashanti. At this big ol' age, if she wasn't interested in a man, she simply told him and sent him on his way.

"It's nice to meet you, Vanna," Tyson said. "You look amazing in that outfit."

She was definitely down for compliments—not that she couldn't or didn't give them to herself often. Nice words just hit different coming from someone else.

"Thank you," she replied. "It's my birthday suit."

Tyson's eyes widened, and her cheeks warmed.

"I mean, it's one of my birthday suits."

He raised a brow.

Dammit. She gave him a terse smile then. "It's one of the outfits I bought to celebrate my birthday." There, she'd finally gotten it right. Even though she wasn't sure why she'd tripped over the words in the first place. Men never made her nervous. Not before or after Caleb. She'd always been able to talk to guys, handle their come-on lines, and put them in their place when necessary.

To be fair, this had been a rough week, so she decided to show herself some grace.

"Oh, okay," he said with a more relaxed look crossing his face. "I see you, then. When's your birthday?"

"August thirty-first," she replied. "But I plan to celebrate all month."

"That's what's up." Tyson nodded. "Hopefully I can join in the celebration."

He was fast, but she didn't mind. Life was short, as evidenced by why her week had been so trying. And hadn't she come here tonight to find herself a good candidate?

"Maybe," she said, and cut another bite of cake before putting it into her mouth.

"You always come out alone to celebrate your birthday, Vanna? Where's your man?" Tyson had brought his drink with him. It was some type of dark liquor, which Vanna didn't do because it hit too fast and too potently for her liking.

"You probably should've been wondering where my man was before you sent over this drink." She nodded toward the mojito.

He shrugged. "Probably. But I was thinking that if you had a man, he had to be a real dumbass to let you come out looking like that by yourself."

She finished the bite of cake. "First, I'm a grown woman who has no problem coming out by myself." Which was straight facts. Even though she'd planned this entire month of events to be spent with her friends and loved ones, make no mistake about it, she would do each and everything alone if necessary. Vanna was comfortable in her own company. Blame that on being an only child. "Dinner, movie dates, weekend getaways, I can pay for and attend alone. And second, I'm not mad at a man who can appreciate when a woman looks good."

"My bad," he said, placing a hand on his chest. "You shootin' daggers over there, but it's cool. I get it—you're independent."

"You say that like it's a bad thing?"

"Not at all," he replied. "I can definitely get with that. So, you don't have a man, is that what I'm hearing?"

She shook her head. "Nope. I don't."

"Cool," he replied. "Then let's dance, 'cause I know you didn't come here dressed like that just to sit in this dark corner alone."

He stood and extended a hand to her again. She looked at it, then took another sip from her glass. Her purse was small enough to hold her phone, lip gloss, and the keys to her rental and house. It had a long chain strap, which she crossed over her body when she stood. "You are right about that," she said, and accepted his hand.

Two hours later, Vanna's feet hurt like the devil. The strappy open-toed silver sandals she'd worn tonight were fly as hell, but they were the kind of shoes that were meant to look pretty, not cut up on the dance floor. Which was exactly what she and Tyson had done. One song after another, fast ones and slow ones, they'd stayed on that dance floor for what felt like an eternity. A blissful, hard-earned eternity that she'd enjoyed every second of.

Except the parts where the straps of her sandals began to cut into her skin and the tips of her toes started to feel numb.

"You don't leave anything at home when you come out, baby," Tyson said. His hand was at the small of her back as they returned to one of the highboy tables on the outskirts of the space.

The bright lights down here didn't bother her as much as they had when she'd first entered—probably because she needed them to help her stay awake now. Last time she'd glanced at her phone, it was nearing midnight, and both Jamaica and Ronni had checked in with her.

Ronni: You still dancin' with Big Daddy?

Jamaica: You takin' him home with you or nah?

To their texts, she'd replied:

Vanna: Yes and maybe, respectively.

A variety of laughing, water droplets, and eggplant emojis came through from both of them, and Vanna chuckled heartily.

"You have a beautiful smile," Tyson said.

She beamed as she replied, "Thank you."

That was probably the moment she decided to let him take her to a hotel tonight. She didn't take randoms to her house, nor did she frequent theirs.

It was one thirty when she and Tyson left the club.

"Let me walk you to your car," he said. "Then I'll run around the back, get my car, and meet you here so we can head out."

She nodded her agreement, counting down to the moment she was sitting in the driver's seat so she could kick off these shoes. They'd just made it to her black rental when Tyson halted her urgency to the door and sweet relief. He snaked an arm around her waist in a move that didn't bother her, since he'd touched her more than a few times while they were dancing. And once, while they'd been at the table, he'd pulled her into a hug that was tight and strong and had made her nipples hard.

So no, she wasn't alarmed by his arms going around her this time, nor did she want him to release her. Even though he was stalling the shoe removal. Instead, she melted into his embrace and tilted her head up for the kiss she just knew was coming. And he didn't disappoint—not in that way, at least. He lowered his face to hers slowly, touched his lips to hers ever so gently, and then . . .

"Oh, no the hell you not out here about to get some other poor woman pregnant," came a woman's voice.

Vanna froze and blinked in question into Tyson's caught-ass gaze. The way his brow had furrowed, his eyes looked equal parts apologetic and apoplectic, and his lips remained parted. Well, now they were parted in more of an *Oh shit* formation, rather than the *I'm about to kiss your panties off* posture.

"Turn the fuck around, Tyson," the woman stated.

She had to be close, because her voice was loud and seemed like she was right next to them. But when Vanna glanced to the side, she didn't see her. Okay, so she was standing behind Tyson. Probably ready to pop him in the back of his head if he didn't do as she said. Well, he didn't move.

Punk ass.

Vanna pursed her lips and shook her head. Then she eased out of his grasp and took a few steps to the side. The movement put her closer to the door handle of her SUV, which was a relief. "I'm going to go now," she said, and meant that to be her only comment to a situation she no longer wanted to be part of.

"Oh, you leavin' so soon?" the woman asked. She had her hands on her hips and wore black legging shorts and a white Nike T-shirt that did nothing to hide her very pregnant belly.

"I am," Vanna replied, since the question was obviously directed at her. "You two have a nice evening."

"How exactly is it supposed to end up 'a nice evening' when you were just about to screw my man in the parking lot?" The accusatory tone was acceptable. This time. Hell, the woman wasn't wrong in her assumption. Still, Vanna didn't have time for these types of encounters, especially not with somebody she'd just met.

"Look, I didn't know he was in a relationship," Vanna replied. "And yes, I did ask. So, my bad for believing the lie. But the rest of what you're tryin' to toss at me is unnecessary. Like I said, I'm leaving, and you can deal with your man however you see fit."

"Vanna," Tyson said, finally turning around and looking at her like he thought for one second she was the one he needed to be addressing right now.

"Uh-uhn," she told him and pressed the button on the key fob she'd been holding. "Save the explanations for the woman I presume is carrying your child. You kept me company tonight, we danced and laughed, and now it's time to say good night." Even though not five minutes ago, she'd been ready to end it in a totally different—and hopefully more satisfying—fashion.

She had the door open and had climbed in before Tyson could say another word to her. That was probably also due to the fact that the woman had taken that opportunity to step to him and slap the next words straight out of his mouth.

That was definitely Vanna's cue to leave, so she started the truck and peeled out of that parking lot as if the police were chasing her. A glance back in her rearview mirror showed Tyson grabbing the woman's wrist before she could land another slap, and Vanna thought the police would probably really be coming along soon.

She was halfway home when the laughter started. *It's better than crying,* she thought, and continued to chuckle until there were tears in her eyes. This hadn't been how she pictured the night turning out. On her agenda, especially since she'd ventured out alone, was at the very least one good-ass orgasm. And she was okay with it simply being good—this time—just to take the edge off.

It hadn't escaped her that this desire to be with a man had probably been amplified—like her entire mood—by the events of this week. That thought sobered her.

It had taken almost a year after separating from Caleb for her to get back into the dating scene. For all intents and purposes, she was still a married woman. But that really wasn't as big of a deal as it seemed. Conversations with Granny and her friends during Sunday-afternoon card games at the senior building revealed they'd known more than a few couples who had gone their separate ways but never bothered with making the split legal. That had been for a variety of reasons—some financial, where the women wanted to remain wifey by law long enough to be eligible for half of his pension and/or social security benefits, some where he left and she was cool with it as long as he still paid all the bills in her house and took care of the kids. The reasons were always personal and often judged by others, but as Granny had frequently said, "Whatever floats your boat."

A heavy sigh as she gripped the steering wheel had guilt stirring in the pit of Vanna's stomach. If she had divorced Caleb, she wouldn't have the responsibility of burying him on her shoulders right now. Or perhaps not. Gail wasn't much smarter—or responsible, for that matter—than her son had been. So it was likely—if Vanna had still decided to keep that insurance policy—that this would've fallen in her lap anyway. Would she have said no then? She didn't know, and it was futile to consider it now.

What she did let her thoughts roam to was the fact that she had terrible luck with men. That thought had her shaking her head and chuckling again at the scene that had played out in that parking lot. Wait until she told Ronni and Jamaica about this. A red light brought her to a stop, and she took that moment to turn on the radio. She was about to bypass the oldies R & B station to find the classic hip-hop one she had automatically programmed in her vehicle, but stopped when she heard a familiar song.

"Yaaasssss!" she shouted, then started bobbing her head to the beat. *"I don't want no scrub."* She sang that line and the rest of TLC's hit tune "No Scrubs" like she was part of the phenomenal singing trio herself.

Chapter 5

Vanna slipped on her sunglasses as she stepped out of Ronni's Atlas. They were at the cemetery; the hour-and-a-half-long funeral service had ended about twenty minutes ago.

Almost finished, she told herself as she tightened the belt to the navy-blue jumpsuit she wore. Since they would only be a short distance away from the car and she already had a glob of tissue in her hand, she slid her purse under the passenger seat and closed the door. After leaving the funeral home, Ronni had cut in front of the black town car carrying Gail, Cher, Cher's husband, Ezekiel, and their twin daughters so that they were riding directly behind the hearse.

"How you gonna act like you're VIP when you didn't put up a dime to pay for this?" Ronni asked with a shrug when Vanna stared at her in disbelief.

She wasn't lying, so Vanna stayed silent for the remainder of the ride.

Granny drove her own car, and so did Jamaica. They'd pulled up right behind Ronni and were now climbing out of their vehicles as well. It was the brightest and hottest day of the summer—or at least, that's what it felt like—and Vanna couldn't wait to get home, take a shower, and lie across her bed. Every second of every day since Monday had been a task, one that Vanna was beyond ready to be done with.

Gail had called her multiple times each day, with one insensitive remark or twenty ridiculous questions each time. At one point, Vanna seriously considered blocking her, but she knew that would only result in the pain-in-the-ass woman showing up on her doorstep, and that was the absolute last thing she wanted.

"Right this way, Mrs. Carlson," Katherine Greenwood, the funeral director, said when she came to stand beside Vanna.

Behind Katherine was Minister Alita Stevenson, who led the women's ministry at Vanna's church and had agreed to officiate the services. Vanna stepped carefully over the grass, silently chastising herself for not changing out of the black pumps she'd worn. Ronni stood directly to her left, and Granny and Jamaica were behind her. She didn't bother to look back to see who else had followed them from the funeral home, because she didn't care.

Sitting in that room earlier, just a few feet away from the smoke-gray casket she'd selected for Caleb, had been the most unnerving thing she'd ever done in her life. Yesterday, she'd had to force herself to make the trip to the funeral home to view his body. Katherine had insisted it had to be done but had also asked if Vanna wanted Gail to do it. To that, Vanna had given an adamant no. If Gail hadn't signed any checks, she had zero consent abilities. She'd told her former mother-in-law that more than a dozen times this week, and the woman continued to push the envelope.

So, Granny had come with her.

"He looks good," Granny said as they'd stood beside the casket.

In all her life, with the numerous funerals she'd attended, Vanna had never heard anyone say the dead body didn't look good. She supposed this was the standard comment. Still, she was frozen to that spot, her gaze locked on the man dressed in a black suit and bow tie in the ice-blue and slate-gray colors of his fraternity. She'd recalled the names of a few of his frat brothers and, with Jamaica's help—because she kept in touch with everybody and their mother after college—had been able to get word to them about Caleb's passing. Her heart thumped wildly, tears pooling into her eyes immediately, but she couldn't look away. Couldn't glance at him, give a nod of approval, and then run out of that place like she'd planned to do. No, she'd simply stood there, shaking all over.

She'd loved this man. Had kissed him, made love with him, planned her adult life with him, and now he was gone. And she shouldn't care. She shouldn't hurt. Yet she did.

"They did a good job with his face, considering how puffed up you said it was the first time you saw him," Granny had said, interrupting Vanna's sadness.

"I want a closed casket," Vanna announced. "He wouldn't want this to be the last memory of him people had."

The mortician had done a good job on Caleb's face, just as Granny said, and the clothes he wore were new. Caleb used any occasion to get a new outfit. His lineup was crisp, the low beard he'd been wearing cleaned up as well. But there was obviously swelling at his neck and around his ears. Katherine had called her on Monday about some mark on his neck that Vanna hadn't recalled seeing at the ME's office. She couldn't see it now either, probably because the collar of his shirt was covering it. But this wasn't the Caleb she'd known. Not the handsome man she'd married.

"He was a conceited little bastard," Granny had quipped. "So I guess that makes sense."

"I won't ever see him again," Vanna said quietly then, as the tears had rolled down her cheeks.

Granny had moved in closer and wrapped an arm around her waist, since she was shorter than she was and didn't try reaching up to her shoulders.

"He's at peace now, Vanna. You deserve to be too."

Those were the words Vanna had been telling herself since she'd gotten up this morning and prepared to say her final goodbye. Caleb had lived his life—whether it was in a way she approved of or could live with, he'd done it. And now she had to continue to live hers.

Minister Stevenson began reciting scripture, and Vanna sat holding a long-stemmed white rose in her hand. Beside her, Jamaica, Ronni, and Granny held one too. Vanna didn't cry again as she stared at the casket for what she knew would be the last time. Instead, she let the corners of her mouth lift lightly as she recalled some of the good times she'd had with Caleb.

The Saturday mornings he would bring them both a bowl of Cap'n Crunch cereal to bed, so they could find the cartoon channel and watch the way they used to do when they were kids. Or on Christmas Eve, when they would each open one gift together. Those were good moments, and they filled her chest with a lightness she hadn't felt this week.

"You're up here laughing, and my son's about to go into the ground," Gail said, her tone—as well as the look on her face—agitated.

Before Vanna could reply, Granny stood. "Look here, Gail. Don't start no shit today."

The graveside service was complete. The minister had prayed and come by to hug Vanna one last time. Others had gotten up to put their flowers on top of the casket, which was why Gail was near Vanna at all. Vanna hadn't moved at the conclusion of the service, and so Jamaica, Ronni, and Granny had remained seated beside her while everyone else moved around. But now the confrontation Vanna had prayed wouldn't happen was about to pop off. She could see it in the way Granny was standing, with one fist on her hip, her chin lifted, eyes narrowed at Gail.

"Nobody was talking to you, Mabeline," Gail shot back. "Your grandchild has done nothing but disrespect me and my child since the day they met. But it ends today! Sittin' up here in that loud-ass outfit when she knows Caleb always wanted everybody to wear white for him."

Vanna only sighed at that last statement, because out of everything Gail had just said, that part was the furthest from the truth. Caleb had hated those Easter Sundays when she would remind him that they wore white at their church. He would attend the ever-popular white parties, but he'd always throw on tennis shoes that had a pop of color. So, while Gail, Cher, and the rest of their family had shown up today wearing all white, some of them—the younger ones—wearing white pants and T-shirts with a picture of Caleb on the front, Vanna never had any intention of wearing that color. Nor had Gail bothered to ask her to wear it during the hundreds of times she'd called Vanna in the last week.

"Nobody cares what y'all got on," Granny continued. "That boy of yours sure don't care no more."

Gail took a step closer to Granny, and immediately Vanna stood. Ronni was right behind her. Jamaica got up from her seat too, but she moved so that she was standing directly in front of Cher, who had decided to join her mother in this ridiculous confrontation.

"You will not stand here and speak ill of my child," Gail said. "Not you or your granddaughter, who never deserved him."

"That's enough," Vanna said. "The services are over, so we can all go our separate ways now."

"Oh, like you called yourself doing when you put my baby out on the streets," Gail shot back.

"Your baby was grown!" Granny shouted. "And if you'd taken half the energy you do in runnin' your mouth to teach him how to be a decent adult, my granddaughter wouldn't have gotten rid of his ass."

"C'mon, Mama," Cher said grabbing her mother by the arm. "Let's just go."

But Gail ignored her daughter. Instead, she opened her mouth to say something else to Granny, but Granny put a hand up in her face.

"I don't have any more words for you after this, 'cause you ain't worth my time," Granny told her as she shook her head. "Stay the hell away from my granddaughter after today. Don't call her, don't text her, don't even speak her name. If you do, I swear I'll come to your house and beat you like you stole somethin'. You hear me?"

Again, Gail opened her mouth to speak, but just as she did, she dropped her gaze and screamed. "Ewwwww!!! Get this little mutt!"

All eyes fell to Gail's open-toed white shoes, which were now being sprinkled by Frito's urine. Jamaica burst into laughter, and Ronni clapped a hand over her mouth. Gail was about to raise the now-soaked foot to kick Frito, who by now had finished doing his business, but Cher grabbed her arm more forcefully this time.

"Mama, I told you to come on. Out here making a scene when none of this is necessary," Cher told her. She was shaking her head now too, her honey-blonde goddess braids swishing with the motion.

Granny bent down and scooped Frito up, then dropped him right back into the oversize brown leather bag she always carried. Vanna hadn't even seen the dog escape, but knowing Granny, she'd probably discreetly let him out during the service so he could relieve himself elsewhere in the grassy area. Not on Gail's feet. Then again, Vanna didn't put anything past her grandmother.

"I hate all of you no-class hoes," Gail snapped at them just before she turned to follow her daughter's directive.

Cher hadn't spoken a word to Vanna, and she hadn't really cared. She'd only seen her sister-in-law a handful of times in all the years she'd known Caleb because Cher only half dealt with her family in any capacity. Which was probably why the woman hadn't engaged in this current argument, instead opting to get her mother out of here before Frito's pissing stunt was the least of what happened. One of the cousins—at least, that's who Vanna thought the younger girl with her *RIP Caleb* T-shirt tied in a knot at the back so that the front of it was stretched over her full breasts was—did look over at them and yell, "Y'all ain't got no class, and my cousin was better off without your fake-bougie ass anyway!"

Jamaica laughed even louder this time. "Girl, go on before I forget I'm too old to put hands on somebody else's child."

"Who comes to a funeral to cut up?" Ronni asked when most of Caleb's family had found their way to their cars. It was a good thing they'd been toward the end of the funeral procession so they could pull right off and not have to wait for Ronni, Jamaica, and Granny to make their way to their cars.

"People with no money to pay for funerals but still wanna flap off at the mouth," Granny snapped. "Get on my nerves!"

"Well, I bet she didn't plan on you sending Frito after her ass," Jamaica added with another chuckle.

Jamaica was the jokester of their trio, but make no mistake, she would forget herself and put hands on a person if provoked. Which Caleb's cousin knew not to really do, based off the way she quickly turned around and hurried herself to that car.

"I can't believe it, though," Ronni said. "If we're too old for this mess, you know Gail's simple ass is."

"Well, I'm not," Granny said, and then patted her bag. "I've got my gun right here for whenever somebody steps too far out of line."

Vanna rolled her eyes.

"Really, Granny?" Ronni asked, her face scrunched up. "You carry a gun in the same bag as your dog? Frito acts like a whole grown person. It's a wonder he never pulls the gun out and starts poppin' people himself."

Again, Jamaica laughed, but it was quickly cut off by a man who was approaching them.

A fine af man wearing dark sunglasses and a black suit that looked like it was designed, cut out, and sewed right back up especially for him. His bald head shone in the glaring sunlight as his long legs brought him closer. The silver-and-diamond watch at his wrist glittered, the sprinkle of gray in his full goatee popped, and when he was close enough, the warm summer breeze delivered a whiff of his amazing-smelling cologne.

"Good afternoon, ladies," he said in a deep voice. "May I offer my condolences to you, Savannah?"

He hadn't even paused, just stepped right up and offered her his hand. When she stared down at it, then back up to him, his medium-thick lips spread into a smile, and he lifted a hand to remove the sunglasses. "My fault. I thought you'd remember me," he said.

And Vanna's mouth fell open. "Aden?"

"Aha, you do remember me," he said, and that smile turned into a full-fledged grin. One that she specifically recalled always making her insides flutter.

"Um, yeah, how could I forget you?" she asked, then cleared her throat. "I mean, it's been a really long time."

He nodded. "Yes, it has." Then he sobered. "I was really sorry to hear about Caleb. I can't believe it, actually."

Caleb. Right. She was standing at her husband's gravesite, recalling how much this other man had always turned her on. She could ask the Lord to forgive her, but until Aden Granger was out of her sight again, she was positive this reaction would remain the same.

"I can't believe the two of you are gonna carry on a conversation while the rest of us stand here and wonder who this is," Ronni said, her gaze steady on Aden.

Jamaica, on the other hand, had folded her arms across her chest and now looked Aden up and down. "Aden Granger. Finance major. Was on the basketball team but cared more about his grades than show-ing off on the court. Dated Yvette Gowans our sophomore and junior year. But since you were a year ahead of us, that was your junior and senior year."

He looked shocked as he gazed at Jamaica. "Correct," he said, then narrowed his eyes at her. "And you're Jamaica Brown. You didn't stay at the same dorm with Savannah, but you two were together all the time." He returned his gaze to Vanna. "That is, until Caleb stole all her attention."

"What?" she asked, but she was certain he didn't know the origin of that question. At least, she prayed he didn't. She wasn't asking *what* in reference to Caleb taking her attention, but rather *what* in the whole hell was happening, because the way he was looking at her was strange. Different. Tempting.

Not to drastically go off topic, because he had shown up at this funeral and offered his condolences just like many other guests had done at some point today, but the way his gaze seemed to be boring into her was alarming. But not necessarily in a bad way—or at least, she didn't think it was bad. It was like he was shooting those red Superman lasers from his eyes and peeling back every layer of her life until her soul was bared to him, or some other wild nonsense like that.

"Ah, c'mon, don't act surprised," Aden continued, oblivious to the confusion now searing through her. "Once you and Caleb hooked up, none of us really saw y'all. I mean, I saw him during frat stuff and in the two classes we had together during my senior year. But that was it." He shrugged. "Y'all stayed cuddled up."

"Ain't that the truth," Jamaica said. "I had to wonder for a minute if I'd ever get my bestie back. But then he started acting like the fool he'd been born to be, so my world went back to normal."

Vanna sighed. "Okay, y'all, let's not speak ill of the dead. Especially while he's still technically aboveground."

They all glanced over at the coffin.

"Then we shouldn't be standing here like we're about to have a picnic with the sonofabitch," Granny said, and started to walk toward the car.

When she saw the surprised looks on each of their faces, Vanna tried for a nonchalant tone: "That's my grandmother."

Aden glanced back at Granny, then returned his gaze to Vanna's. "I can hear the resemblance." He grinned.

And Vanna did the same. "Oh, shut up."

"So, ah, I didn't see any details about a repast on the program. Are you just heading home, or do you have some other private plans?" he asked.

"No, there's no repast. This"—she gave a wave of her hand toward the casket—"is over." *In so many ways,* she thought.

"Great," he replied, then cleared his throat. "I mean, that's fine. Can I buy you a cup of coffee?"

"Is that how they ask for dates now?" Ronni asked.

Jamaica shook her head. "Nah, what you want to ask is if that's how frat brothers ask their deceased brother's wife out on a date?"

Vanna's eyes widened as heat creeped onto her cheeks. Aden didn't look bothered by either question. He simply replied, "It's how I ask a woman I haven't seen in a long time out to catch up."

Well, that shut them up. All three of them.

Until Vanna thought the silence was rude and way too uncomfortable, so she opened her mouth to reply, only to have it quickly clap shut again when she heard, "Savannah Carlson?" in a deep male voice she didn't recognize.

It had come from behind her, so she turned to see who it was. Probably another guest who wanted to offer their condolences before leaving. There were actually two men approaching her now: one, a medium-build Black man whose salt-and-pepper hair was badly in need of a cut; and the other, an older Caucasian man, with thinning brown hair and black-framed glasses.

"Yes," she replied. "I'm Savannah Carlson. Were you friends of Caleb's?" she asked because she didn't recognize either of them.

They were both dressed in suits—a muddy brown and a gray pinstripe. Both could use new shoes.

Mr. I Need a Haircut stepped up first. He moved his hand so that it pushed back the side of his suit jacket to reveal a badge attached to his belt, and said, "I'm Detective Andy Parish from the Metropolitan Police Department, and you're under arrest."

Chapter 6

Conspiracy to embezzle money from the Lennox Casino.

That's what she was being charged with. The words, followed by her Miranda rights—which, after hearing them so many times on TV and in movies, were more like a litany than a warning—now replayed in her mind.

She sat in a room that wasn't as dark as she'd imagined an interrogation room at a police department would look. The walls were painted that government-beige color and had scuff marks in various areas around the room. The floor was a basic tile—again, very government issued. As was the dark, brown-topped table and the three chairs around it. Well, two chairs were on one side, and the chair she sat in was on the other side by itself. That's how she felt, like she was by herself—which she literally was.

On the ride from the cemetery to here, she'd sat in the back seat, alone. Her purse was still in Ronni's car, which meant her phone was too. Which was probably for the best. She didn't want anyone in here in possession of her personal items. The detectives hadn't cuffed her; instead, because she hadn't yelled and screamed her innocence or tried to run through the cemetery in an effort to get away from them, they had simply walked her to their twenty-something-year-old town car and opened the back door for her. She slid onto the seat, willing herself not to cry. Her hands had immediately fallen into her lap, and she clasped her fingers to still them. Her stomach had twisted as she crossed her legs and looked out the window, trying to find the calm that refused to come.

Now, with her hands flat on this table, she could only stare down at them. They'd put her in this room and left her here for who knew how long. It seemed like an eternity, but she figured it may be going on an hour. She hadn't requested an attorney yet, hadn't spoken a word to them since asking, "Are you serious?" at the cemetery. Their stoic faces had been the answer to that question, while Jamaica and Ronni held Granny back after she'd tried to charge the detectives the moment she saw what was happening.

Vanna knew Jamaica and Ronni would take care of her grandmother. They would see that she got home safely, and then they would get on the phone and find her an attorney, find out how they could get her out of there, and all that. They were her best friends—no way they were going to let her rot in jail.

Oh, gracious, was she going to rot in jail?

And for a crime she was absolutely oblivious to?

She'd been to the Lennox Casino, which was located in the National Harbor area, maybe twice in the three years since it had been open. It was the smallest and newest of the casinos over there, so when she did desire to visit a casino, she normally chose the bigger, more well-known ones in the area. Overall, though, Vanna wasn't a gambling person. She would much rather spend her hard-earned money on home improvements, helping Granny, and her hair. Clothes, shoes, nails, et cetera—those were at the bottom of her top-five money-priority list, right after saving for her dream trip to Ireland—which nobody understood why she had in the first place.

So, just how she would've managed to conspire to embezzle anything from a place she barely frequented was beyond her. That had her thinking of HC Sr. and Jr. She prayed Jamaica and Ronni knew not to call either of those jokers to help her. Since she'd worked for them, she'd learned all that was behind the reputation of so-called ambulance chasers. Their priority was always their bottom line and the quickest way to it, which was why their percentage of settlements was twice as high as their litigation stats. Still, she would definitely need a lawyer to reiterate what she planned to say the moment those detectives came back into this room: that she was innocent.

She was drumming her nails on the table, her knee shaking violently beneath it, when the door opened and, as if she'd summoned them, the two detectives stepped in. Detective Stuart Beaumont—he'd introduced himself in the car—pushed his glasses up on his nose and was the first one of them to take a seat. Detective Andy Parish closed the door and, with a folder in one hand, took the second chair across from her.

"Mrs. Carlson," Detective Beaumont said, "we have some questions to ask you, and if you answer them all correctly, this interaction will go a lot easier."

So, he was going to be the bad cop. Okay, she could roll with that. Actually, she couldn't, because she was scared out of her mind, but she wasn't about to show them that.

"How about I answer truthfully?" she asked, then told herself to remain silent.

She could sit there and just let them talk. Then sit even longer while she waited for her attorney—whoever her friends found for her—to appear. Or she could at the very least try to find out what the hell was going on.

"That's a good idea," Detective Parish said.

He had a smirk on his face that told her he wasn't exactly going to be the good cop in this scenario. Whatever. She already knew to trust them only as far as the next question or bogus charge they could toss her way. While she generally trusted most cops to do their job and protect and serve, all that went out the window when she was falsely accused.

"You were married to Caleb Carlson," Beaumont said. "Correct?"

"Yes." Because whether or not she answered, they already knew that to be true.

"When was the last time you saw your husband? Before his unfortunate demise?" Beaumont continued.

She didn't want to answer that, didn't want to risk incriminating herself in a way she was absolutely clueless about, so she folded her hands together and asked, "Can you explain these charges to me?" She had a right to know what she was being accused of; whether she decided to answer any of their questions, she knew she had that right.

"Like I stated at the cemetery," Detective Parish began, "you are charged with conspiracy to embezzle money from the Lennox Casino."

"What evidence do you have?" she asked.

Parish tilted his head, one corner of his mouth lifting. "Oh, that's right, you work at a law firm. So I'm guessing you figure you know how to handle this."

She raised a brow at his comment.

"I know how to handle myself, period," she replied. "That has nothing to do with where I work." One thing she couldn't stand was someone underestimating her, whether it be because she was a woman or because she was a *Black* woman. She was mature, educated, and unintimidated by a title or a badge.

Beaumont nodded and rubbed a finger over his chin. "I see why he married you."

"What?" Vanna asked, her ire rising.

Parish chuckled. "You're here because we found the bank account you and your husband shared. The account that currently has a balance of approximately $173,000 in it. But I guess you already know the balance."

She was two seconds away from screaming *What. The. Hell?* But she sat there blinking at the detective instead.

One hundred and seventy-three thousand dollars. In a bank account with her and Caleb's name on it. A joint account.

Her temples throbbed, and her breathing came just a little quicker, anxiety slamming into her with an iron fist.

"Cat got your tongue?" Beaumont asked with a wide grin.

"Why don't you go ahead and tell us what the plan was, Mrs. Carlson. We can make this process short and sweet." He pulled a pen out of the inside pocket of his suit jacket, then opened the folder in front of him. "Or we can make it long and painful. Emotionally, I mean, because we certainly wouldn't do anything to harm someone as . . . ah, I mean, someone like you."

This bastard. She'd thought his gaze was lingering just a little longer than necessary on the cleavage displayed by the low cut of her jumpsuit. Which actually would've been a lot lower if she hadn't pinned it this morning because showing up at her estranged husband's funeral with miles of boob on display hadn't seemed like a good idea. Still, with the little bit that was showing, it didn't mean the detective's lecherous gaze was welcome.

"Or . . . ," she said, and took a deep breath. While her knee still shook beneath the table, not enough to have her heels clicking on the floor but still enough to remind herself she wasn't as calm as she would like to portray, she released that breath as slowly as she could manage. "You can get me a phone so I can call my lawyer."

August 9

Thirteen hours and a trip to see the commissioner later, Vanna was released on citation. As she didn't have any belongings to retrieve from the evidence room, she clenched the paperwork she'd been given in one hand and walked with her head held high through the double doors at the back of the facility.

It was almost 2:00 a.m. now, but when she'd called Jamaica—three hours after she'd told the detectives she wanted to make the call—to see if they'd found her an attorney, she was told that they were already on their way and would be waiting for her when she was released.

The temperature had dropped a bit so that the balmy atmosphere that had hung over them during the burial service was now a damp, chilly air. The puddle she splashed with her first step outside told her it had rained. With a murmured curse, she continued across the dark parking lot, where she saw Granny's black car and Jamaica's white Lexus NX right beside it.

They looked like a trio hanging out in a high school parking lot, with Granny sitting on the trunk of her car, large-framed prescription glasses she needed for night driving on her nose, cigarette between her lips, and Frito in her lap. Ronni leaned her backside against Granny's car, while Jamaica was across from her, relaxing against her truck.

"You cannot be serious," Ronni said to Jamaica as Vanna grew closer. "You're really going to start making wedding plans with him?"

"Wait a minute, now," Jamaica said with a shake of her head. "I know you're not about to tell me I shouldn't get married. You've been married since I met you, and about five years before that."

Ronni, who was five feet three inches tall and never wore heels because then she would be taller than her five-foot-five-inch husband, Croy, propped both hands on her hips. "I've been married for seventeen years."

"And considering you're only forty years old, you've been married the majority of your adult life. So, tell me again why me deciding to marry the guy I've been dating and living with for the past three years is a problem?" Jamaica was the same height as Vanna, with a mahogany complexion and a penchant for fake eyelashes that were way too long and often left her looking cartoonish.

"I didn't say getting married was a problem," Ronni argued. "I said marrying *him* was a problem. He doesn't love anyone more than he loves himself, J."

"Well, I love myself too, and so do you—or at least you should," was Jamaica's retort.

"Both of y'all hush, 'cause neither of your men is worth a damn," Granny said, and blew out the smoke from the puff she'd taken. "Well,

I'll give Croy points for taking care of his house and kids. But he still works you like an employee, Ronni. And you, Jamaica—that man doesn't do a damn thing but beg, cry, and play the victim with you. But look, if y'all like it, I love it, and my grandbaby's coming, so hush it up."

She tucked Frito under an arm and hopped down off that car with way more speed and ease than Vanna would've imagined a seventy-eight-year-old woman could. Granny had changed from the long, dark-gray linen dress she'd worn to the funeral into a pink-and-black tie-dyed caftan. Rows of chunky bracelets—Granny's favorite jewelry—jingled at her wrist as she plucked the cigarette away and extended an arm toward her.

Vanna walked into her grandmother's embrace. Granny always gave the best hugs, and tonight, when she needed it most, wasn't any different.

"You're not supposed to be smoking," Vanna said, and inhaled the scent of Granny's signature White Diamonds perfume.

"You had my nerves bad, babygirl. Are you all right?" Granny asked as she continued to rock Vanna in her tight one-armed hold.

"Yeah. I guess," Vanna said. "I just want to go home, burn these clothes, and then sear my skin with the hottest water I can survive."

Frito gave a grumbly rumble in what Vanna considered his approval as she eased away from Granny. With upturned lips, she glanced down at the dog she swore was the funniest-looking pooch she'd ever seen up close and scrubbed behind one of his tall ears.

Jamaica was the next one to pull Vanna into a hug. "Girl, I know that's right. It's dirty as hell in there, and you know I know."

Vanna was nodding when Ronni came in to make their hug a threesome. "I was praying so hard for you, V. So hard."

"Thank you," Vanna said, and took a step back away from them. "Thank y'all for coming down here. I hope you weren't standing out here too long. But I didn't have any idea how long this process would take, and they wouldn't let me make another call."

"Oh, no, we had somebody on the inside giving us the scoop," Ronni said.

Vanna gave herself a gentle smack on the forehead and said, "Duh. That's right, J, I'm sure you've got COs that are down here tonight. Thank whoever kept me alive in there for me."

"No, ma'am," Jamaica said, and grabbed Vanna's shoulders to turn her around. "You can thank him yourself."

"Hey, Savannah," Aden said as he stepped out from around a sleek silver Audi.

"Aden? What are you doing here?"

He came closer, in that walk that seemed more like a saunter. He'd changed out of his suit as well and now wore dark jeans and a black T-shirt that fit his muscular torso way too well. "I've got a buddy who's a defense attorney. I called when those detectives drove off with you. One of his associates was already down here seeing to another client, so he got the scoop, relayed it to my friend, and he got here just before you were scheduled to see the commissioner."

"I didn't see anyone in the courtroom when I was there," she said. "I mean, there were lots of people in there, but nobody came over to me to say they were my attorney. I just figured they let me go because I had no prior record."

"He was already taking care of the paperwork for you. His wife is in the last month of what has been a difficult pregnancy, and he barely likes leaving her to go to work during the day, let alone in the middle of the night. So he wanted to get back home. But while you were being processed out, he told me to tell you to call him first thing tomorrow morning." He handed her a card.

She took it and, thanks to the floodlights on the building behind them, could read the name Jovani Kincaid on the front.

"He was fine too, V," Jamaica said from behind her. "Even in that slim-fit suit he was wearing. I think I've seen him down at the jail too, probably visiting with his clients or whatever."

Aden, who was still staring at Vanna, nodded. "He's had his own practice for ten years and is one of the most reputable defense attorneys in the District."

"And you called him for me?" she asked. "Why?"

"Because it looked like you were in trouble," he replied.

She tilted her head and narrowed her eyes. "And? Who are you, my knight in shining armor?"

"You're rude," Granny said, and came up to loop an arm through Vanna's. "Thank the man, and let's get you home."

Vanna resisted the urge to stare quizzically at her grandmother, because if she wasn't the pot calling the kettle. She sighed. "Right. Sorry. It's been a rough day," she said, then tucked the card into the side pocket of her jumpsuit and extended her hand to Aden. "Thanks for all your help. I'll give him a call in the morning."

Aden accepted her hand in a stern but gentle grasp. He held on to it as he continued to watch her. "No problem. I'll check on you tomorrow."

She was just about to say he didn't need to do that when Granny yanked on her arm. "That sounds good. Let's go. I don't want none of these fools coming back out here and tryin' to take you away again."

"I know that's right," Ronni said. "Let's go home."

Vanna eased her hand out of Aden's grasp and gave him a small smile. "Thanks again, and good night."

His response was a nod before he turned his attention to Granny. "Good night, Granny. Ronni, Jamaica. You ladies drive safely."

After the rest of the *good nights* and once Vanna was belted into the back seat of Granny's car—because her grandmother insisted she was going to drive her home—Vanna said, "You just met him today . . . or rather, yesterday, at the cemetery. Why's he calling you *Granny?*"

Mabeline was insistent about respect and people addressing her properly. Vanna had witnessed her correct a young nurse at the vein clinic who came into the room one morning and referred to her as Mabeline. "That's Ms. Jackson to you, little girl."

Vanna hadn't bothered to tell Granny that referring to the nurse as *little girl* was disrespectful too, because she knew her grandmother was aware of exactly what she'd done.

Granny started the car. "He got my grandbaby a lawyer and brought his fine self down here to sit and wait for you with us. He can call me *Granny* all he wants to."

Well, all righty then, she guessed that was a good enough point. Still, she couldn't help but wonder on the ride back to her house why Aden Granger, whom she hadn't seen in fifteen years, would turn up at Caleb's funeral and help get her out of jail all in the span of twenty-four hours.

At nine fifteen, with her venti caramel macchiato—extra caramel and extra steam—on a napkin beside her desk blotter, Vanna stared down at the business card and punched the numbers on the keypad of her phone.

"Good morning. May I speak with Jovani Kincaid, please?" she said in her professional voice.

Then she sat up straighter in her chair and smoothed down the floppy bow on the purple blouse she was wearing.

"May I ask who's calling?" asked the perky receptionist who answered.

"Savannah Carlson, and it's in reference to my . . . ah, my upcoming court appearance." The last thing she wanted to say was *my incarceration last night*, because she was still trying to digest that whole interlude.

"Please hold," came the receptionist's next response.

Vanna closed her eyes to the thoughts that had kept her awake long after she returned home from the police station. She'd insisted that Granny and Frito stay at her house since it was so late, and despite Granny's obstinance, Vanna didn't want her driving at night, glasses or not. And after they were settled into the guest room down the hall, Vanna had gone into her bedroom and closed the door. She'd hurried to get that shower, tossing that jumpsuit in the trash can, because she never wanted to see it again.

She'd been to jail in that outfit, and the memory would forever be emblazoned on her mind. She'd been to jail. Had literally sat in a cell. With bars around her. Bars with a lock to keep her in. Now, she hadn't been in there alone, but that was beside the point. She didn't know those other women in there with her, even though, by the time she'd left, Kita was reminding her that she thought her weave was gorgeous.

The one place Vanna had never imagined seeing herself was in jail. Sure, she, Jamaica, Caleb, and some of their friends had been in possession of and smoked their fair share of marijuana during their college years and for a good few years after that, until Jamaica started working at the jail and Vanna feared what was once their recreational use was turning into something a little more frequent for Caleb. And while back then, before District voters had approved the legalization of possession of minimal amounts of marijuana for personal use, they'd definitely had a supplier from the old neighborhood hooking them up, she'd still never considered that those puffs of entertainment would land her behind bars.

"Good morning, Mrs. Carlson," a man's voice said on the phone.

"Good morning," she replied. "You can call me Vanna. And thank you for your help last night."

"You can call me Jovani, and there's no need for thank-you's."

"Okay. Well, if you'll send me your invoice, I'll take care of it right away." She'd thought about that too, last night. How she was going to pay for a lawyer.

Vanna wasn't destitute by any means. She made a decent high five-figure salary at the firm; she had some small investments that Croy, Ronni's husband, who worked some entry-level position at an investment firm, had coached her on; and her credit was good. She would also get a check from the life insurance company, even though that funeral bill had been a lot more expensive than she'd imagined. But she didn't have extra thousands just lying around, waiting to be tossed toward legal fees.

"No need to worry about that; it's been taken care of," Jovani said. "But I'd like to set up a time for us to meet. I have to be in court within the hour, and I have another appointment this afternoon before I need to head home, but how does Monday morning look for you? Can you be in my office by seven thirty? I know that's early, but I have to be in court at nine. Providing my wife doesn't go into labor this weekend."

That last part was said with a hint of excitement, and Vanna couldn't help but smile. "Right. Aden told me you were expecting. Congratulations," she said.

"Thanks. While I've mastered being a defense attorney, the reality that I'll be a father very soon is scaring the hell out of me." He chuckled.

"I'm sure you'll be fine," she replied. "It's a blessing."

"You're right about that," he told her. "Definitely a blessing, and my wife and I are so grateful."

Vanna continued to smile. That had been her fifteen years ago, happily married and excited about the future. That parade had been quickly rained on. "Seven thirty on Monday is fine for me. I usually try to get into my office by that time even though I'm not due here until nine."

"Okay. Cool. I'll put that on my schedule, and I'll have more information by then so we'll have a better picture of what's going on."

"I was just about to ask if you knew what this was all about. Because I don't have a clue. I've been thinking about it and trying to figure out where this money they're talking about could've come from and why they think I have access to it," she said, a rush of anxiety creeping back into the place it had resided all night.

"Don't worry about all that right now. I've already got my assistants looking into this, so we'll talk about it on Monday. In the meantime, don't discuss this with anyone else, Vanna. Not the police, not your friends. Put it out of your mind for the next few days, and we'll map out our next steps when we meet." He sounded so confident, so relaxed. Like he helped middle-aged women out of weird-ass conspiracy charges every day.

She frowned when it dawned on her that he actually did get people out of legal dilemmas for a living. "Okay," she said, and sighed deeply. "I'll try."

"You're going to be fine," he told her. "We'll take care of this, and you'll move on with your life—I promise."

And, damn, she wanted to believe him. Wanted to trust that this was all going to go away and she could get on with her birthday-month celebration, her plans for the future—all of it. But hadn't she just thought this same thing a few days ago when she'd been preparing for Caleb's funeral? Life seemed intent on tossing everything but the kitchen sink her way, and she was getting weary of fighting the battle.

"Thank you, again. And wait, did you say your bill was taken care of? How? By who?" she asked, but her heart skipped a beat as the answer echoed in her mind before Jovani even said the name.

"Aden took care of it."

Chapter 7

August 9

The only thought that got Vanna through what felt like the longest Friday of her life was the dinner and company she expected the moment she walked into her house.

And she wasn't disappointed. After two steps into the foyer, she smelled the delicious scent of pot roast. She slid her purse strap from her arm and set it and her keys on the small round table by the door before stepping out of the taupe wedge sandals she'd worn today. After retrieving her phone from her purse, she bent down and picked up the sandals, then made her way up the steps to the main level of her house. Motown tunes blasted from the cordless speaker on the stand in the living room. Vanna had curated the playlist for Granny and shown her how to cue it up whenever she came over.

"It smells like heaven in here!" Vanna yelled as she dropped her shoes near the stairs leading up to the bedrooms. Then she walked through the open space to get to the kitchen, where Granny was stirring something on the stove.

"Roast, baby gold potatoes, and onions over there in the Crock-Pot," Granny said without turning to face her. "Greens are almost done. Got the ones from that new market because I couldn't get to the farmers market last weekend. But these'll be fine. Macaroni and cheese just came out of the oven."

Vanna's stomach growled, and she moaned. "I love you so much, Granny."

Going to stand beside her grandmother, she leaned in and kissed her on the cheek. "So, so much."

Granny chuckled. "Sure you do. Especially when I cook everything you put on that list. Even though you know I don't need you to tell me what your favorite foods are."

Vanna opened a drawer and found a fork. She pulled back the foil on the pan of mac 'n' cheese and stuck her fork into a crispy brown corner. Granny always cooked it until the thick layer of cheese she piled on top was golden brown, just like Vanna loved. "Mmmmmm," she said, and chewed the forkful, which almost scorched the roof of her mouth. "I know, Granny. You know all the things."

"Indeed, I do," Granny said, and returned the top back to the large stainless steel pot she had almost filled to the top with collard greens. "Just like I know what happened last night has something to do with that raggedy man you married after I told you not to."

Vanna didn't even bother rolling her eyes or attempting to find an excuse to leave this conversation. She'd known it was coming. Last night, when she'd told Granny to stay here and there'd been no argument, she'd thought her grandmother might start this talk then. But, blessedly, she hadn't. They'd both gone straight to bed. Granny was not a morning person, unless there was a man in her bed she wanted to hurry out—as was the case whenever her "little boy toy," as she referred to Sam from the senior center, paid her a visit after dinner. So when Vanna had gotten up to get ready for work, Granny and Frito were still in the guest room, snoring.

From the day Vanna had settled on this house—yes, it was in her name only because Caleb had been unemployed and she'd been pre-approved for a home loan based on her own income—Granny'd had a key. Caleb had been perturbed by that thought, claiming he didn't want her popping up on them unexpectedly, but Vanna quickly ended that remark by flashing the mortgage-payment book with only her name printed on it in front of him. Granny was wearing different clothes from what she'd worn last night, which meant whenever she'd gotten up, she'd gone home, showered, changed, and then went to the market to get all the food she needed for tonight's meal.

"You might as well go ahead and tell me the details," Granny prompted when Vanna hadn't replied.

"I think it involves Caleb," she said, and tossed the fork she used into the sink. "The detectives didn't tell me much before I asked for a lawyer."

"Well, that was smart. But you need to find out what that man has dragged you into, because now that he's in the grave, you've got to answer for it by yourself." Granny crossed the room to the refrigerator and yanked it open. "And don't think I can't see how much of a coincidence this is that he floats up in the water dead as a doornail one day, and not a week later some dusty cops show up and put you in cuffs."

She pulled out the pitcher of iced tea and set it on the counter. Vanna went to the cabinet to get them both a glass. With glasses in hand, she went to the island and set them down. Granny went back into the refrigerator and pulled out the carton of lemonade.

"I don't think that's a coincidence either," she said quietly. Absently, she ran a finger along one of the gray marble lines in the island top. "They said something about a bank account that had both our names on it. But I know Caleb, and I talked about splitting everything when I put him out. He even brought me some papers to sign and get notarized from the credit union so that we could make it happen."

Granny picked up the glasses and went back to the refrigerator to use the ice machine. When she returned, Vanna picked up the pitcher of tea and poured some into the glasses first. Granny always poured too much tea in the half-and-half mixture, so Vanna wanted to be in charge of that part. Granny poured the lemonade. Then she stuck a finger into the glass in front of her and stirred.

How many times had Vanna seen her grandmother do that with a mixed alcoholic drink? The thought had a ghost of a smile appearing on her face.

"He was always a sneaky bastard, Vannie. I don't put anything past him, not even now that he's gone," Granny said, and took a sip. "He did something bad, I just know it."

Vanna could only shake her head before sipping from her own glass. She didn't disagree with her grandmother. Not about anything she'd just said. It had taken Vanna a long time to come to terms with the truth about the man she'd married, and in the months leading up to this birthday, she'd realized it was time for her to accept that she'd made a mistake and finally, totally, move on from it.

"Well, unfortunately, I'm gonna find out all the details soon enough. But for now," she said, recalling what her new attorney, Jovani, had instructed, "I'm going to continue with the second FFSF weekend celebration."

It may have been too late for her to start the belated divorce proceedings, but it wasn't too late to focus on her new beginning.

Granny smiled when she looked over at her. "That's my girl," she said. "Keep your head up."

"I plan to," Vanna told her. "I'm going up to shower and change. Jamaica and Ronni will be here in an hour, and we can get our dinner-and-a-Madea-movie night started!"

"Lawd, I don't know why you like those movies. That man don't know how to be a woman. Looks a holy mess on that screen."

"But you laugh right through each movie," Vanna said before she drank from her glass again, then stepped away from the island.

"Sure do," Granny said. "Funny is funny."

Vanna chuckled as she walked toward the stairs.

"That shit was not funny at all," Jamaica said. She was sitting in the corner of Vanna's royal blue sectional with her legs stretched out on the long portion of the furniture. "Every time I watch this part, it makes me angrier and angrier."

Which was why Vanna had saved this movie for last. She'd known exactly what Jamaica's reaction was going to be and figured it would be better to send her home pissed off to Davon instead of having her sit through another movie here. This was the third and final Madea movie they would watch tonight, since it was already ten forty and they were only five minutes into it.

"If Davon ever thought he was going to drag me out of my house and toss me on the porch, I would burn that shit down with him in it," Jamaica proclaimed.

Nobody responded because everyone in the room believed her. Vanna sat at the other end of the sectional with her legs curled at her side. Ronni had set up a blanket and pillows she'd retrieved from the couch in the basement on the floor at the foot of the sectional where Jamaica was stretched out. Granny, who was laid out on the recliner Vanna had bought especially for her, had asked Ronni if she thought she was having a picnic with her children.

"Men like him need to be shot in the balls," Granny said, and crossed one ankle over the other.

"Exactly!" Jamaica chimed. "And I'm the right one to do it."

"I always feel so bad for her in this movie," Ronni said. "It took her so long to recover from everything he did to her, and then he goes and gets shot and he guilt-trips her into taking care of him."

"She should've pushed his ass into oncoming traffic while he was in that wheelchair," Jamaica snapped.

"Well, she did get her lick back," Vanna added, before forking another piece of the lemon meringue pie Granny had bought from the bakery.

"I guess that's worth something," Jamaica replied. "Speaking of which, you ready to talk about what happened last night?"

For the second time this evening, Vanna settled into a sense of dread over a conversation she knew she would have to have sooner or later.

"Don't look at me," Granny said. "I already said my piece. These two been hanging tight with you for a long time. I don't know why you didn't think they'd want the details too."

She had looked to Granny without noticing it. Had she thought her grandmother would say or do something to deflect this conversation? She should've known better.

"So, wait, you were really planning not to tell us?" Ronni turned her attention to Vanna, her brow creased. "I thought we were giving you space."

"That space thing was your idea," Jamaica said. "I wanted to call her when I went on my break earlier today. But since I knew we would be here tonight, I waited."

"Well, now I know why the two of you didn't bail on me tonight," Vanna said. She leaned over and set her small paper plate with the last chunk of her pie on the end table.

"Not fair—your nephew was sick last week. And besides, we did the spa day and church. Plus, we promised not to miss any more of the birthday activities," Ronni replied, her tone almost a whine.

"She's avoiding the question," Jamaica said through pursed lips. "Spill it."

Vanna sighed. "Since we're obviously not interested in this last movie . . .," she began.

"We've all seen this movie a dozen times, and I told you it wasn't that good the first time," Granny said, and smacked a hand to the button on the side of the recliner until it brought her up to a sitting position. "I need something else to drink."

And since she and Vanna had already had this conversation earlier, Granny wasn't trying to stay for a replay.

"Again," Jamaica said, "spill."

"Okay, okay," Vanna replied. "I don't really know that much. The charge was embezzlement, which you heard at the cemetery. You know I was gonna take advantage of my right to remain silent, so my conversation with the cops was quick. There's a bank account with a crazy amount of money in it. They say it's in me and Caleb's name. They asked me when was the last time I saw Caleb, and I requested my lawyer." She shrugged. "And that's it."

"Wait, you and Caleb still have a joint account?" Ronni asked.

"No," Vanna replied quickly. "We don't. The checking and savings accounts we had together at my bank, I closed before I even told him to leave. All the money in those accounts was mine, so I just opened new solo accounts. He had credit union accounts from when he worked for the city, but I filled out all the paperwork to have my name removed a few months after he moved out. So I don't know what they're talking about."

"Sounds fishy," Jamaica said.

"Real fishy," Ronni echoed.

"Right. So I talked to the lawyer this morning, and he said he was looking into it and that we'd talk about it in more detail on Monday and make a plan." She shrugged. "That's it. I've been fingerprinted, had a mug shot taken, sat in a cell with Kita and some of her friends, and have some papers upstairs with a next court date printed on them. All in the same twenty-four hours that I buried my estranged husband."

Ronni got up from where she was sitting and came over to drop down onto the couch beside Vanna, who quickly moved her legs out of the way. Ronni pulled her into a hug. "Oh, sweetie. I'm so sorry this happened."

"I don't like this," Jamaica said. "I know you don't have all the details, but I don't have a good feeling about this."

Easing her head up from where she'd momentarily let it rest on Ronni's shoulder, Vanna replied, "And you're the one who gets to stand on the other side of the locked cell door. Imagine how I'm feeling."

"I did imagine it," Jamaica replied. "All last night while we were waiting to hear from you, I was picturing you in there, and my stomach twisted. But what I'm saying is, I don't feel good about where this might lead. Caleb obviously got you mixed up in something."

"We haven't even been talking that much these last few months. I mean, not like the every couple of weeks he used to hit me up, asking if we could talk." She'd been amazed that all these years after their separation, Caleb had still thought they had something to talk about. She always declined, and when he'd finally stopped completely, she couldn't lie—it had been a weird change for her.

"Is this lawyer any good?" Ronni asked.

"I asked around about him at work today," Jamaica said. "He's damn good. If I'd heard anything different, I would've called you and told you to find someone else. He's pretty expensive too, so let me know if you need anything to get this taken care of."

"Oh, yeah, right. I have some money in my private account too," Ronni said. "I can help out."

Ronni worked as a part-time secretary at the elementary school where Wyatt, her seven-year-old, attended. Her middle child and only girl, Tasia, was four and attended the church day care, along with Jonah, during the hours she was at work.

Vanna shook her head. "I don't want you dipping into your private stash," she told Ronni, and prayed they would avoid the conversation of whether women should keep a separate bank account from their spouses. They'd had it so many times, and where it had exhausted Vanna before, considering the present circumstances, she definitely didn't want to go through it again.

"Don't get all proud on us," Jamaica said. "You know how we roll. If either of us are in need, we've got each other's back."

And that was true, had been for as long as Vanna could recall. But just as she'd never imagined herself being in jail, she couldn't even fathom accepting money from her friends to get her out of this legal trouble.

"Aden paid for it already," she blurted out, and noted the raised brows and widened eyes of both her friends seconds before the doorbell rang.

Vanna jumped at the sound and so did Frito, who'd been sleeping at the edge of the blanket where Ronni had been sitting. Now he jumped his compact little body up and charged through the room and down the couple of stairs to the door, barking like he was a pit bull instead of a noisy little runt.

"Who in the world?" Granny said, echoing everybody's thoughts as she came back into the living room area. "It's eleven o'clock at night. You got a booty call you ain't tell us about, Vannie?"

Standing, Vanna ignored that question.

Jamaica snickered. "Lord knows, she needs one right about now."

Granny made it to the door just as Vanna started down the stairs, and they both froze in shock once they saw the person on the other side.

"Hey," Aden said, giving Granny a surprised smile. Frito was at his feet, dancing around and continuing his barking greeting. "Hey, little guy. Good to see you again."

Vanna watched as Aden eased down into a squat and scrubbed behind Frito's ears the way she sometimes did.

"Boy, what are you doing here at this time of night?" Granny asked, taking the words right out of Vanna's mouth again.

When Aden stood once more, his gaze found Vanna's, and he waved. Then he returned his attention to Granny. "Ah, I was in the neighborhood, coming back from a networking event, and thought I'd stop by to see how Vanna was doing."

Granny folded her arms over her chest. "You know what time it is?"

"Yes, ma'am, I do. And I apologize for the late hour. I thought about getting in touch with Vanna earlier today, but I didn't have her phone number." He was actually standing there answering Granny's questions, like he was a teenage boy knocking on her door at this time of night.

When she was a teenager, all Vanna's boyfriends and boy *friends* (romantic *and* platonic) had known of Granny's wicked tongue and were trained not to knock on her door after eight at night.

"So, you don't have her phone number, but you have her address? Tell me how that works?" Granny asked.

Vanna walked down the last step and came to put a hand on Granny's shoulder. "I can take it from here," she said, giving her grandmother a light smile, then turning the same to Aden.

"I know you can, but I have questions," Granny continued.

"And I'll get the answers," Vanna told her. "Now, please get your dog before he wakes up the entire neighborhood or runs out into the street. Neither of which I feel like dealing with tonight."

"*Hmpff,*" was Granny's only response, before she bent down and scooped up her dog, then walked back up the stairs.

Vanna waited until she heard her grandmother's slippered feet shuffling across the living room floor before she spoke again. "How *did* you get my address?" she asked him.

He gave a little nod and pushed his hands into the front pockets of his dark-brown slacks. "Caleb invited me to a get-together he was doing for the brothers a while back, and I couldn't come. But it had been some time since I'd heard from him, so I saved his number and address in my phone so we could get better at keeping in touch."

She narrowed her gaze at him, forcing herself to watch him strictly as a friend of Caleb's and nothing more. It occurred to her then that she'd done this on previous occasions.

Aden pulled his phone out of his pocket. "Do you want to see the saved contact?"

When she didn't immediately respond, he swiped a finger over his phone, then leaned in closer to put his phone up to her face.

She read the entry for Caleb Carlson and relaxed her stance just a bit. "It's still pretty late for a wellness check."

"You're right," he said, pulling the phone back and slipping it into his pocket. "But like I told Granny, I was worried about you all day."

"Why?" It was a clipped question, and she instantly felt weird about it, so she continued, "I mean, we haven't seen each other since college."

He hadn't attended the big cookout-style reception Granny had thrown for them after the wedding. And Caleb hadn't mentioned him at all during that time, so she was a little shocked that he'd reached out to Aden at some point. She remembered the get-together Caleb had suggested, and she'd done all the legwork for. It was during the summer, and she'd rented tents, tables, and chairs; hired a DJ; and helped Granny cook all the food. Two months later, she put Caleb out of her house.

"I know." His expression sobered, but his gaze remained intent. "I've been feeling a way about that too. So I wanted to make sure you were good."

She wanted to ask what that meant because it felt like it meant more than just those words. Was she serious right now? This was so out of bounds, from him being here to her even attempting to entertain that it might mean something more than what it appeared. She felt like the twenty-two-year-old she'd been when she first met him.

"I'm fine," she said, and cleared her throat. "Just having a movie night to celebrate my birthday with Granny and my girls."

"Oh, it's your birthday?" He looked genuinely surprised.

"No," she said with a shake of her head. "Not today. At the end of this month, but I'm celebrating with activities every weekend." And why had she just told him all that? "Look, thanks for stopping by. I appreciate your concern, but like I said, I'm fine."

"Good," he said. "I'm glad to see you're holding up."

"She is because we've got pie and Moscato," Jamaica said from the top of the stairs. "Why don't the two of you stop letting the mosquitos in and come get some."

Jamaica walked away as quickly as she'd seemed to appear, and when Vanna returned her attention to Aden, it was to see him grinning.

"Your people don't play about you," he said. "I like that."

"Yeah," she admitted. "I like it too."

"So, I'd planned to ask if you wanted to go out and grab a cup of coffee, catch up or something. And before you say it, I know it's late. I just . . ." He shrugged. "I don't know, I just really wanted to see you."

And that was different. It was odd and she knew it; she just didn't know what to do about it. Just like she hadn't known how to handle it when they'd had these awkward interactions while she and Caleb were dating back in college.

"I don't . . . ah . . . I'm not sure that's a good idea," she said.

"Well, he did pay for your lawyer," said Ronni, who was now at the top of the stairs. "The least you can do is go get coffee with the man to say thank you."

She didn't know how she'd forgotten about that. Perhaps because he looked just as good as he had in that suit at the funeral—and the jeans in the parking lot of the police station—as he did standing here right now, dressed in shades of brown.

"Right, I should thank you for that. Even though I don't know why you did it. I can pay you back. Just tell me how much it was and I'll—"

"Have coffee with me," he said. "That's how you can thank me."

Chapter 8

Twenty minutes later, Vanna reminded herself that it was *just* coffee. She hadn't even bothered to change out of the gray leggings and pink off-the-shoulder T-shirt she was wearing. She'd simply slipped her feet into a pair of Crocs, grabbed her phone, keys, and purse, and walked out the door. All while he waited in the living room with three women and a surly dog staring at him.

"I can't believe it's been so long since we've seen each other," he said when they were settled in a booth toward the back of one of the few diners open at this hour.

"I know," she replied. "And right about now, I feel like those nights after we'd hit the club and we were all starving, so we found a spot to eat." The memory made her smile.

He chuckled too. "You're right. It was usually IHOP, though, and you always ordered breakfast food."

"Well, it was morning." She reached for the thick menu on the table in front of her. "It was in the wee early-morning hours, but still. Plus, I can eat breakfast food at any time of day or night."

"Yeah, I remember that about you."

Her head snapped up, and she saw that he hadn't picked up his menu but was watching her. She sighed and thought, *Fuck it.* Setting the menu down on the table again, she eased back against the seat. "What is this, Aden? And don't tell me you just wanted to check on me again, because I think we both know that's not totally true."

He mimicked her moves and sat back against his seat. "You wanna do this right now? Tonight?"

"If by 'this,' you mean be honest with each other? Yeah," she said with a nod. "I want to do this right now. I'm too old for games, and tomorrow's not promised, so say what you have to say."

She sounded like a combination of the cards from her affirmation and motivation box. She should've pulled one out tonight when she'd gone up to her room to grab her shoes. But now she'd have to wing it.

"Okay, I wanted to see you again," he said. "I just wanted to see you."

"Why?" She toyed with the hem of her shirt.

There was a moment of silence between them. Their gazes held, but neither of them spoke. Then his shoulders rose and fell as he sucked in a breath and released it.

"I met you first," he said. "You remember that?"

Oh, wow. She did remember, so she nodded.

"We were at that rally in the park, and you dropped the flyers," he said.

"And you picked them up like we were a meet-cute scene in some romance movie." Why in the world did she say that? They didn't have a meet-cute, did they?

His grin was slow to spread this time, and he dragged his tongue over his lower lip. Something no man who looks like him should do at this time of night when he's sitting across from a woman as sexually deprived as she'd been these past few months.

"Yeah, it did feel like that, didn't it?"

No. No, it did not, her mind screamed, but she nodded.

"You smiled when you said thank you, and I thought my heart was gonna stop," he told her, and shook his head. "I was like, what the hell is goin' on? Having quick physical reactions like that to a shorty wasn't my thing."

"Oh, come on, now, you are not gonna sit here and try to tell me you never had a purely physical reaction to a woman before. Especially not when you were in college."

"Well, I mean, if you're talkin' about did I see a fine girl and I got aroused, hell yeah, that used to happen. But this was different."

The way his tone shifted when he'd said that last sentence had her pulse quickening. *Stop it! Stop it, Savannah!* Screaming at herself was the best reminder of who and what she was at this very moment. A grown-ass woman who'd just buried a man she'd dedicated way too much of her time and energy to. A man who had, once upon a time, happened to be this guy's close friend.

"Y'all like to toss that word *different* out there," she replied. How many times had one of those early conversations with a new guy included "You're different from the women I'm used to meeting," or "I like you because I can tell you're different," only for them to end up treating her the same way they'd treated all the other women before? Too damn many.

"That's what Caleb said about you too," he told her. "When he came back over to our table that night at the step competition. We asked where he'd been for so long because he'd said he was just going to the concession stand. And he said he'd met this girl, and that just the way you looked at him when you talked was different."

Why did he remember that? Of course Vanna remembered every detail about the night she'd first met Caleb, but why would Aden remember it?

He dragged a hand over his neatly cut goatee. "I was like, word? And then when we were leaving, he pointed you out and I felt sick to my stomach."

"Me too," she said. "Those jeans were so damned tight I was afraid I might faint from poor circulation." She tried to joke because the look on his face was too serious, too potent. But she hadn't lied—when she'd finally peeled those jeans off that night, the etchings from the seam, zipper, and snap were red marks along her skin.

"Nah," he said, half his mouth lifting in a sad smile. "Those jeans looked fuckin' perfect. Everything about you looked perfect that night, just like it did that day I met you a week before the step show."

She cleared her throat because his potent look had just ratcheted up the heat in this joint. Aden had root beer–brown eyes, but as he'd been talking to her, they'd gone almost black, the timbre of his voice dipped just a tad lower, and something flipped and flopped in her stomach that she knew wasn't hunger because she'd eaten enough at home.

"Then Caleb and I became a couple, and Jamaica and I became a part of your circle," she said, because what the hell else was she supposed to say?

That she'd thought he was fine that day they first met too? And that she'd been a little jolted by seeing him again at the step show, but Caleb had already sent her pulse into a frenzy with his attention and goofy demeanor? She'd always been a sucker for a man who could make her laugh.

"Nah," he said with a slow shake of his head. "You wanted honesty, don't pull back on me now."

She sighed. "You're right." Now she settled her hands on top of the menu, clasping her fingers, which just didn't want to remain still. "I thought there was something between us that day in the park. But the interaction was so brief. There was so much going on that day. We didn't even get each other's names." Which, later that night, she'd thought was kind of romantic. Again, like something in a movie. They had this encounter and then walked away without knowing how to get in contact with each other, but they were both longing for the other. Such wild nonsense that she almost cringed at the thought now.

"I know. I kept looking for you on campus that week, hoping I'd bump into you again. I was definitely going to get your name and hopefully your number that time."

His phone rang and he pulled it out of his pocket. He glanced at the screen momentarily, swiped to dismiss the call, then put it back. All the while she watched him move, her gaze transfixed by the deep-mocha hue of his skin, bared by the short-sleeve beige shirt he wore. There was a tattoo on his right bicep—the Greek letters of his frat, she recognized by the bottom half she could see. She wondered if he had more ink on his beautiful skin.

"You had a girlfriend," she blurted out. "When we all went to the movies together that first time, she was with you."

"She was a date, not a girlfriend. I was still nursing some feelings of regret for not making a move on the girl with the pretty smile and great taste in jeans," he said.

Vanna had been thick all her life, and she'd never lacked for attention from guys. She knew how to dress to accentuate all her best features and loved the admiration she received for her efforts. Yet she hadn't forgotten the way Aden had looked at her that first day, or many times after that.

"You and Yvette eventually became a couple," she said. "You dated her until y'all graduated. What happened after that?"

"We stopped dating," he said with a shrug.

"Did you ever get married?"

"No," was his quick reply. "And I wished you hadn't either. At least, not to Caleb."

Oh. That was a turn she hadn't expected in this conversation she'd never imagined having, and she couldn't have been more thankful for the server who approached them at that moment. They turned their attention to the menus at that point. He ordered food, and she requested that coffee that he'd offered her because she was going to need something strong to keep her wits together during the rest of this interlude. And not alcoholic strong, because that, coupled with the hum of sexual tension circling them, would surely make a dangerous combination.

"So," he said after the server left them to put their order in, "tell me what you've been doing these last fifteen years."

She was just about to say *living through an emotionally exhausting marriage*, when he held up a hand. "Tell me about what *you've* been doing, not about who you were married to or what that relationship was like."

"The two are intricately entwined," she said, then huffed. "Even after death, it seems."

"Hey," he said, and reached a hand across the table to take hers.

She stared down at this connection, his fingers moving along the back of her hand, turning it around until their fingers linked. It was meant to be a casual touch, she knew, but it felt deeper, more intimate. That thought didn't scare her as much as it probably should've.

"Jovani's a great lawyer. He's going to get to the bottom of whatever is going on," he said.

"Why did you pay him for me? Why are you here now?" She frowned as she looked up at him. For as much as she'd always known she could take care of herself, she wasn't averse to men doing nice things for her. She just hadn't experienced that interaction frequently.

"This is the weirdest reunion, Aden," she said honestly. "First, we meet and there's this buzz of . . . I don't know, something. Then we meet again, and I'm with Caleb and you're with Yvette. We spend a couple of years around each other more than we were around our family, and then we don't see each other again until fifteen years later. When Caleb dies." She released a heavy sigh and felt the prick of tears. "This has been an eventful first two weeks of my birthday month."

He squeezed her hand. "Then how 'bout we focus on making the next two weeks better?"

Bowling on Saturday was definitely a better excursion than Vanna's solo club venture last weekend. Jamaica and Ronni had laughed till they had tears in their eyes as she told them about how she'd skedaddled out of that parking lot when Tyson's baby mama showed up. And she would be forever grateful that even though she'd been ready to follow him to that hotel and ride him like a racehorse, she had yet to give him her phone number, which meant they'd had no further interaction since that night.

Bowling was something Vanna didn't do often, but she did enjoy it. For a couple of years, Caleb had been part of a league, so she'd spent some time at bowling alleys, trying to support him. And on weekends when he would practice, she would join him. She didn't want to feel like tonight was paying any homage to him, but from the moment she woke up this morning, he'd been on her mind.

And not just Caleb, but also their college years, their friends, the life they built together. Aden.

Vanna had always treated her experience with guys as an adventure. It was fun flirting and meeting them, nice when she allowed some of those meetings and flirtations to turn intimate, and, more often than not, disastrous when their end came. Caleb hadn't been her first run of bad luck with a guy. He had just been her longest. Still, each time had seemed to hammer home the fact that she wasn't meant to be in a lasting and loving relationship. She wasn't meant to be loved and cherished.

A heavy sigh followed that observation.

One small positive thought in the morning can change your whole day.

The favored words from one of her cards in the box popped into her head like an alarm reminding her that she could choose to be happy.

Not yet ready to get out of bed, she rolled onto her back and stared up at the ceiling, returning her thoughts to the man she'd spent two hours talking to at a diner last night. Or rather, earlier this morning, because it had been almost two thirty when he'd dropped her off at her house. Jamaica had texted her not long after she'd left the house to let her know they were leaving, and that, yes, she would follow Granny home to make sure she got there safely. And Vanna had texted their group thread to let Jamaica and Ronni know when she'd arrived home. Jamaica's reply had come quickly.

Jamaica: We want all the details at first daylight

A slow turn of Vanna's head showed that the large, bright numbers on the clock on her nightstand read 7:23 a.m. She'd always been a morning person, even though she woke up groggily; she couldn't sleep late into the morning unless she was sick. The sun was up, she could see the golden rays trying to peek through the closed blinds at her window, but she made no move to pick up her phone and give her friends the details she knew they were both waiting for.

There weren't any details to give. Unless they wanted to know that she'd revealed to this man—who had once been a very close friend of her husband's—that a long time ago, she'd had a crush on him. And he, apparently, had had a crush on her too. She still didn't know how to feel about that. For a brief moment after she'd arrived home last night and climbed into bed, she'd allowed herself to wonder what her life would've been like if she and Aden had exchanged names and numbers that day at the park. She would've never met Caleb under the circumstances that they had and would have gone on to become romantically involved with Aden, because that man was just as fine back then as he was now. Would they have gotten married? Had children? Would he have been the happily ever after she craved but was afraid to hope for?

She dropped an arm over her eyes and groaned. That line of thought had been pointless last night and was even more so in the morning. Especially since there *had* been Caleb, and she *had* loved that man to distraction. Why else would she have given him all those years? More importantly—and the point she kept trying to push out of her mind, but because it was such a big damn deal, it kept resurfacing—what the hell had Caleb gotten her involved in?

In two more days, she would hopefully find out more, but damn if she didn't want all the answers now. Was she actually in danger of being sentenced to a long term in prison now? She knew what embezzlement was, but since she'd only worked in torts and litigation during her career in the legal field, she didn't know the specifics on the actual charge, and the sentences that went along with it. So she'd researched, and succeeded in scaring herself even more at the implications.

Being charged with conspiracy to embezzle, she could get some crazy fines, probation, or a combination of all the above. What in the world was her life now? This was supposed to be her birthday-celebration month, she was supposed to be in a perpetual good mood from the first of August until the big birthday-dinner party she had planned for the 31st. Yet here she was, getting another headache from worrying over some mess she hadn't gotten herself into, nor could she get herself out of on her own.

For as much as she cherished the people closest to her—Granny, Jamaica, and Ronni—and knew they were her ride-or-dies until the very end, Vanna hated depending on anyone. As a child, she'd depended on her mother for love and affection, and Diane had paid her dirt. Vanna vowed she'd never need someone like that again. There'd been a part of her that had even held back from Caleb. While she'd given their marriage 98 percent, the 2 percent she'd kept locked tight was a result of having been disappointed far too many times before. Now, if she ever even considered another serious relationship, unfortunately that person would only get part of her. At this point in her life, she wasn't willing to risk any more than that.

Her bladder wouldn't let her lie in that bed with racing thoughts a moment longer. She pushed the sheets off and got up.

Just as she came out of the bathroom, her phone chimed from the nightstand with a notification.

"All right, y'all, it's barely eight on a Saturday morning. So damn impatient," she said as her bare feet padded over the wheat-colored carpet on her bedroom floor.

But when she picked up the phone and swiped to view the text, she was surprised to see that it wasn't from the *J&R* thread, as she'd named it.

Aden: Good morning, beautiful.

"Oh. My. Gracious," she whispered.

Aden Granger, whom she'd learned last night was a former adviser at one of the largest financial firms on the East Coast and now owned a gym and a nutritional supplement line, was not sending her "Good morning" texts. But yeah, he was, she thought again, this time with a smile spreading across her face.

Vanna: Good morning.

She was not calling him *handsome* via text. Or *fine af.* Or *damn delectable.* Nope. She was not.

Aden: Did you sleep well?

Vanna: I did. You?

It wasn't really a lie. When she'd finally been able to fall asleep, it had been that deep, restful type of sleep. Which was probably why she'd been able to sleep until seven.

Aden: I did. Can I take you to dinner tonight?

Oh no! Last night had been a coffee to say thanks, and everyone had agreed she should go because she owed him that much. So she'd gone and it had been fine, but dinner? Tonight? What would that mean? Her worrisome thoughts were growing louder and louder, and she really needed them to calm down. The butterflies that had immediately awakened at the sight of Aden's first text weren't helping the situation. And now she had to figure out how to get out of . . . Oh, wait, she had an excuse.

Vanna: Sorry. Can't. FFSF Week #2 is Bowling Night.

Aden: FFSF???

She managed another smile as she whispered and typed the words that instantly came to her mind.

Vanna: Freakin' Forty and Still Fine. It's my birthday mantra.

Aden: 🖤 I love it! And I'm a pretty decent bowler. What time and which location?

She dropped onto her bed, holding the phone in both hands now as she stared down at it in shock. Was he inviting himself to her birthday celebration? Should she tell him no, he couldn't come? Why would he even want to come? He hadn't celebrated a birthday with her before. This was weird as hell.

Twisting her lips as she tried to think this through, she held the phone tighter. She and Aden had admitted they'd liked each other last night. But that was *liked*, past tense. And he'd shown up at her husband's funeral. She had to stop saying that like she and Caleb were happily married. They'd been separated, just not legally divorced; so not technically an ex—or estranged, as she most often thought of it. Still, Aden didn't know that. Or did he? She had no clue what Aden knew about her marriage to Caleb; he'd admitted himself that they hadn't kept in touch. So him turning up at the funeral was odd. Well, maybe not. He was in the fraternity with Caleb, so him turning up at the funeral wasn't that strange. Him showing up here last night was. Unless he liked her now too.

Her fingers flew over the screen to open the J&R text thread, the one she used most.

Vanna: Help! Aden wants to come bowling with us tonight. How do I tell him no, stay the hell away from me?

She bit her bottom lip and tapped her nail on the screen of the phone while she waited for one of them to reply. It would probably be Ronni first. She'd definitely be up at this time of morning, with her house full of kids. Plus, she did her market run on Saturday mornings because that's when she could leave the kids with Croy. She usually sat at a Starbucks for forty minutes either reading or just people-watching because she said she had to build her self-care time into her other responsibilities. Granny would say she did it so Croy wouldn't call her lazy and selfish and chastise her like she was the child. Vanna tried really hard not to tell her friends how to live in their relationships, especially not after her marriage turned out the way it had.

Jamaica: WTH did you put on him last night? Did you give him head on the first date?

Whoa! What?

Vanna: First, last night wasn't a date. It was coffee. To say thanks.

Ronni: That was a long ass coffee date. You home alone, or is he still there?
I can be there in 10

They couldn't see her shaking her head, and she wasn't about to type *smh*. They'd know exactly how she was side-eyeing this conversation.

Vanna: No head. Just coffee. And now he wants to go bowling? I don't think so.

Ronni: Well, it is a group outing.

Vanna: It is not! It's my birthday outing.

Jamaica: Tell him to bring a gift.

Vanna: I don't want no gifts from that man

Ronni: Technically, he already gave you one. The lawyer.

Now Vanna rolled her eyes. She shouldn't have even told them this. She should've just answered Aden on her own.

Aden: You still there?

Oh, damn, she'd forgotten he was waiting for an answer. On a sigh, she got out of one text thread and opened the other.

Vanna: Yeah. Just got up. Had to go potty.

Well, that was definitely TMI. She groaned.

Jamaica: If you want him to come and don't want it to feel awkward, I can bring Davon

Ronni: Yeah, I can bring Croy too. But you gotta let me know now so I can see if mama will babysit

She was just about to answer them with a resounding *no* when Aden replied:

Aden: Bowling?

Now she closed her eyes and resisted the urge to scream. This wasn't what she'd planned at all. It was just going to be the three of them, Granny, and maybe her neighbor Joanne, but she wasn't sure about her because Joanne never remembered anything. Which was partially why Vanna had invited her. During one of the weirdest coincidences, Joanne had been in the party store when Vanna was picking up items for her dinner party later this month, so she'd had to tell her it was her birthday. Luckily for her, Joanne said she had plans most of the weekends, except this one, so she'd felt compelled to invite her. But that had been three weeks ago. Joanne hadn't said a word about coming since then.

Jamaica: Davon is cool with coming. He wants to know if we need to bring our own drinks or is there a bar at the bowling alley

Ronni: Let me text Croy right now

Vanna groaned again. She hated feeling like things were spiraling out of control, and for the past two weeks that's exactly how she'd felt. After another heavy sigh, she went back to the first text thread and replied.

Vanna: 7pm Larabee Lanes on Canal

Aden: Cool. See ya then

And since that was how all this started, there was no way for her to know how great the night would turn out.

By their final game, the third one after they'd consumed two of those awful pizzas, a bucket of french fries, and a couple of pitchers of beer and fruit punch, she was relaxed and laughing. Even though her birthday celebration had turned into a triple date. Granny had canceled, preferring to stay at the senior center, where they were playing strip bingo. Vanna prayed her grandmother had just said the wrong thing and that wasn't exactly what was happening at the high-rise building, where the minimum age of each tenant was sixty-five. And, as Vanna had expected she would, Joanne had forgotten.

So Aden, who had arrived dressed in a gray running suit, tennis shoes, and a smile, made Davon's bright idea of boys against girls an even better-looking one now that they were even. And instead of being overwhelmed by the entire setup, what she probably should've been chanting was, *Oh, hell yes, Aden showed up wearing gray sweatpants!*

But she'd been able to remain focused enough to help her team beat the socks off the guys for the first two games.

"Yeaahhh!" Davon yelled, pumping his fist after he gave his team a much-needed strike.

"We got this, man. We got this!" Aden dapped him up and nodded.

Croy clapped a hand on Davon's shoulder as he passed him to step up and take his turn. "This one is ours."

"That's right, y'all pump each other up!" Jamaica said from where she sat on the edge of the bench.

"It's a little late for all that morale-boosting, though," Ronni said, and laughed.

Vanna tried to keep her giggles to a minimum, especially since Aden had dropped himself onto the bench right beside her.

"You think that's funny?" he asked.

She shrugged and chuckled again. "I mean, she's not lying."

He gave her a playful nudge. "We can play another game or two, just to see who's really the best. We had to get warmed up."

"Oh, that's what it is, huh?" she asked.

"Yeah. You ladies had the advantage; you've played together before. This is my first time with the fellas, so we had to find our rhythm," he said.

"Oh, I'd say you are finding a rhythm just fine, sir," Jamaica said, and Vanna knew she wasn't talking about bowling.

Clearing her throat, Vanna stood and walked over to the table where their food and drinks were since they couldn't have them down on the game floor where the benches were. Luckily, the table was close enough for them to keep an eye on, so she picked up her glass and finished the fruit punch she'd poured a while ago. She didn't like beer, and when the bartender on duty had fixed her the worst mojito she'd ever had when they first arrived, she'd decided to stick with juice.

By the time she made it back to the bench, Jamaica was still talking. "So, what are your intentions here, Aden?"

Vanna almost choked at the question. She froze and considered turning around and making a trip to the bathroom until this conversation was over.

He frowned at Jamaica, then looked up to meet Vanna's gaze. "I'm here to help Vanna celebrate her birthday."

Why did that make her feel all warm and tingly inside? Like, really, they were just words, and yet . . . "He's right. We're all here to celebrate my birthday. The big four-oh," she said, and tried to act like those damn butterflies weren't back and having a whole party in her stomach.

"Not what I meant, and both of you know it," Jamaica said with a smirk. "You haven't been around in fifteen years. Where have you been, and why pop up now and suddenly want to celebrate her birthday? She's had a lifetime of them without you."

Jamaica could be as bad as Granny with her slick mouth, and usually it didn't bother Vanna because she didn't normally bite her tongue either. She also tried not to embarrass the hell out of her friends when she could help it. There was also the fact that the question she'd just asked had been one gnawing at Vanna too. So instead of penalizing her friend, she kept moving until she was seated again.

Aden looked from her to Jamaica, then gave a small nod. "That's a fair question," he replied. "As I told Vanna last night, I worked for Tomlin Karn at the office here in DC for five years. Then I moved down to their Miami office for seven years. Just came home three years ago and opened my gym."

"Really?" asked Ronni, who had been sitting at the scoreboard table but was still listening to their conversation. "Croy works at Tomlin Karn. He's been there for two years."

Aden nodded. "It's a great firm."

"He also has a nutritional supplement line he's launching next month," Vanna added, because he had already given her his career rundown. And she had to admit to being extremely impressed with how much he'd accomplished and how much more he set out to do.

Jamaica narrowed her gaze at him, but she crossed one leg over the other and finally nodded. "Good, you're not broke, so she won't have to pay your car payments and buy your clothes."

"And that's enough now," Vanna told her, immensely embarrassed. She prayed Aden wouldn't take Jamaica's words to heart. While her friends knew all that she'd put into her marriage emotionally and financially, she didn't want that information broadcast. Didn't want anyone knowing just how much of a fool she'd been for love.

Ronni leaned over and slapped Jamaica's knee down. "You never know when to shut it off. Get up there and take your turn."

Jamaica had the decency to toss Aden an apologetic look. "You know how I am about my girl."

He nodded. "I do. But you don't have to worry—I've got her now."

Ah, what?

Her expression must have screamed those words, because when he turned back to her, he gave her a tentative half smile. "I just meant I can pay your bills and mine if that's what's required. But I'm definitely not here to use or hurt you in any way."

When she didn't immediately respond, he reached for her hands, holding them both in his. "I didn't know it was your birthday when I showed up at the funeral. But the one thing I did know was that if this turned out to be another shot with you, I wasn't missing it again."

Chapter 9

Later, after bowling and drinks and dancing at Glitz because Ronni had mentioned missing it last week, Vanna walked into her house recalling Aden's words about not missing another shot with her.

"You sure about this?" he asked from behind her as he closed the door.

She turned to him and took a deep breath before replying, "Remember I told you tomorrow's not promised?"

"I do." He remained where he was and folded his arms over his chest. "And I agree. I'm just trying to be certain the three mojitos you had at the club weren't making decisions for you."

She closed the distance between them and reached out to push the hem of his hoodie up enough so that she could grasp the elastic band of the joggers he wore.

"First, I'm no lightweight—literally or figuratively. I can hold my liquor." And because she'd already learned, when she'd tripped coming out of the club and he'd easily wrapped an arm around her waist to steady her, that Aden was a lot stronger than his athletically built body portrayed, she didn't attempt to pull him to her. Instead, she took the final step, which had his folded arms pressing against her breasts and his growing arousal to her belly. "And second, I've never been an indecisive person. When I want something, I go get it."

He let his arms fall down to his sides, slowly enough that the backs of his fingers brushed over her nipples, and she sucked in a breath.

"Earlier today you and your friend wanted to know what my intentions were toward you. Why I was back here after all this time. Now you're ready to, what? Take me to bed because your body says that's what you want?" he asked.

"Exactly," she replied. "And look, it doesn't have to be a big deal. We're both consenting adults. I'm assuming you don't have a wife or girlfriend that would make this an absolute no. So, unless your real reason for standing in my foyer instead of following me upstairs to my bedroom is that you don't want me, I'll lead the way."

She stared at him, pulled her lower lip between her teeth, then smiled as she turned away and headed up the steps. But he grabbed the wrist of the hand that was just about to release his joggers and held her still.

"Wanting you has been an affliction for me since that day in the park," he said. "But I'm not interested in being a Band-Aid or an itch you need to scratch."

She huffed and rolled her eyes. "Really, Aden, the door is right behind you. It's been a long night—hell, it's been a long two weeks. I'm going to bed."

This time when she tried to move away, he laced an arm around her waist while still holding her wrist in his other hand. Then, in a few steps, he turned her to the left and walked them back until her ass brushed the wall beside the table that held her keys and purse. "You should know before another minute ticks by that I stand on my business too. I know what I want from you and with you, what I've wanted for a very long time. So when I ask you to be sure, I mean I want you to be sure you're ready for this."

The edge to his words, the bass in his tone, the simmering heat in his eyes, kept her body still and sent her hormones soaring. When she'd planned this bowling event, she never would've imagined it could end this way—not even when he'd invited himself to come along. She hadn't expected to ever see him again, and if she were being totally honest, she was still reeling from the funeral, his appearance, her arrest, all that dramatic shit that should've had her teetering on the brink of a nervous breakdown.

But none of that seemed to matter in this moment, nor did the point she suspected he was trying to make. All Vanna wanted was a blissful sexual release. She wanted . . . no, *needed* it, like an addict needed whatever it was that they craved. And dammit, it was her FFSF month, so she was gonna get it!

"I hear you, Aden," she replied. "Now, are we going upstairs, or are you leaving?"

He didn't leave, and moments later they were walking into her bedroom. She went straight to her bed to sit and untie the tennis shoes she'd worn with her jeans and white bodysuit. She had just set them to the side when she felt his presence more than saw him. When she'd come into the room, she'd known he was right behind her, but he'd stopped in the doorway to look around. Now, as she sat up, it was to see that he'd crossed the room and was standing directly in front of her.

"Stand up," he told her, and again, there was something about the deepness in his tone. It was different from his usual voice, tinged with just a hint of dominance that she had to admit turned her all the way on. So she stood.

His arm was around her waist again, but this time he didn't stop there. With that one arm, he pulled her into him, his hand snaking down beneath the band of her jeans to rub directly over the bodysuit she wore. With his other hand, he cupped her cheek and whispered, "Savannah," before his lips touched hers.

It couldn't exactly be described as a touch—it was so brief that maybe it was more of a brush—but he didn't even give her the time to figure it out. His tongue was extended in the next second, licking her bottom, then her top, lip, then pressing between them both to take her mouth in a deep, tumultuous assault that had every nerve in her body standing at attention. Arousal had already been brewing just beneath the surface for her all night. Aden was fine, he smelled good, he had his own money, he got along with her friends, he'd paid for her lawyer. Check. Check. Check. Check! He'd checked every damn box she could've imagined if she were the type to have a checklist for the kind of man who turned her on. Of course, she'd never been that type, but he was fitting the bill, and if he kept kissing her like he was, he would have her ringing the bell to satisfaction in no time.

When he finally tore his mouth away from hers to drag wet kisses down her neck, she panted and whispered, "Um, I was . . . I was gonna . . . ahhhh . . . take a quick shower."

His hand moved from her cheek to lightly grip her neck now as he kissed the swells of her breasts just above the neckline of the bodysuit. "Mmmm-hmmmm," he moaned. "Let's take that shower."

It was hot and soapy and as erotic as people loved to imagine a shower with a sexy man should be, but it was what happened after the shower that Vanna was certain she'd never forget. The moment he'd gently pushed her still-damp body onto her bed and watched her with a sexy grin as he sheathed himself with a condom. Her knees were pushed back until they were near her face, and she was panting his name before he was fully buried inside her. If her FFSF celebration were to end here tonight, she would declare this as the best birthday present ever!

"I talked to Caleb when I first came back to town," Aden said after their second shower.

Vanna lay on her back, wearing a pair of her favorite night shorts and tank top, with him right beside her in his boxers. It was almost three in the morning, and she felt like she was floating on a cloud. Her goal had been sexual satisfaction, but Aden had been an amazing overachiever. She probably should've suspected that from his swagger and confidence, but she was more than happy to have found out from firsthand experience.

"So he knew you were here," she said, and continued to stare up at the ceiling. "I guess he wouldn't have told me, since we were separated."

And she was sure Caleb had no clue about the times when they were in school and she'd stared at Aden a little too long. Hell, Aden probably didn't even know that.

"We hung out a few times. And a few of the brothers were planning a trip out to Sedona for a week around Thanksgiving. Caleb was excited for the trip," he said.

"He loved to travel," she said absently, and wondered how abnormal it was that her husband was the topic of their after-sex discussion.

"I almost told him that I wanted you," he said, and her head jerked in his direction.

"You what?" They'd forgotten to turn off the light in the bathroom, so the golden hue partially illuminated the otherwise dark bedroom.

He was lying on his side, an arm tucked under his head as he stared at her.

"Back in college, about a month or so after he started dating you. He was bragging about how good things were going and about how you might be the one, and I was getting so pissed with him. I almost shouted that I'd seen you first and that you should be mine."

She didn't know what to say to that. Hearing it now, all these years later, she was torn between whether to think it was creepy-obsessive or endearing because his crush on her had been reciprocated. She just wasn't being as open with him about it as he was with her. No way was she putting herself out there for this man, whom she'd technically known for twenty years but at the same time had only really known intimately for about two hours.

"Seeing me first didn't mean anything," she replied.

His mouth curved into a small smile. "You don't believe that," he said. "I knew you still felt it too. Whenever we were in a room together, I felt your gaze on me. When I was trying desperately not to look at you, not to want to touch you, to talk only to you—hell, to take your ass out of whatever room we were in and go someplace so we could be alone." He reached out and ran a finger down her cheek.

"It was wrong to look at you like that," she said.

He sighed. "I saw you first."

She grinned and turned over onto her side so she could face him. "You're just gonna keep saying that, aren't you?"

He nodded. "'Cause it's true. And if I hadn't been tongue-tied and afraid I might just pass out and make a complete idiot of myself, I would've claimed you right then."

"Nobody claims me," she said. "I only go willingly."

He let his finger glide down her neck to trail along the breast that had escaped the confines of the tank top. One thing was for certain: after being trapped inside a bra for more than eight hours, when her girls were finally let loose, they had a mind of their own.

"I mean, we could go another round to prove my point, but I'm pretty sure during the last round, you were already admitting to being all mine," he said, then licked his lips.

She swatted playfully at his shoulder but didn't make any move to stop the tiny circles his fingers were making on her breast. "Sex talk doesn't count."

He paused then and stared at her. She wanted to look away. To say she was thirsty and get the hell out of that room for just a few minutes because his gaze was making her uncomfortable. Not like she wanted him to leave right this moment uncomfortable, but definitely like she was rethinking some of the things she'd said since being reunited with him.

"If you knew Caleb and I weren't together, why didn't you let me know when you came back to town?" she asked.

"I was determined to get my gym opened, find a house, do research and development for my supplements. It took a lot of my time."

"Oh," she said, and started to move so she could lie on her back again. Staring into his dark eyes was starting to be too intense.

But he moved his hand from her breast and had both his arms around her waist before she could make it. He pulled her to him until almost every part of his body was touching some part of hers. "When I'm with a woman, I like to give her as much of my attention as I possibly can," he said, his face so close to hers that his breath was warm against her cheek.

"All those years you were away, I know you weren't thinking about me. Or still wanting me. You had to date other women." Her mind seemed to be all over the place, rattling off some of the things she'd meant to say last night.

He paused for a second, and she wondered if he might actually pull away or perhaps decline to answer. He did neither.

"I had girlfriends, Savannah. Just like I did when we were in college. But I never forgot about you. Never stopped wondering what if."

She sighed, recalling having been caught up in that *what if* question earlier yesterday.

"How do you know I wasn't already with someone else?" Obviously, this question was a bit too little, too late, but she wanted to know what he'd been thinking all these years, what he was thinking now.

"I didn't when you were at the funeral," he said, and kissed the tip of her nose. "But you definitely would've been more resistant to me paying for your lawyer if you had a man, and you certainly wouldn't have gone out for coffee with me." He kissed her cheek.

"If I had a man, he wouldn't dictate which gifts I accept or who I can have coffee with," she replied, and eased an arm around his neck.

He kissed her other cheek, then her forehead, then back down to drop another kiss on the tip of her nose. "You didn't pick the right man, Savannah," he whispered, then touched his lips to hers.

"You did *what* with your mouth?" Ronni practically screamed when they took their seats in the alto section of the choir on Sunday.

They'd just marched around for the offering, and in a few minutes would be singing the sermonic selection, but Jamaica had to finish telling them about her night with Davon.

Vanna smacked Ronni's arm. "Girl, you too loud," she whispered.

"Yes, you are," Linda, who thought she was the best singer on the choir, said and rolled her eyes.

Jamaica, sitting on Vanna's left side, leaned forward to give Linda, who was on the other side of Ronni, a stank look. With her lips twisted and another roll of her eyes, Linda set her gaze forward.

"Yeah, that's what you betta do," Jamaica whispered.

Vanna sighed and wished she were anywhere besides trapped between them as they faced the entire church.

"Anyway," Jamaica started, but Vanna shook her head.

"No, let's not finish that story," she said.

"Fine," Jamaica said. "Y'all know how me and Davon get down, anyway. Let's talk about you and Aden. 'Cause I know you gave him some last night."

"You don't know anything," Vanna argued, but her thighs were pleasantly sore, and if she hadn't worn the high-neck sleeveless white blouse with her black skirt today, everyone would've easily seen the passion marks he'd left on her chest. There were more on her breasts and thighs, but they wouldn't be seeing those either.

"I know you were smiling when you came in this morning, and you've been checking your messages and smiling at that phone every second we haven't been singing," Jamaica said.

Ronni leaned over and said, "Yup, she sure has." She gave Jamaica a low five, since not only were they not supposed to be talking about sex while sitting with the choir in Sunday worship service, they certainly weren't supposed to be having such a good time doing so.

"Y'all act like we're in high school," Vanna said with a shake of her head.

"Nah, we're much better at it now than we were in high school," Ronni said.

Jamaica chuckled. "You certainly are, with the baby factory you've got at your house."

Vanna was grateful when the choir director had them stand and they began singing. She let herself fall into the lyrics of the song, to let those lyrics minister to her in a way that only good gospel could. Tomorrow would be here soon enough, and no matter how good last night—and three times this morning before Aden had finally, reluctantly, left her house—was, she couldn't shake the trepidation.

Was the lawyer going to tell her there was no chance and she was definitely going to prison for something she didn't do? Or was there a way out of this mess? A mess she still wasn't clear on how she'd become involved in. But, honestly, she'd much rather Jamaica and Ronni continue their banter about her sex life and their sex lives, instead of either of them worrying about her and this new situation. She would handle whatever it turned out to be, the same way she handled everything else—with strength and faith.

Chapter 10

Vanna kept her hands tightly folded as she sat in the guest chair across from Jovani's black lacquer desk. As an annoying coincidence to already feeling like she was going to be in the hot seat, the weather was suffocatingly humid on this bright and sunny Monday morning. Thankfully, the air conditioner in Jovani's office suite was fully operational. Otherwise, she might've been a puddle of sweat. As it was, anxiety had her heart thumping, and she was about to rub the skin right off her own hands.

"Your husband—"

"Ex-husband." She quickly corrected Jovani as he began to speak.

After he'd let her into his office since it was too early for any of his staff to be in, he'd ushered her to this seat, and they'd exchanged the initial pleasantries. Jamaica hadn't lied: he was fine, with a honey complexion just a shade darker than hers, a full and healthy black beard, and close-cut hair. He wore navy-blue dress pants, a baby-blue dress shirt, and a white tie with faint navy-blue stripes. The jacket that completed the expertly tailored business suit was neatly draped over the back of his chair.

Jovani looked up from the files he had spread open on his otherwise sparsely decorated desk with one brow raised. "I didn't see a divorce decree in my file. Naomi is usually very thorough in her background research, but we were operating within a short time span."

Vanna shook her head. "We weren't officially divorced, just separated for five years."

"Okay," he said, and reached into a black mug with the word His in a thin font across the front to pull out a pen.

She gnawed at the inside of her lip as he scribbled that information onto the bright-white legal pad.

"At the time of his death, Caleb had been working at the Lennox Casino," he said. "Did you know that?"

"Yes," she replied.

"How did you know? Were the two of you still close even though you were separated?"

"No." She forced herself to take a breath, then began again. "We were cordial whenever we saw each other. He called or texted me every few weeks, wanting to meet up and talk about our relationship. But I was over it, so I never accepted any of those invitations."

"When was the last time you saw him?"

"A few months ago, I guess. It was after church one Sunday, at the Cheesecake Factory. He was on a date, and I was with my friends." She wondered if Caleb had known then the trouble he was getting her into.

"And how did you know he was working at the casino again?" Jovani asked.

He'd slipped on a pair of gold-rimmed glasses after he sat across from her. They added a scholarly look to his otherwise *GQ* aura. Now he stared through them at her with a pointed glare.

She sighed. "I think he told me or one of our mutual friends." She thought about it for a moment. "Yeah, a woman at my grandmother's senior building used to live next door to Caleb's mother, so she knew me from the times when I would be over there. I was visiting Granny one day, and Ms. Evelyn mentioned that Caleb was doing good and that he had a steady job at the casino now. That was right before Christmas, because she was sitting by the bulletin board in their community room, and I remember the garland somebody had tried to tape up there was falling down."

"Good memory," he said. "I have a hard time recalling what I had for dinner two nights ago, let alone remembering something almost nine months ago."

She shrugged. "Conversations tend to stick with me once I think about it a little."

He sat straight up then. "Ever have a conversation with Caleb about stealing money from the casino?"

Her eyes widened. "What? No! Is that what they think I did?"

"Charging documents state you conspired to plan and execute multiple robberies from the Lennox Casino. Didn't they give you a copy when you left the station last week?"

"I stuffed them into my purse as soon as I got into my grandmother's car," she said. "I went home, showered, and went to bed after that. Then, the next morning, I talked to you, and you said to put it out of my mind until today. So I did. I focused on my friends, my birthday celebration, my . . ." Her words trailed off then because she was certain he didn't need to know that a portion of her attention this weekend had thankfully shifted to finding some much-needed physical pleasure.

"On what?" He nudged.

She cleared her throat. "I had plans with my friends Friday and Saturday nights; then it was the Women's Ministry anniversary at church yesterday, so we had to sing."

"What church do you attend?" he asked, and she blinked at what felt like a random question.

"Glory Sunrise Baptist," she replied.

"Yeah," he said with a deep nod. "I know that church well. My uncle is the pastor at Greater Hope, so I grew up there. We may have celebrated some usher anniversaries together back in the day."

She smiled. "Okay, I know that church. We probably did." Her next breath came a little steadier, her heartbeat just a tad slower, as she started to relax. Which she figured was Jovani's intention in that quick diversion from the subject.

"Look, Caleb and I weren't beefing, but we weren't best friends either," she said. "He went his way and I went mine. We were married for fifteen years, together two years before that. A lot of people know us as a couple, so even after the separation I still get unwanted updates on his life. But that was the extent of our connection."

"Good to know," Jovani said, and scribbled on the legal pad again. Then he set the pen down and sat back in his chair.

"Three months ago, there was an armored truck robbery that went wrong. Two guys pulled up on the truck; driver got spooked, started shooting. Killed one and wounded the other. Cops got a hit on the dead guy's prints—prior robberies, some drug arrests. They link him to a previous codefendant, find that guy and question him. Codefendant rolls 'cause he's not built for real jail time, even though he's now looking at a felony robbery and handgun charges because of this last job. That codefendant named Caleb and a few of his coworkers at the casino as being part of the plan."

"What?" Vanna whispered, although she didn't need any of the words repeated. "Was all of that in the charging documents too?" If so, she definitely needed to dig those papers out of the bottom of her purse and read them.

Jovani kept watching her. "No. Right after our call last week, I had my staff start to investigate. The cops gave us minimal information, but we've got a lot of ears on the street. This was the fourth robbery of this kind."

She felt herself shaking her head, but everything else was a blur. This office, Jovani, the words—everything just seemed to melt and mold into one big ball of disbelief. "I didn't know," she finally said. "I didn't know about any of this."

His elbows rested on the arms of the chair, fingers steepled and touching his bearded chin. "There's a checking account at the Freedom Financial Credit Union in the names of Savannah L. Carlson and Caleb J. Carlson. That account has a balance of $173,000. In the last six months, there's been a monthly deposit of $25,000."

"No," she said, her voice steadier. "No. I signed the paperwork to get my name off that account right after we separated, five years ago. I had it notarized by the paralegal in my office. My name shouldn't be on any accounts with Caleb's."

"You didn't go into the credit union and request to have your name removed from the account?"

She shook her head. "No. We had a huge case at work during that time—a bus and three vehicles were involved; we represented multiple plaintiffs. Settlement talks didn't work, and there were depositions, endless discovery, pretrial motions, trial. I was lead paralegal on the case at the time, before I became office manager, so I was working late and leaving the house early. I didn't have time." She sighed. "So Caleb brought the forms to me at the office one day, and I signed them. He said he would take care of everything after that. Should've known not to believe his ass."

Jovani didn't speak for the next few moments, and neither did she. Her mind was reeling, her heart once again pumping wildly, but this time from rage.

"Their case against you revolves around that bank account," Jovani said. He dropped his hands and leaned forward to look at the papers on his desk again. "That's it. They've been investigating this case for months, trying to put together the full picture and possibly catch Caleb and his crew in the act of another robbery before they arrested him. But his body turned up first."

"So, wait? The police have been investigating me too?"

Jovani looked up at her and nodded. "Watching your accounts as well as his for any more big deposits. I'm guessing that's why they didn't immediately bring you in when his body was found. They waited to see what you'd do."

"The only deposit into my account is my direct deposit every two weeks. Oh no, wait a minute, my name is on my grandmother's checking and savings account. Please don't tell me they're watching that too."

Don't tell me she's at any type of risk because of Caleb's ass and my foolishness for not making a cleaner break from him."

"No," Jovani said, and held up a hand to stop the rant she was definitely about to go on. "No. They could only get subpoenas to monitor your accounts. Not accounts that you share with someone else who wasn't also involved in this case. So your grandmother's money is safe."

It felt like a *for now* was lingering in the air, and Vanna began to feel sick. She brought her hands up to cover her face as she tried to take the next calming breath.

"So, here's our position. To be successful on this conspiracy charge against you, they have to prove that one, you entered into an agreement with at least one person connected to this case to steal the money, and two, that at least one person in that agreement performed the act that furthered the agreement." He was giving her that pointed glare again. "As long as they can't prove you agreed to be a part of the robberies with Caleb and his crew, this case fails. We win, you go on with your life."

"We win? So there has to be a trial? I have to sit in a courtroom while they accuse me of conspiring to steal money that I never even saw? This is bullshit!" First there'd been fear. Then worry had settled in. Now, with all the facts on the table, anger was quickly taking over.

"Not if I can help it," he said. "Like I said, my team is already on this. With Caleb's death, two of the key players in this scheme have disappeared. Their case is falling apart, which is why they finally decided to bring you in. They want you to give up the two who're on the run; then they'll offer you probation and probably a fine. But we're not giving them a damn thing. They're gonna have to prove this case to win, so we're just going to build our own case that will ensure they lose."

"If he wasn't already dead, I promise you I'd kill Caleb Jeremiah Carlson. Then you'd get an even bigger fee to represent me."

Jovani gave her a half smile. "While I totally understand where you're coming from, let's not say that anymore outside of this office."

Then, when she didn't agree, he continued, "How 'bout we just don't speak those words again. Ever."

She sighed and rolled her eyes. "Fine."

By noon, Vanna's day had gone from bad to horrendous, when HC Jr. barged into her office. If he'd opened that door two minutes earlier, she would've been still eating the steak burrito bowl from Chipotle that Sanni had brought back for her. And that would've pissed her off. On the days she didn't leave the office for lunch—which were few because she really did need to get away from this place for a short period during the middle of the day—she would hang a sign on her office door: OUT TO LUNCH. That's what the sign said—nothing ambiguous, printed in bold block letters, in the English language, which everyone in this office spoke fluently.

And yet, HC Jr. had clearly decided to ignore that sign and walk in unannounced. It was a good thing she didn't take after him when it came to office etiquette, otherwise he might have found her in a compromising position with the UPS delivery guy. He was currently the finest man to come in and out of this office, as noted by her, Sanni, and Neshawn.

"Why hasn't this expert been paid?" he asked as he stalked up to her desk, then stood there glaring down at her, waiting for a response.

One that she was in no hurry to give because his rudeness was growing with every passing second, and she had to start counting down from five hundred to keep from going off on his annoying ass. HC Jr. was a few inches taller than his father. He was in his early fifties, and his thick hair was still chestnut brown, his eyes an eerie green. He had the slim and polished look of a legacy student at Yale and the arrogance that often came with it.

She continued wiping her hands with her napkin, then made a production out of leaning to the side and tossing that napkin into the trash. Then she angled her chair so that she was facing the computer more than HC Jr.'s scowling face.

"Which experts are you referring to?" she asked, purposefully keeping her tone even, her gaze directed at the computer.

Vanna had an inkling of which expert in particular he was referring to, and the two cases she hadn't been paid for yet. But he was going to have to ask for everything he wanted today. She wasn't in a generous mood.

"Rayna Postmore, the registered nurse on the Forney and Hayes cases. She provided written reports, sat for depositions, and testified at trial in the Hayes case. Both those cases settled last month; she should've been paid by now," he blustered.

Rayna Postmore was an attractive woman—if pixie-like, raven-haired nurses were your thing—with multiple degrees in the medical field. She was a great expert witness both on paper and on the witness stand. In addition to her job at the Johns Hopkins Hospital, she had a thriving consultant side business. She was also one of HC Jr.'s latest side chicks. Which, in Vanna's estimation, had knocked her worth down tremendously.

"The Forney case settled on July second. Check was received on Friday and hasn't cleared our account yet," she said after pulling up a spreadsheet.

She'd lowered the font size on her computer while he'd been talking so that when the spreadsheet came up on the screen, he couldn't easily see the numbers. He would've had to lean over her desk to get a good look, but she knew he wasn't going to do that. HC Jr.'s and his father's names might be on the door and the stationery in this office, but Vanna controlled the money, and both men knew it. She looked out for them and this firm in a way neither of them would've ever been able to do. She'd done it to an extent as their paralegal, when they'd both acted like their law degrees had been another one of those gifts passed down, but not earned in the least bit, and worked some of their highest-netting cases. Which was why they eventually promoted her to her current position. They knew she was capable of managing every aspect of this firm on her own, and they respected that. They respected her. To the extent that they could respect a Black woman who was younger than them.

"Hayes just settled last week. The defendant's insurance company in this case is notorious for taking up to seven weeks to pay. I've already got it on my calendar to do a first follow-up on payment next week," she told him. "So, you can tell Rayna her $4,200 from Forney should go out by the end of this week. When the Hayes payment comes in, it usually takes three to five business days for those checks to clear. So, the $5,875 she's due from that case will come after that."

His brow furrowed, and he pushed his hands into the front pockets of his khakis. "Can we cut her a check today?"

Vanna sat back in her chair. "We can, but are you prepared to do that for every expert who calls crying for money?"

The question was on the borderline of being insubordinate. No matter how good she was at her job, they were still her employers, and on most days Vanna respected that. Today was not the day for this man to be in her office, worrying her about his mistress. Not when Caleb was still wreaking havoc on her life from the grave.

"Nobody has to know what we're doing here, Vanna. She needs that money now," HC Jr. said.

Vanna gave a little nod. "Okay. So, you want me to cut a check for ten thousand to Rayna today. Because that's the total amount she's owed for both cases. What should I put in the memo portion?"

"What are you talking about? What do you normally put in the memo portion?" he asked, obviously irritated with Vanna's questions.

"I normally add the case name and number, which will coordinate with the deposit and clearing of the settlement check. This is how we handle all cases and the settlement sheet that goes into each digital and paper file. Now, if I cut these checks before that happens, it messes up my recordkeeping. So I just need to know how you want me to adjust what will be a discrepancy in the event the accountants decide to audit our accounts."

His phone buzzed in his pocket, and Vanna wondered if it was Rayna or Paula, his wife of twenty-three years. When he pulled the phone out and scowled down at it, she surmised it was Paula. The woman who'd given him four children and treated him like he was the king of the world.

"Look, I just want her to get paid for her services," he said, stuffing the phone back into his pocket. "Is that too much to ask? Don't you expect to get paid for your work?"

She nodded. "I do. Every other Friday and twice during performance appraisals and holiday-bonus time. Which is why I'm always on time to call the payroll service and give them the information they need to process the checks." When he only blinked at her, his lips going into a tight line, she continued, "And why I am attempting to follow procedure with handling our accounts. But again, your name is on the checks, not mine, so just tell me what you would like me to do and I'll do it."

She knew he wasn't going to tell her to write that check. For one, the last thing he wanted was any discrepancy in their books, because that would certainly bring forth his father's ire. As a result, Vanna would certainly cover her ass and tell why she'd cut those checks and at whose request. Then, the senior's anger would be directed at his philandering son. They'd been through this song and dance before, and each time she'd presented him with the same facts. She really wished he'd start thinking with the head that had supposedly gotten him all the degrees that hung on the wall in his office. Because his other one . . . well, that one was as dumb as a bag of rocks.

"Well, just call her and explain all that to her," he said with a huff. "I guess she'll understand."

"She will," Vanna said. Just as she did every other time she'd explained when her check would get there.

It took everything in her not to shout, *Why don't you write her a check out of your own account to pay for the extra services she's giving you?* Because that's exactly what he was doing. None of their other experts made the money Rayna did, and he knew it.

A few minutes later, he stalked out of her office, and she picked up the phone to call Rayna and let her know when she would receive her money.

At twenty minutes after four, there was a knock on Vanna's office door. "Come in," she yelled without looking up from her computer.

She'd readjusted her font because she'd been barely able to see those small-ass numbers earlier herself. Now she was working on another settlement sheet, and she needed to see to make sure all her tabulations were coming out correctly. She only half trusted the computer to do the job.

"Hey, you got a minute?" Sanni asked as she came into the office.

Glancing over at her, Vanna saw that Sanni, a normally easygoing woman, looked stressed. Her shoulders were rigid and her brow furrowed. Vanna could so relate to that feeling, but since she was older than Sanni and Neshawn, she'd become accustomed to acting like the surrogate mother in the office.

"Sure. Close the door," she told her.

Sanni came in and dropped down into the chair across from Vanna's desk. "I'm pregnant," she said without preamble, and Vanna immediately stopped typing.

She turned her head away from the computer screen and looked at Sanni again. She was a pretty young woman with expressive chocolate-brown eyes. Her parents were from Haiti, but Sanni and her two sisters had been born here. She'd had a son, Mikal, when she was in undergrad and thus changed from attending law school upon her graduation and had instead gotten a paralegal certificate. She was twenty-six years old and rented an apartment about twenty minutes away from their office. Mikal's father wasn't part of his life, so parenting was solely on her, except for when they went to New York to visit her family.

"Jawan?" Vanna asked, knowing he was the guy Sanni had been messing with for the past few months.

Sanni nodded.

"How far along are you?" Sanni wore a size 0 or 00, a fact that never failed to make Vanna roll her eyes. She didn't look like she'd gained an ounce yet, so Vanna figured she couldn't be that pregnant.

"Eight weeks," Sanni said, and crossed one long leg over the other. "What am I going to do with another baby?"

It almost slipped out that it was maybe a little late to consider that question. Vanna had a full-blown headache from a day full of thinking, worrying, and, since she'd been in the office, biting her damn tongue. What she desperately wanted to do was go home, where she didn't have to talk to or see anyone. That way she could sit in her thoughts in peace.

"What do you want to do?" she asked her.

Sanni's eyes widened. "I want to buy a house. I want to take Mikal on nice vacations. I want to pay off these student loans and my car." She ran her fingers through the silky weave that stretched past her shoulders. "I don't want another bill."

Vanna eased back in her chair again, measuring her words. There was so much she could say to Sanni in this moment, but she sensed that listening might be her best bet right now.

"You know how much I make here," Sanni continued. "It's barely enough for my rent, day care, car, loans, insurance, and for Mikal and me not to starve. How am I gonna afford another mouth to feed? And day care again? For an infant? That's going to take half my check!"

Sanni dropped her hands into her lap. "And you know how our PTO works here. How am I going to afford taking off to have this baby?"

From all that Sanni was saying and from her past, Vanna figured Jawan wasn't going to be an active part of this baby's life, similar to Mikal's father. The bastards. And on some level, she really did sympathize with Sanni. Men really weren't shit. On another, more mature and probably motherly level, she wanted to go right back to her initial thought—it was a little too late to be considering all this now. Because birth control was a thing. Now, it may be a thing that some ridiculous people thought they could dictate to women, so it might not be a thing for long, but right at this moment, and eight weeks ago when Sanni's baby had been conceived, it *was* a thing. So why hadn't this bright, independent woman considered that?

"Have you told your family?" Vanna asked when Sanni had gone quiet.

Sanni shook her head.

"What can I do, Sanni? How can I help you right now?" Because Vanna was certain the words she felt compelled to offer weren't what this woman needed or wanted to hear at this moment. She'd rather just ask what Sanni wanted and follow her lead than say something that might offend or hurt and cause this situation to be much worse for her.

One thing Vanna knew for certain was that Sanni wanted to be a good mother to Mikal. The younger woman had talked before about how she didn't want him to suffer because of what his father refused to do. Vanna could wholeheartedly relate to that situation. Having children hadn't been a consideration to her for just that reason. What if she couldn't be a good mother?

But that wasn't the case with Sanni. Vanna saw how hard Sanni worked to take care of her son. She heard about all the things Sanni did for him, the sacrifices she made to ensure his well-being and happiness. If ever she'd witnessed what a good mother—even a single one—could be, it was Sanni. So she was certain Sanni would be the same for this new baby. And in that moment, Vanna decided that she would help her. Whatever Sanni needed to make this experience less stressful, to ensure that she was always able to give her children the very best of herself— without having to be worried or stressed about anything—that's what Vanna would do. It's what both Sanni's children deserved.

Sanni shook her head. "I don't know," she said quietly. "I just needed to say it out loud. To tell somebody." She sighed. "I know I have a lot to think about, a lot to work out. But I figured you would need to know eventually anyway, so why not let you be the first." She gave her a small smile then, and Vanna returned it.

"Well, I'm honored for that privilege." Then she glanced at the clock and noted it was time for both of them to get off. "Hey, why don't I cook us something nice for lunch tomorrow? I think I have the makings for lasagna at home. I can whip that up and bring it in tomorrow, and we can sit in here, eat, and watch Netflix for an hour."

Sanni rubbed her nonexistent stomach. "You tryin' to feed this baby already?"

Vanna chuckled. "Absolutely. The same way I'm always trying to feed its mommy. I'm gonna take good care of this little one, you just wait and see."

At that, Sanni smiled. A slow, genuine smile that touched her pretty eyes and warmed Vanna's exhausted soul.

Chapter 11

At seven forty-five that night, Vanna eased the glass dish containing a bubbling and delicious-smelling lasagna out of her oven. She'd gone straight home from work and hopped in the shower, then came downstairs to cook. With the music on one of her favorite playlists titled *#rbthrowback*, she relaxed enough to sing and move about the kitchen, cooking the food she knew would help soothe a young soul tomorrow. And probably another night this week, since she planned to put some in a separate container for Sanni to take home. She also made chocolate pudding for Mikal because he loved it and Sanni didn't know how to make it.

Dressed in legging shorts and an old New Edition T-shirt—because she didn't dare wear the one she, Jamaica, and Ronni had gotten last year when they'd seen the group in concert—she put the dish on top of the warming pads she'd set on the island. She sang along to the lyrics of one of her oldie-but-goodie favorites, Deborah Cox and Whitney Houston's "Same Script, Different Cast," and had just moved to the refrigerator to grab the bottle of wine to pour herself a second glass when there was a knock at the door.

Setting the bottle on the island, she grabbed her dish towel and made sure her hands were wiped clean as she went to answer it.

"Aden?" she asked in surprise when she saw him standing on her porch, dressed in blue basketball shorts and a gray sleeveless T-shirt.

"Hi, Savannah," he said. "I would think after the weekend we shared, you'd stop seeming so surprised to see me."

His tone was light as he spoke, but she was still confused. "Um, I'm not . . . Well, yes, I guess I am surprised. Were we supposed to see each other today? I mean, with the day I've had, I definitely could've forgotten. But I usually put all my appointments into the calendar on my phone."

"So, I would be an appointment?" he asked.

"Well . . . ," she started to say, then closed her mouth.

He chuckled. "On second thought, don't answer that. Can I at least come in?"

"Oh, yeah. Sure," she said, and stepped aside to let him into the house. Once he was inside, she closed the door and walked up the stairs behind him.

He followed the music back to the kitchen and leaned against the island in a way that was far too familiar for her liking. Yes, they had a good weekend together, but this was still her house and hers alone. But he'd come in and now looked like he belonged here. She didn't even want to consider how much that possibility frightened her.

"Okay, I have to be honest, I'm not used to this," she said. "You just popping up whenever you feel like it and coming in here like you've been coming here forever." She stopped and sighed because she didn't know what else to say to articulate how confused she was feeling at the moment. Today was just a roller coaster of emotions, and she was ready to get the hell off right now!

"That's fair." His hands were clasped in front of him, and he looked annoyingly calm . . . and sexy. "I'll call or text before I come next time."

"There's going to be a next time?" she asked.

Now he raised a brow. "I'm going to ignore that question because we already had this conversation."

She didn't know which conversation he was referring to. They'd had their after-sex discussion early Sunday morning, then another after-sex chat before he'd left and she'd gotten ready for church. Throughout the rest of the day yesterday had been full of text messages that she'd been unusually excited to return. So technically, there were several conversations he could be referring to.

"And I had lunch with Jovani today. He told me about what was going on with Caleb. I figured you'd need a distraction this evening, and I meant to get here earlier, but I had a meeting with my marketing people that lasted way longer than planned," he said.

She folded her arms over her chest. "Isn't that a violation of attorney-client privilege? Jovani telling you about my case?"

Now she was certain the look he was giving her was one of mild annoyance. It was unfortunate for her that he still looked hot when he was getting pissed.

"We talked about Caleb, who was a frat brother to both of us," he told her. "So there was no privilege violation."

She didn't have a response for that.

"But since you seem so tense and obviously bothered by me being here, would you like me to leave?" he asked.

Damn. She was not in the mood for Aden's Superman routine tonight. All day long she'd planned for this quiet time—well, her alone time, since Faith Evans's "Love Like This Before" was now blaring through the speaker. Sanni's dilemma had altered the lie-back-and-relax part of her evening a little, but she hadn't minded that because she needed to eat too. But now, he was here, and while her immediate feeling about that was, *Wow, this man must really be into me, and damn, doesn't that feel good for a change?* she was having a hard time figuring out if she *should* be feeling that way.

Like, was it smart to let herself get swept away by this man from her past? Wasn't part of her FFSF celebration to start this next phase of her life anew? To leave all the things in her past—including the feelings, disappointments, and expectations—behind?

"I didn't say that," she replied, in answer to his question, not all the ones popping into her head right now.

"Then what are you saying, Vanna?" he asked. "I stopped by to check on you and to maybe take you out to clear your mind a bit. Nothing serious, nothing nefarious. Should I have called or texted first? Yeah, I can admit that, and I'll do better next time. But if there's something else you want me to stop, now's the time to let me know."

Great. Just great. Now he wanted her to put her cards on the table when what she really felt like doing was crawling under the table and sleeping until all the mess in her life was resolved. But as she inhaled deeply, Vanna knew that wasn't how this worked. Every second of every day, she was on duty. There were no breaks or getaways from life, and she knew that well. So even though her frustrated mind instinctively wanted her to yell *Get the hell out and never come back*, a bigger part of her—the needier part she tried so damn hard to keep hidden—warned her that this was a mistake. It was reactionary and she'd regret it later.

"I was just about to have dinner and a second glass of wine," she said. "You can join me if you want."

She dropped her arms and walked past him to pick up the bottle of wine again. He didn't move at first—or at least, she didn't notice him moving—so she removed the cork from the wine and was about to pour it into her glass when she felt him behind her. Like, directly behind her, so close that his breath brushed over the side of her face as he leaned in and covered her hand that held the bottle with his. "How 'bout we skip the second glass of wine and head to the gym?"

She spun around so fast the bottle wobbled on the island. "The what?"

He took a step back. "The gym. I figured we could go and get a short workout in and—"

"And you could what? Get me to lose some weight?" She gave a derisive laugh. "Man, this has been one unbelievable day. No, bump that, an unbelievable two, almost three weeks." She stared at him, at the calm gaze he was giving her as she spoke. "Is that what all this was about? You claiming to want me all this time, finally getting me, and then deeming me too fat for your tastes? But instead of leaving me alone, what? You're up for a challenge. Want to step in and change my whole life around? I shouldn't have married Caleb, but that's okay because now he's gone and you're here. I shouldn't drink this wine? I should go with you to the gym and get in tip-top shape like you. Boy, please," she hissed, and pushed past him.

He grabbed her wrist before she could get completely away, but he didn't pull her back to him. Instead, he simply held on to her.

"I liked you just as you were back in college, and I still like you just as you are now," he said. There was an edge to his tone, though. She'd definitely pushed a few of his buttons, but so the hell what? He was irking her nerves, adding to all the other things that threatened to push her over the brink. She had to stop it, stop him, and preserve her peace—or the peace she struggled to maintain each day.

Yet she didn't pull her wrist away from him, didn't turn around and tell him he could either let her go or get punched upside the head. Didn't threaten to call the cops or worse, Granny with her dog and gun.

"Physical activity does more than just foster weight loss, Savannah. It relieves stress, helps you to maintain sound sleeping habits, clears your mind." His grip loosened just a little. "I know you've had a rough day and, as you've said, a rough couple of weeks. I'm just trying to give you an hour or two of not-so-rough time. That's all."

She sighed and wanted nothing more than to get away from this man. To run upstairs and close herself in her room so she could be alone with all these conflicting thoughts and emotions. The latter having definitely been brought on by him. Her emotions toward Caleb right now and in the past years were clear—dislike, disinterest, and disdain.

But where Aden was concerned . . . Hell, it had only been a few days since he'd popped back up in her life. And now she'd slept with the man and argued with him. She released a heavy sigh, knowing that running away was not an option. For one, this was her house, so if anybody was leaving, it was going to be him. But honestly, she didn't want him to leave. What she wanted was for him to stop confusing the hell out of her, but she wasn't about to tell him that. He was holding too many of the cards in this hand of her personal life as it was.

"I'm cranky," she said quietly.

He chuckled. "And don't say it's because you're hungry."

She looked over her shoulder at him. "Shut up."

His grin grew wider, and this time he did pull her to him. He pulled her until she was positioned directly in front of him and his arms had snaked around her waist. She reluctantly rested her hands on his chest.

"Forty-five minutes at the gym. A light workout, and then we'll come back here and eat," he said.

"And have my glass of wine," she said. And when he raised a brow, she continued, "Well, if I've gotta go walk on a treadmill or lift some weights, I might need something stronger by then."

He kissed the tip of her nose, and she blinked at how tender the action was. "I'll make you a stronger drink if you really feel like you need it when we come back. Deal?"

She stared at him, wanting to protest but also wanting to get this gym nonsense over with. "Deal," she said.

"Good," he replied, and moved one hand down to slap her ass. "Go get yourself a bag with a towel and a water bottle. I'll meet you in the car."

Vanna didn't comment on him slapping her ass; he'd done that the night before. And she didn't say a word about him walking through her house again and going out the front door. And, a few minutes later when she had her duffel bag packed with the towel and water bottle he'd suggested—as well as a change of underwear and clothes because if she was too sweaty, she wasn't even sitting in a car for a ride home like that—she found herself walking out her front door and climbing into the passenger side of his car.

Aden's gym was amazing. Everything was state-of-the-art. The space was huge, in a building she'd passed hundreds of times but had never wondered what was inside. Of course, it hadn't always been Aden's gym, but she never imagined there was this much space in here either. There were two levels. A brightly lit reception area just inside the tinted windows at the front of the building; rooms for spin, Pilates, kickboxing, yoga, and some other classes he'd rattled off as they passed them; and the pool and sauna area toward the back. Upstairs was a more open-floor concept, with all the machines she supposed were usually found in a gym. Since she preferred pulling up one of those in-home walking videos on YouTube when she was in the mood and walking to the beat of one of her many playlists, she didn't know what half the stuff in this place was.

But that was just fine when her escort was the owner and a certified personal trainer.

"Relax," he said as he stepped closer to her and reached for the strap of her bag, which she'd crossed over her body.

She sighed heavily and lifted her arm so he could remove it.

"That's easy for you to say," she replied. "You look like you belong here, like you actually live here." She huffed. "I don't know what I'm doing."

"But you have an excellent trainer," he told her with a grin and a wink. "So just relax."

She tried, but that wink had set off a whole other—not fit for a gym—set of thoughts. At least, until he'd finished with what he called "stretching exercises," one of which had required her to bend as far forward as she could go comfortably. She knew this was really the touch-your-toes exercise and hadn't wanted to embarrass herself so quickly in the process, by one, not making it nearly close enough to her toes, and two, being out of breath when she stood up straight. So she'd given it only half the effort, until Aden stepped up behind her and placed his hand at the small of her back, where he applied just enough pressure to push her down farther.

She groaned at first, but then, when that same hand started to move slowly, back and forth over her back, she relaxed, took a deep breath, and tried to go lower.

Later, when she was on the treadmill and he was leaning against the wall across from her, arms folded over his chest, she frowned. "You should be on that other machine, not watching me like you think I'm gonna hop off here and make a run for the door."

The twenty-minute session he'd programmed into the machine had just started, so the stride was slow enough that she could still talk normally.

"Nah," he said with another one of those slow, sexy grins. "I like the view from here."

"I'm starting to think this wasn't about me feeling better, but more about you getting free looks at me stretching, bending, and jiggling all over the place."

He laughed then, a hearty sound that ripped through the air and had a couple other people in the space looking in their direction.

"You might know me a little better than I thought," he said when he was finally able to contain some of his chuckling.

She shook her head. "Actually, I don't," she said.

Sobering slightly, he asked, "Do you want to? Get to know me better, I mean."

At one time, before that step show and the meeting of the man she did not want to think about any more tonight, her answer would've been a quick-ass *Hell yes*. Now, though, she needed to be cautious. And while it might be a little too late for that train of thought in the physical sense—considering they'd both gotten to know each other pretty well in that area over the weekend—on a bigger scale, she had to practice some common sense where he was concerned.

"I want to know why me," she said. "Why now?"

"Maybe our time is now," he replied. "And a better question might be, Why not you? Why wouldn't I be interested in a smart, beautiful woman who's loyal and ambitious and a pretty decent bowler?"

"I'm a good enough bowler to have helped beat your team in two games," she replied, and felt the burn in her thighs as the machine beeped and she had to pick up her pace.

"Touché," he said. "Is it my turn to ask a question?"

"Sure," she said, because she wasn't certain how much longer she'd be able to talk normally.

"Have you been involved with anyone seriously since you and Caleb separated?"

Oh, wow, she hadn't expected that question. And really, she could probably use the fact that this inclined uptick in pace was hindering her conversating abilities, but that would be cowardly. "No," she replied, and knew exactly what was coming next.

"Why?" he asked.

She wouldn't look at him. Kept her gaze forward to the window that overlooked this corner of the city. From the outside, all the windows were tinted, which she personally liked. She never understood why people would want to be all hot and sweaty on a treadmill *and* be in a window on display at the same time. This way, she could see out, but nobody could see her sweaty boobs bouncing and thighs swishing as she struggled to maintain the next steps on this thing.

"I didn't want to," she replied.

"Why didn't you divorce him?"

Damn. Damn. Damn. She hadn't expected that question either.

"I don't know," she said.

"Yes, you do." His words were a challenge, and she hated each one. Hated that he was calling her on a point she'd battled with for far too long.

"I planned to," she said, still not looking his way. "This birthday is my new beginning, so one of the things I'd planned to do next month was get a lawyer and start the proceedings. I probably could've just filed the paperwork myself and had him served, but he might have fought it, so I wanted to be prepared."

And look at her now. Caught off guard by Caleb's death and the other legal problems he'd sent her way.

"You're right," he said. "He would've fought it."

Her head jerked in his direction then. "How do you know? Did he tell you something about it?"

He shook his head. His hands were pushed into the front pockets of his shorts now. "Right after I came back to town, one of our brothers mentioned Caleb was living back with his mother and that you had kept the house. That's how I knew I could find you at the address he'd given me a while back. But Caleb also didn't like to lose, at anything. Losing you, forever, would've definitely been a problem for him."

She was out of breath now, but that didn't stop her from asking, "So, that's how you knew we weren't together. That's why you had no qualms about shooting your shot at the cemetery?"

Their gazes held for a few seconds while she waited for an answer and she supposed he contemplated which one he was going to give her.

"I already told you I wasn't going to let another opportunity pass me by," he said, then shrugged. "So I didn't."

"And now . . ." She huffed. "Now you feel like you've . . . accomplished something?"

He tilted his head. "Now I feel like we're on our way to something."

"Oh," she said, because she didn't know how to respond to that admission. And because she couldn't say much else while her thighs burned and her heart felt like it was going to thump right out of her chest.

"I feel energized," she said two hours later—after the gym and after they'd each had a plate of lasagna and water when they returned to her house. "Like, I'm still kinda tired. Definitely ready for bed since it's almost eleven, but I've got energy. You know?"

He nodded. "I do know. And I'm not gonna say I told you so."

When they'd returned from the gym, Aden had brought his duffel bag into the house with him. When he'd placed it at the bottom of the stairs leading up to the bedrooms, she hadn't said a word. Was he planning to stay the night? Or was this just his take-a-shower-and-put-some-fresh-clothes-on bag? She didn't ask, wasn't sure what she would do with the answer if she did. But after dinner, when she declared it long past time she took a shower, he agreed on his own behalf and climbed those stairs with her. And joined her in the shower.

Vanna hadn't taken a shower with a man since Caleb. Not one of the men she'd slept with since her separation had she showered with. Hell, she hadn't even slept with any of them in this house because this was *her* house now. Her space, and hers alone. Except Aden had been in her bed, her shower, and he was sitting on the side of her bed again.

How was this her life?

"It's about feeding your body the right things," he said. "And no, I'm not just talking about food. Although we both know the benefits of a healthy lifestyle."

She'd just finished putting on her lotion and had stood to return it to her dresser when this conversation began. "Are you insinuating that I don't lead a healthy lifestyle?" she asked, and propped one hand on her hip.

"Woman, you love to argue, don't you?" he asked, and tossed his head back to laugh.

"I'm not arguing, but trying to clarify what you're saying," she countered.

"Come here," he said, and patted the space on the bed next to him.

After their shower he'd put on another pair of basketball shorts and a ribbed white tank top. Again, like he belonged here. Like this was his bedroom, *their* bedroom. She shook that thought away as she walked over to the bed and sat where he'd told her to.

"I said, I don't like to—"

He put a finger to her lips to halt her words. When she only glared at him, he smiled again. "Are you comfortable with your weight, Savannah? Are you fine with how you look?"

"Yes," she said without any doubt or dishonesty.

"Okay. Are you happy with how you feel on a daily basis?"

She opened her mouth to respond, then closed it. Then she tried again. "Not all the time. I get stressed and tired, and that's when I don't feel like myself."

"Good, that's fair. So maybe you start doing some things to work on that."

"Are you trying to fix me again?"

"You're not broken," he told her. "In fact, I think you're perfect," he said, and took her hands in his. "But we're all a continuous work in progress, especially as we go through things and get older. So, if you want to, I can set you up with one of my reps at the shop, and we can maybe find some holistic supplements that might help you feel better physically."

She pursed her lips. "And if I say no . . . ," she replied.

He shrugged. "I'm cool with that." He leaned in and kissed the shoulder left bare by her sleeveless nightshirt. "Just as long as you don't tell me no when we're here, like this."

Those kisses continued to rain over her shoulder until they landed on her collarbone and then her neck. "You're not slick," she said. "Ever since you showed up at my door tonight, you've been getting your way. And I don't like it."

"Hmmmm," he said, and kissed his way up to her ear, where he nipped her lobe and she moaned. "You sure you don't like it?"

He was grinning as he licked her ear again—she could hear it in his voice—but she didn't bother to deny it. "Oh, I like that well enough. It's all this other *Go to the gym, drink this water instead of the wine, take some supplements* that's rubbing me the wrong way."

"Because you're used to being in control," he said, moving a hand up to cup her breast while his kisses returned to her neck. "Used to making all the suggestions and decisions where you're concerned."

"Um, I think that's called being an adult," she said, and tried not to moan again. The combination of his mouth on her in one place and his hand on her in another was making her warm all over.

"It's called being controlling and not being open to suggestions." He squeezed her breast in his strong hand, then pinched her nipple and she hissed.

"I seem to be letting you suggest an awful lot right now," she replied.

"You are," he said, then pulled his mouth away from her neck. "And I'd like to reward you for such good behavior."

His smile was enigmatic. His tone husky. His touch, when she hadn't bothered to stop him, was addictive. In the next moments, her nightshirt and underwear were on the floor. Aden was naked, and they were in her bed, again.

This day that had started out so irritating, and had only grown worse by the hour, was ending on a blissfully sweet note.

Chapter 12

Keep glowing. Keep growing.

Vanna read the affirmation card she'd randomly selected this morning one more time.

She was pretty sure she was still glowing from the past few nights with Aden. And no, the glow didn't totally come from the way that man had mastered every part of her body in such a short span of time. Speaking of which, her smile widened as her skin tingled at the memory. But there were little things that had her feeling some type of way about these last few days. Like when he texted her.

Now, on any given day, Vanna's notifications kept her phone buzzing, whether it was her personal emails, text messages, or the couple of social media apps she was on. So that wasn't new. And her J&R thread stayed poppin', even while Jamaica was at work and not supposed to be on her phone. So receiving and replying to texts wasn't that big of a deal, until Aden began texting her. It wasn't just the normal new-dating messages, like, *Good morning, hru, wyd*—which she hated, by the way—*you wanna do something tonight?* No, his were more like *Hey, beautiful. You make it to work okay?* and *Just heard that nasty Tank song you love so much on the radio, you remember that time we . . .* , or her favorite, *Thinking of you.* Well, *Thinking of you* was a close second to any words of encouragement or scriptures that seemed to come right on time that he would send. And she would hurry to respond, enjoying engaging with a man in a way she hadn't in far too long.

She knew that wasn't exactly the type of glow this affirmation card was referring to—still, it made her steps a little lighter this morning as she put the card back in the box and turned to leave her room. In the grand scheme of things, she had every right to glow in all the possible ways. She was successful in her career, was paid well for her efforts, owned her own home, had healthy and thriving friendships, and had a meaningful family connection. For all intents and purposes, she was well-balanced and living her best life. And if anybody asked, she wouldn't deny one word of that statement.

The parts of her that wanted to push back against the declaration, she ignored. Especially this morning. Today she wanted only positive vibes. It was the last day for RSVPs to her birthday dinner at the end of the month, so that was something to get excited about. Women from her church, her coworkers, and a few she'd met by extension of her work and had clicked with over the years would be in attendance. She'd included plus-ones as if this were a wedding and was genuinely pleased at how many couples she already knew would be attending. Love had always been a positive beacon in her mind. A goal she'd thought she reached, only to be slammed back down again. Not that she didn't continue to believe in the institution of love, committed relationships, and, ultimately marriage, because she did. It probably just wasn't for her.

With her thoughts light, she walked down the stairs and went into the kitchen to grab one of the fruit smoothies she'd watched Aden make when he came over last night. It was full of some of her favorite fruits: strawberries, cherries, and blackberries. Then there was the healthy stuff he insisted on adding: steel cut oats, honey, turmeric, and two spoonfuls of powdered protein. He promised it would keep her full until lunch, when she definitely planned to enjoy the rest of the grilled chicken, onions, and cheese she'd cooked for dinner last night. Like she'd told him, she wasn't averse to being healthy—hell, she wanted to live a long and prosperous life—but she also knew that she only had this *one* life to live. She had no intention of denying herself the foods she loved while living it.

It was supposed to rain later today, so she double-checked her purse to make sure her travel umbrella was still inside. While digging, her fingers brushed over the charging documents she'd gotten last week. After her meeting with Jovani on Monday morning, she'd been determined to read the papers for herself. Other things had taken her mind right off that task, and she sighed because she wasn't about to read them this morning when she was in such a good mood. Subconsciously she knew it was a self-preservation move, and that from the outside looking in, it was probably smarter to just read them and get it over with. But she wouldn't. She desperately needed every shred of peace she could maintain. Besides, Jovani was handling this for her; adding her own worries to the mix wasn't going to make the investigation or impending court process go any faster.

With that in mind, she grabbed her purse and keys with her free hand and juggled all the things she was carrying to make it out the door. After checking the knob to make sure the door was locked, she turned and made her way down the porch steps and over to her driveway. Her car was still in the shop, and the rental SUV was actually growing on her. She pushed the automatic door opener on the keychain, and was about to reach for the handle on the passenger side so she could put her purse and lunch bag on the seat when she paused. A shiver eased down her spine, and she looked down the street to see if there was a reason why. The feeling that came next was indescribable, at least for her. *Eerie* was the best she could do as she slowly turned to look in the other direction.

Nothing she saw was out of the ordinary. More single-family homes occupied the block on both sides. Cars in driveways, a few parked on the street. Most were already gone for the workday. There weren't many kids in this neighborhood; the ones who had been here when the area had been appealing to Vanna and had ultimately led to the purchase of the home here had grown up and gone away to college or moved out.

So even though it was the middle of the summer, the block was still quiet, except for the occasional barking dog, a siren of some sort in the distance, and now, her rapidly beating heart. Because something wasn't right. She couldn't readily see it, but she felt it and she didn't like it. She didn't . . . There.

Right there, on the corner at the top of her block, was a car she didn't normally see in her neighborhood. Not that she was a car connoisseur or anything like that, but there were mostly couples, former families on this block, so the vehicles were SUVs, an old-ass Toyota minivan all the way at the other end of the block, and hybrid vehicles. This was a sedan. An older model, dirty-brown color with Maryland tags. From the distance of three additional houses on each side of the street, she could almost make out two people sitting in the front seat. Men, she supposed, but couldn't be totally sure.

Men she didn't know, sitting in a car that she didn't recognize, on her block.

She thought about going back inside her house and calling . . . who? The police? What would she say? *Hi, I don't think I've ever seen this car on my block before. Can you come and check it out?* They wouldn't take that seriously. Hell, how many real calls for help went disregarded by law enforcement these days? Too many, as evidenced by so many restraining orders that ultimately ended with the petitioner dead. Plus, she wasn't really feeling the police right now. What if she called them and they came running over here just to see if she had more of Caleb's stolen money? No, thank you.

Would she call Aden? Funny how he was the second one she thought of after the cops. Well, no, it wasn't that funny. He'd been intent on acting like he had a solution to her every problem since he'd been back in her life; it was no wonder she thought of him. Then again, she wasn't totally comfortable with that particular part of his position in her life right now. Besides, he would be at the gym now—or no, he had another meeting with the marketing department to go over glitches in the new website for the supplemental products and the print ads they would start running at the beginning of next month. Yeah, she knew what was going on in his business because that was one of the many things they discussed when they were together.

So what the hell was she going to do about this car?

Nothing, she decided. She was going to get herself away from the strange car. That seemed like the best action to take. So she opened the passenger door, set her purse and lunch bag on the seat. She kept the keys in her hand because they also had her can of Mace on it, and continued to hold the tumbler with her smoothie in it. At the driver's-side door, she opened it and slid onto the seat. Pressing the buttons to lock the doors was immediate; then she set the tumbler in the cup holder, started the truck, and backed out of the driveway. She had to pass the car to get off her street, and she told herself not to look to see if she knew the men.

Did it matter if she recognized them? Would she get out and talk to them if she did? What if it was someone she knew through Caleb? Yes, her husband was on her mind again. Dammit! Fear had been a steady part of her diet lately, and it was because of him and this nonsense he'd gotten her mixed up in. Jovani said there were codefendants with criminal records who had given Caleb's name as part of the robberies. What if they thought she had some of the money too?

What the entire hell?

Her mind screamed those words as her fingers gripped the steering wheel. Of course there was a stop sign at the corner, so she had no choice but to pull up and stop right alongside the ugly brown car. And because curiosity killed the cat—but she prayed it wouldn't get her—she turned her head slowly until she glimpsed one of the two men in the car.

She yelped when she saw he was staring right back at her.

Then she pressed on the gas and took off, making the widest, wildest right turn she'd ever made and then speeding down the street. She didn't dare look through her rearview mirror or take a breath until she was three blocks away and had made another turn to get on the highway.

By the time Vanna made it to her office, she'd calmed down somewhat. She hadn't called anyone while she'd been in the truck, preferring instead to listen to one of her gospel playlists in search of that peace that had been shaken by the ugly brown car.

It was probably nothing, she told herself an hour later as she stared at her computer screen. She hadn't done a thing except sip on that smoothie since she'd been in the office. That car and that guy, who had been staring at her like he wasn't a bit surprised to see her glance at him, couldn't possibly mean anything. But wait—he had looked at her with a sort of smirk, hadn't he? Now her hands began to shake again, and she cursed.

She reached down and opened the desk drawer where she kept her purse and pulled it out. Digging down to the bottom where she'd felt them this morning, she retrieved the papers she'd gotten last week. They were a mangled mess, so she smoothed them out on her desk, separating them so they looked like a miniature train on the surface. Then she sat back and stared at them.

Her gaze lingered on the caption on the first page, which read: *Superior Court of the District of Columbia v. Savannah Laniece Diane Carlson.*

In all the years that she'd been working in the legal field, never had she imagined seeing her own name on this type of official court document.

With a heavy sigh, she leaned forward so she could see the words. Then she began to read, her chest hitching when she saw some of the details Jovani had given her in his office. The ears he had on the street had definitely provided him more information than was typed on these forms; still, none of it gave any indication that two men would be sitting in a car on her block this morning.

Because it wasn't related.

Right?

She desperately wanted to believe that, but the commonsense part of her just wouldn't allow it to be so. She'd never seen the guy before, and couldn't see the person in the passenger seat at all. Her glance had been too quick, her foot on the gas pedal too fast, to give her any type of real description of the man. Except that he was Black. That was undeniable, as was the immediate feeling that he knew exactly who she was.

This was ridiculous. All of it was. How in the hell had she gotten mixed up in a robbery, or conspiracy to embezzle, or whatever these papers were calling it? She'd never stolen anything in her life. The office supplies she took from work didn't count, even in as much as they technically did. Everybody did that, and unless she was taking a computer or some other big item like that, neither HC Sr. nor Jr. was going to be pressing charges against her.

Still, that's what she was being accused of—stealing.

On a whim, she turned to her computer and pulled up her online banking login. She went into the system and viewed the balance of her checking, savings, and the IRA account she'd opened as a backup to the 401K plan she had through the firm. With today's current political climate, there was no way in hell she was depending totally on the social security she'd been paying into against her will since her first job when she was sixteen years old.

All the balances looked correct, and as she stared at the numbers on the screen, she wondered who else was looking at these numbers today. Who else was viewing her private financial information?

The phone ringing on her desk jerked her quickly out of those thoughts.

"Hello? Yes?" The two words spilled from her mouth even though she had no clue who was on the other end of the phone, whether it had been an outside call, to which this was the absolute wrong and unprofessional way to answer, or an inner-office call—in which case, her annoyed tone was only marginally problematic.

"Hey," Sanni said. "You ready for lunch? Want to go out and get some air first?"

A quick glance at the bottom of the screen told her it was indeed almost one o'clock. She hadn't realized how long she'd been sitting there reading those court documents and thinking about all this mess.

"Yeah, sure. Some fresh air sounds good," she said. In fact, it sounded amazing.

She needed to clear her mind and get on with her life. Whatever was going to happen with the case was going to happen whether she sat at this desk worrying about it or not. She'd just hung up with Sanni and reached down into the drawer for her purse when it started to vibrate. Not her purse, but the phone inside it.

When she found the phone, she was shocked to see that it was on vibrate. She never kept her phone on vibrate when she was in the office, even though she probably should've. And she definitely didn't put it on vibrate when she was driving. So when had she done it? When she realized the phone was ringing and not just vibrating from a notification, she hurriedly swiped it.

"Hey," she said a little breathlessly, even though she hadn't moved from that chair.

"Hey," Aden said, confusion clear in his tone. "You okay? I've been texting you all morning and you haven't replied. This is my second time calling. I was about to drive over to your office."

She sat back in the chair and sighed. "Sorry," she said, and closed her eyes. "I didn't know the phone was on vibrate, and it was in my purse, in the drawer, so I'm just hearing it."

"What's wrong?" was his next question.

Her eyes shot open, and she straightened in the chair as if he could actually see her. "Nothing," she replied. "I've just . . . um, been busy this morning. That's why I didn't notice my phone."

He was silent for a beat.

"You don't sound like yourself," he said.

She tried to smile. "Then who do I sound like?"

Another moment of silence. "How was your smoothie?" he asked.

"Tastier than I thought it would be," she answered. And that was mostly true. It had been tasty, but she hadn't really enjoyed it as much as she knew she would have if all that other stuff wasn't on her mind.

"Good," he said. "Listen, I've got a meeting tonight, and I'm not sure how long it'll last—"

"Oh, that's fine," she hurried to respond. "We don't need to hook up every night. We're not that serious. Besides, I have some stuff to do tonight too."

She was talking fast, so she forced herself to take a deep breath. He took those seconds to go silent again. She was just about to tell him she was heading out for lunch, because suddenly this conversation seemed awkward. Or perhaps it was just the mood she was currently in, who knew.

"I was going to ask if it would be okay to stop by when I was finished with my meeting," he continued. "I'd like to put eyes on you just to make sure all is well."

Guilt stabbed at her. She knew she was overreacting and overthinking, and she willed herself to stop both right this minute. "I'm sorry," she said. "It's been a really rough morning. But I did plan to stop by to see Granny after work and maybe take her out for something to eat. So how 'bout you just call me when you're finished with your meeting and we'll see how both of us are feeling then."

"Yeah, that sounds good," he replied, but he didn't sound as certain as he usually did.

Vanna didn't have the energy to question him at the moment. Possibly because she knew that would only end up in a deeper discussion as to what was bothering her. And she didn't feel like that right now. What she wanted most at this moment was to get out and get that fresh air Sanni had just mentioned. To talk to the other woman about *her* problems rather than sit and stew on her own.

"Okay," she said, and closed her eyes for a moment. "I'll talk to you later."

There was another moment of silence, which was starting to irritate her. What was he thinking? What did he want to say that he was holding back for whatever reason? And why did she even care?

"I'll talk to you later," he finally replied. "And Savannah?"

"Yes?"

"You know you can call me if you need me. Whatever it is, whenever you need me, you can just call," he said.

"Ah, yes . . . yes, I know," she said, then disconnected the call.

Chapter 13

Vanna: Can you stop by when you're done with your meeting?

She'd stared at that message for a long-ass four minutes before finally hitting the "Send" button. It was a little after ten in the evening, and she'd been sitting on her couch, pretending to watch the *Murder, She Wrote* marathon for the last two hours.

After work, she'd done exactly what she'd told Aden she would do: she went to visit Granny and suggested they go out for dinner. The comment had been impromptu when she'd been on the phone with him, just something to make it seem like she wasn't going to be sitting at home, waiting for him to decide to show up or not. And yes, that was petty. She prided herself on not being about games in any relationship—never again. So when she wanted to see a man, she would see him, and when she didn't, she would make that clear. She wanted that same courtesy from whatever man she was dating. But there'd been something in Aden's tone, something in the way he looked at her each time they were together, that had her feeling a little edgy where they were concerned. It was like she was in uncharted territory with him even though she'd clearly dated before. Hell, she'd been married before, so this, what they were doing, shouldn't be at all complicated.

And yet, it was.

Or at least, it felt like he was making it complicated. Or was she the one doing that?

"You seem distracted," Granny said when they were seated across from each other at Outback Steakhouse.

Granny loved a Bloomin' Onion and the Bloomin' Fried Chicken. Vanna had chicken last night and for lunch once she and Sanni had returned from their walk, so she'd ordered salmon instead.

Vanna's response had been to shrug because, just like she hadn't wanted to unload all that had happened this morning on Aden earlier, she didn't want to put that on her grandmother's shoulders either. "I'm okay," she said.

"You're not," was Granny's absent-minded reply as she pulled another piece of the onion off and put it into her mouth. "You shouldn't keep it all bottled up. I've been telling you that since you were a little girl."

She had, and Vanna had been ignoring the comment since then. "I'm not keeping anything bottled up. But I'm also not going to dwell on every time I have a hard day. It's counterproductive."

Granny finished chewing and reached for another piece. Her bracelets jangled and clunked as they hit the table. She wore wood-and-bronze earrings to match the jewelry at her wrists and her necklace today. "It's a shame how easily you sit at this table and lie to me," Granny told her. "But like I said, I'm used to it. You've been doing it since you were a child."

"Maybe I get it from my mama." The words slipped out before she could stop them, and her eyes widened as Granny stilled before she could get the food into her mouth. "I'm sorry, I didn't mean . . ."

Granny shook her head so hard and fast, the long earrings slapped against the side of her face. "Don't apologize for saying what you mean. Diane is a liar. Has been for most of her life. Neither of us can change that fact."

Unsure of what to say or do next, Vanna opted to scoop a pile of rice onto her fork and put it into her mouth to chew.

"But what my only child never seemed to have a problem doing was saying whatever she wanted," Granny said after she finally put that next piece of onion into her mouth, chewed, and swallowed. "No, that girl was a chatterbox from day one. Think she started talking before she started walking. She was lazy like that." Granny gave a wry chuckle. "Always wanted to be on my hip, like I hadn't carried her for almost forty-two weeks before those doctors finally decided to get her stubborn behind out of me."

Whenever Granny talked about her daughter, there was a lightness to her tone. Or at least, it usually started out that way. Vanna hated that she'd even brought this topic up. One thing she knew for certain, though: once Granny began talking about her child, she didn't stop until she was ready. So Vanna just continued to eat.

"Yes, she was a pretty little thing too. Eight pounds and four and a half ounces of screaming baby." With a shake of her head, Granny picked up her knife and fork and cut into her chicken. "Always had something to say. Thought she knew everything, even when she wasn't taller than my kneecaps. But you know I didn't let her get away with it—no, indeed. I tried to teach her how to respect me and others. How to respect herself."

Silence fell over the table as they both chewed.

"But somewhere along the way, I guess she forgot everything I taught her." Those words sounded so forlorn that Vanna wanted to reach out and touch her grandmother's hand. She wanted to apologize for bringing up what she knew was a painful topic for both of them. But she didn't. That's not how they dealt with the conversation about her mother.

"You, on the other hand," Granny said, and pointed her fork at Vanna, "know better, so I expect you to do better."

That Maya Angelou quote was printed on one of the affirmation cards in Vanna's box, so she knew it well.

"You keep everything you're feeling buried inside. You think if you pack it all up and never show it to anybody, people will only see what you want them to see," her grandmother said. "The beautiful, confident woman you've worked so hard to become. Well, I see her, Vanna. But

I also know you. So whether you tell me now what's going on or you call one of your girlfriends and chat their heads off with your problems, you need to let this mess out. You've got a lot going on; nobody's gonna judge you for venting every now and then."

"I vent to them plenty of times," she said. "And to you. How many times did I call you complaining about Caleb?"

"Not enough," Granny replied with a huff. "Not a damn 'nough. And you definitely didn't listen to my warnings about him—but you know folks in love can't hear a train rushing to mow them down."

"Definitely not," Vanna replied. "Seems like I just lay there on the tracks and let it run me right over."

"But you got up, didn't you?" Granny asked. "You went out there and you tried, you worked at it until you knew you couldn't anymore. Then you fell down, but you got up. That's what really matters, Vannie. People are gonna fall—some of us more times than others. But the true test of character is when you get back up. Don't let this mess that's going on now pull you down again. You've worked too hard to get yourself back on track."

And that was the truth. Vanna had thought on those words long after she'd dropped Granny off at the senior building and drove herself home. Then she ran herself a hot bath and sat in the tub until her fingers and toes were wrinkled.

But she'd been too restless to get into bed, so instead she'd come downstairs and curled up on the couch. Excitement had temporarily rippled through her when she saw there was a marathon of one of her favorite shows on tonight. It was mainly her favorite because Granny used to watch it all the time when she was younger. So every time she tuned in to watch Jessica Fletcher solve a murder that really wasn't any of her business, Vanna was wrapped in nostalgia. She felt comforted and soothed, exactly what she needed tonight.

Only it hadn't lasted long enough. By the second episode, irritability had reared its ugly head again. She detested this unsettled feeling, hated the way worry poked at the calm she attempted to foster, and simultaneously fought to keep these feelings from blossoming into the chest-constricting anxiety that could bring her to her knees. The loud *No!* that screeched through her head at the thought and the memory of her primary care doctor suggesting she start taking an anxiety medication a few years ago, and again each time she showed up for her annual physical, snapped her out of it. Or at least, it signaled that she needed to act quickly in order to prove to herself that her doctor—and Granny—were wrong. She didn't keep things bottled up; at least, she didn't want to this time.

So she grabbed her phone off the cushion beside her and opened the text thread. It had seemed so natural to ignore the J&R one she'd used most often up until last weekend and open the one under his name instead. She'd typed, deleted, and retyped the message multiple times in an attempt to get the words just right. There had to be a balance between sounding needy or clingy and being assertive. She wasn't sure either was what she wanted him to believe she was, but when she finally hit the "Send" button, she figured it didn't really matter now.

He probably wouldn't even respond, had most likely finished with his meeting and gone home. He owned a home in Southeast DC. Had told her it was one of the first purchases he made when he returned to the city. But he hadn't invited her there, and she hadn't asked to go. It was too soon; they both knew that.

And, sure, he'd said he would text her or call when he was finished with the meeting to see if he could stop by, but he hadn't. Another glance down at the phone told her it was too late to still be in a meeting—unless the meeting was with a woman, which was entirely possible. She hadn't asked him anything about the meeting, hadn't even thought to. But now, she wondered. She shouldn't wonder, because it didn't matter. They weren't exclusive. This wasn't a committed relationship. They were just enjoying each other, exploring that thing that had settled between them like a baby elephant when they were in college. That's all.

Twenty-five minutes later, when she still hadn't received a response to either of the texts she'd sent him, she pursed her lips and pushed herself up from the chair. "To hell with this," she muttered, and reached down to grab the remote so she could turn off the TV. She was going to bed. Sitting here waiting up for some guy to text her back was juvenile, and she hadn't been that young in a very long time.

The knock sounded at the door before she could hit the power button, and she gasped.

"Girl, get it together," she said with a sigh. But as she turned to drop the remote back onto the chair, she had a second thought.

A thought that took her right back to this morning, when she'd seen that ugly brown car and the man who'd been staring at her. Now her heart thumped a little wilder, her mind quickly grabbed hold of the fear and was prepared to run with it, when her phone dinged with a notification. She put down the remote and reached for her phone.

Aden: Hey. I'm outside. Are you in bed?

The sigh of relief that soared through her at seeing those words was dual parts annoying and comforting. And instead of replying, she put the phone down again and went to answer the door.

"Hey," she said. "I wasn't in bed. Just watching TV."

He looked at her for what seemed like a long moment before he stepped closer and touched a hand to her cheek. "Hey," he said, his deep voice cocooning her in an unexpected warmth.

They stood there for a few moments, right in her doorway, just staring at each other. Her in the shorts and tank top she planned to sleep in, and him in his slacks and dress shirt, unbuttoned at the neck.

She broke the trance first because it was too intense, sending too many emotions soaring through her and causing a flurry of confusion as it mingled with the other things she'd been feeling tonight. "Come in," she said as she took a step back.

He did, and she closed and locked the door. She knew he was staying. It had become an unspoken thing between them that she would question later. Tonight, she was going to allow herself to lean, just a little, on someone else.

"So, I have no idea who it was," she said a few minutes later after they'd settled on the sectional in the living room. "And it freaked me out."

Aden hadn't spoken a word since she told him she had something she needed to get off her chest. If he'd been worried about what that might be, she couldn't tell because he remained silent the entire time she relayed her story from this morning. Now, however, as she chanced a look at him, it was to see that his brow was furrowed, his lips drawn into a tight line. He sat leaning forward to rest his elbows on his knees, his hands balled into fists.

"Did you see the car again?" he asked. "I mean, any other time today when you were out. When you came home?"

She shook her head. "No. And Sanni and I went walking right after I talked to you at lunchtime. I haven't seen it, but I can't get it out of my mind."

She fell back against the cushions. "I mean, it's strange, right? That I got so worked up about it? This isn't some TV show where viewers have to figure out who the bad guys are before the innocent person gets too caught up in the trouble. This is my life, Aden. And I feel like it's being turned upside down by criminal charges, dead husbands—and now, what? A stalker?"

He turned slightly so that he could reach for both her hands and hold them in his. "Take a breath," he said, and when she looked at him, he hiked his brows up to reiterate the command.

She sighed.

"A deep breath, Savannah," he said.

He held her gaze, and she was reluctant to look away or find another rebuttal to his words. She sucked in a breath slowly, then released it.

Aden was the one shaking his head this time. "Do it again," he said. "Breathe in through your nose, out through your mouth. Slow and steady."

She frowned. "I'm not having contractions, Aden."

He smirked. "Just do it."

She did, and when he said "Again," she obliged, until on the third deep breath, the heaviness that had built in her chest started to subside.

"Now, I want you to listen to me," he said, still holding her hands. "We're going to call Jovani first thing in the morning. I would call him tonight, but I don't want Megan cussing me out for ringing her phone at this time of night again. I already owe her a couple hours of babysitting for last week's call."

"You? Babysitting?" she asked with a frown.

"Fix your face," he said. "I know how to watch a baby. My older sister has a nine-year-old and a set of twins. I've watched all three of them before."

She shrugged. "I'm impressed." Actually, she was intrigued. She would've liked to have seen Aden in action with children. He'd always struck her as the macho I-can't-boil-an-egg type. Learning about his personal input into some of the holistic supplements he planned to feature on his website and at the gym had been a nice surprise.

"Don't change the subject," he said. "This is serious, Savannah. You're not wrong for being afraid. So we're going to let Jovani know what's going on. He has people on the streets; he can get some eyes on you. And if he can't, then I will."

"He told me about his eyes and ears on the street." She sighed. "But I don't want to be watched. Not by anyone."

"The ugly brown car, as you put it, took that option away from you," he told her. "We can't rule out that it was the cops either. Or someone working with them to try and get more evidence against you."

"What evidence? There is none because I didn't do anything!" She hadn't wanted to raise her voice, had wanted to just tell him about this incident and move on with their night, but calling her lawyer, possibly having someone watching her from now on, the police, and this whole investigation . . . it was all working her nerves.

"Look, I just want to be able to get some rest without thinking about this," she said, purposely leaving out the fact that she'd seemed to sleep a lot better the last few nights he'd been in her bed.

Of course, that could've also been because of what they'd done in that bed before falling asleep. Sex with Aden was by far the best she'd had in a very long time. She enjoyed it immensely, just as she enjoyed being wrapped in his arms as she fell into a deep sleep. If she could get just that portion of their relationship tonight, that would certainly be enough.

"Okay," he said with a nod. "Then that's what you'll get. Do you want a glass of wine, some herbal tea?"

A light smile touched her lips. "I see how you slipped that healthy drink in there."

He brought both her hands to his lips for a quick kiss on the back of each. "Of course I did. Now, which one do you want?"

"Honestly," she said, trying hard as hell to resist the warm tingles that eased down her spine at that simple romantic gesture, "I think the tea would be great."

"Good," he said with a wink. "I'll take care of it. You go on upstairs and get into bed."

"You're bossy, you know that?" she said as he stood and used his grip on her hands to pull her up with him.

"No, I'm not," he countered.

"Yeah, you are," she said. "You've been giving me orders since you came in here. Since you waltzed back into my life, actually."

Releasing her hands, he stared down at her. "I like to call it 'taking care of you,'" he said. "Do you know how long I waited for the opportunity to treat you like you deserve to be treated?"

Oh. Damn. This was not the direction she saw this going. She should've just gone on upstairs and waited for her tea like a good little girl.

"All those times I watched you with Caleb, saw him leaving you at the table while he ran around the room, talking to everybody but you. When we were out and he was careful to keep you close to him, but he barely paid you any attention." He shook his head.

And Vanna felt like turning and walking away. This was a reminder of how early on Caleb had begun to show his ass—and how she'd learned to ignore it.

"I'm just doing what I've always wanted to do," he said, and she effectively felt like crap.

This man was too good to be true. Had he really held on to his crush for her all these years? Had he watched her be with Caleb and felt some kind of way about it? Surely that couldn't be true, since he had a girlfriend much of the time she'd known him in school. And she hadn't even thought of him in that way. Well, not as much as he apparently thought of her. Yes, she stole looks at him, plenty of them. And yeah, she daydreamed a time or two about what it might've been like if they'd been the ones navigating through a relationship, but all that was futile, and she'd known that, so she hadn't given it nearly as much attention as it seemed he had.

He scrubbed his hands down his face and gave a dry laugh. "Ah, man, I did not mean to say all of that."

She cleared her throat, almost wishing she hadn't heard all of that. "It's okay. I mean, if that's how you feel."

Letting his arms fall to his sides, he said, "It is how I feel, Savannah. But we don't need to go into that right now. Can you just go upstairs while I fix your tea? I want you to get that rest you need."

All the right words; that's what Aden always seemed to say. All the right words, and he did all the right things—now that his bossiness had been put into perspective. But what did any of it mean? She was still asking herself that question a little while later when he delivered her cup of tea.

"I can leave now that you're all set," he said as he stood on her side of the bed. "If that's what you want. I don't want you to feel like I'm crowding you or moving too fast. I realize all this can be coming off that way, and it's really not my intention."

"I don't want you to leave," she said, and stared down at her hands, now resting on top of the sheets that covered her legs. "I want—"

Her next words died as a loud crash echoed through the air and everything around them shook. Tea spilled over the rim of the mug, splashing onto the nightstand where he'd set it. The lamp wobbled, and Aden moved closer to the bed, ready to shield her from whatever. Seconds later a horn blared, and they both stared at each other quizzically.

Frowning down at her, he yelled, "Stay here and call 911!"

But the second he moved away from the bed, Vanna tossed those sheets back and jumped off the bed.

"Savannah!" he yelled when she was right behind him.

"Don't 'Savannah' me," she countered. "This is my house, dammit! I'm going to see what's happened."

Not bothering to argue with her because he probably figured it was pointless, Aden turned and headed down the stairs. She was right behind him again, until they both came to an abrupt stop at the sight of shattered glass throughout her living room, splintered drywall, her love seat turned over, and the front bumper of a car.

"Stay back," he said, putting out an arm to keep her in that spot in case she planned to not listen to him again.

Which she definitely did, until he followed up with, "There's glass everywhere, and you didn't put on any shoes."

She looked down at her pink toenails smiling up at her and huffed. "How the hell did a car . . . ." Her words trailed off again as memories of that car from this morning popped up in her mind. "Oh. No." She was just about to turn back and run upstairs to grab her phone to call the police when she heard a sound.

Barking.

Aden had already started toward the door. She could hear him open it, and seconds later the barking was louder and the clickety-clack of nails on her hardwood floors filled the air.

"Frito?" she asked as the dog came up the steps and all but skidded into her. Then he was running circles around her, barking and jumping up so that his front paws were on her bare legs. "What's wrong? How did you get here?"

"Them bitches put me out!" Granny yelled.

She was coming up the steps with Aden close behind. "They had the nerve to tell me I had to go," Granny continued. "After they take almost half my check to stay in that filthy apartment the size of a damn closet. Get off of me! I told you I was okay! Get outta my personal space before I let your ass have it too."

With that, she reached into her bag and pulled out her gun, whirling around until she could point it at Aden.

"Whoa!" he yelled, immediately putting his hands up.

"Granny! Wait! What are you doing?" Vanna yelled and—to hell with the glass on the floor—tiptoed over to where her grandmother now stood.

Frito was still barking, which, on top of all that had happened today, was really starting to work Vanna's nerves.

"What? I told him to get away from me," Granny said, then glanced over at Vanna. "Just like I told that stank hoe Sylvia to get her ass outta Sam's bed. And you know what she told me?"

"Granny," Vanna said, reaching out to place a hand on Granny's outstretched arm in the hope of lowering the gun.

But Granny didn't budge; she just kept right on talking to Vanna.

"She told me if I was doing it right, he wouldn't have had to come and get some from her." Granny was shouting now. Her hair was wild, the gold caftan she wore giving her an ethereal glow as she ranted. "Now, you know I knows how to get down," she said, and demonstrated by dropping it like it was hot right there in the destroyed living room while still holding a gun.

"Give me that," Vanna said finally, and reached out to grab her grandmother's wrist. The gun wasn't loaded, which was the only reason she never really pitched a fit at Granny carrying it all around the city with her. One of her worst nightmares had been having to go and bail her grandmother out of jail for catching a handgun charge.

Granny had no permit, and as far as Vanna knew, she'd never been to a gun shop to buy any bullets. About twelve years ago, the man Granny had been messing with at the time had owned several guns, and when Granny put him out of her house, she'd stolen one of them. That, and his entire collection of original Motown albums.

"Just give it here," Vanna said, and grabbed the gun out of Granny's hand. "Did you have something else to drink?"

Granny had ordered a Long Island iced tea when they'd been at Outback, and Vanna hadn't minded because she knew she was driving her right back to the senior building. Now, however, she was second-guessing that decision.

"Maybe we should go to the ER," Aden said, and pointed to his forehead.

Granny was still in her squatting position—probably a lot harder for her to bring it back up than it had been to drop it down. She was picking up Frito, so Vanna tossed a questioning glance at Aden. He kept pointing to his head and then pointed down at Granny. So when Granny stood, clutching her dog to her chest, Vanna gasped. "You're bleeding."

Instead of acting shocked or concerned for her own safety—which, considering the bumper of her car was now peeking through Vanna's front windows—Granny lifted a hand to where the blood was on her forehead. She didn't touch the wound, though, oh no—her grandmother fluffed her hair.

"Sylvia thought swinging that cane was gonna stop me, but when I got hold of her ass, it was on," Granny said with a bleak grin.

Vanna couldn't do anything but sigh. It was that or cry, and she didn't want to do that—not in front of Aden, who was probably thinking he should've just ignored her text message and taken himself back to the normalcy of his own home.

Chapter 14

"You. Are. Lying!" Jamaica basically screamed from outside the dressing room in the department store where they were shopping for swimsuits.

Inside the small space, Vanna shook her head as if Jamaica could see her. "Nope. Not lying. When I left my house today, there were three construction men present, discussing how long it was going to take them to repair part of the front wall of my house."

Jamaica's laughter was just as loud as the screeching she'd been doing since Vanna began telling her about what happened last night. She peeled off the one-piece tummy-control suit and tossed it onto the small bench against the wall. "Too plain," she murmured.

"So, wait, you had to call contractors? How'd you get them to come out so fast? My mother waited a day and a half for a plumber to come out and give her an estimate," Jamaica said.

Vanna picked up the second bathing suit, but not before turning to the side to view herself in the mirror. Of course, she'd kept her panties and bra on while trying on the garments, so she had to take into account how that would skew the look of the suit, but she still had a precise look she was going for—sexy and unapologetic. Hopefully, this one would be it.

"Aden knew a guy," she said, and leaned forward to balance herself on one leg while she pushed the other into the suit.

"Ooooh, Aden knew a guy. He knows a lot of guys that come in handy for you, doesn't he?"

"Stop it," Vanna chastised as she shimmied into the very tight material. A portion of the sides to this one were just a row of strings, like a ladder, so she had to be careful not to get her other foot—or her arm, for that matter—stuck in one of them. "I'm actually glad he was there. Granny was a mess! Did I mention she pulled her gun on him?"

"What?" Jamaica's tone was even louder this time because she pulled the door to the dressing room open at the same time. Her eyes were wide as she continued, "Granny was going to shoot Aden?"

"Girl, get in here before somebody walks by and sees all my goodies," Vanna snapped.

Jamaica squeezed into the dressing room and closed the door behind her. She picked up the pile of bathing suits on the bench and plopped down. "So, why was she going to shoot him?"

"He was trying to help her, wanted to take care of the cut on her forehead or possibly take her to the ER. And she just turned on him." The swimsuit was pulled all the way up, the top adjusted correctly over her breasts. She turned to the side again, then to the back, and looked over her shoulder.

"Your ass looks hot in that," Jamaica said. "Like, ole boy's gonna want to peel that right off you and get busy in the pool."

"Not!" It was Vanna's turn to yell, her eyes going wide. But when she turned to look at herself from the front again, she smiled. "It does look good, though."

Behind her, Jamaica nodded too. "It does, and it's pink. I'm telling you, we're gonna look like a bunch of cotton candy by the end of this month."

"Oh, hush, this is the first event I've asked everyone to wear pink. You have your outfit, right? Or do we need to go over to your size section and pick something out?"

"I've got a pink bathing suit, girl." Jamaica rolled her eyes and started looking through the pile of suits she'd dropped onto her lap. "I ordered it from Amazon," she said.

"Amazon sells bathing suits?"

"They sell everything. I keep tellin' you and Ronni, y'all be missing out." Jamaica held up another suit. "You try this one on? It's a two-piece. Sexxxxy!"

"Oh yeah, let me try that one," Vanna said, and began easing out of the second one. "This one goes in the keeper pile."

"Definitely," Jamaica said. "Okay, now let me get this straight: the senior home is putting Granny out because she threatened two of the tenants?"

"Not just threatened them. She mooned them, then waved her gun in Sylvia Randolph's face. And when the night manager came into Sam's apartment to try and gain some order, she cursed him out too. Told him she'd beat his ass all up and down the halls." Vanna shook her head as she accepted the two-piece suit from Jamaica and handed her the other one.

Jamaica laughed. "Girl, you can't write this shit! I mean, woooowww. Granny's pushing eighty, and she's out in these streets fightin' over some man."

"And she don't even want him," Vanna said. "That's the kicker. She's been sleeping with every man she can in that building, whenever she feels like it, so I don't even know why she's trippin' over Sam doing the same thing."

"It's different, you know that," Jamaica said.

"No. That's the other way around. Men are cool when they cheat but can't take it when a woman cheats. Granny's out here in her feelings over Sam, when she's getting it in with anybody who can get it up." She pulled the bottom piece up and over her stomach, loving how it smoothed out her side rolls there.

"True, true. But that Sylvia woman was runnin' off at the mouth too, right?"

Vanna put her arms through the top piece and took a step back so Jamaica could snap it. If she were in here alone, she would've worked it like she put her bra on in the morning, but since Jamaica had brought her silly self in here, she might as well be of some use.

"That's what Granny said, and she said that's what really pissed her off. If Sylvia wasn't gloating and acting like she'd stolen Sam from Granny, then Granny would've told her she could have him because his breath stank when he didn't clean his dentures properly."

The howl of laughter Jamaica let out from behind her had Vanna chuckling too. "Girl, it's not funny. When I finally managed to leave my house late this morning and get to the senior building to talk to the manager, they told me I had seven days to get all of her stuff out of the apartment. I told them absolutely not, she's paid up until the thirty-first, so that's how long I had to move her out. But I did grab her some clothes and Frito's food."

She started her turns as she surveyed this suit in the mirror. It was a darker shade of pink than the first one—which she would never admit to Jamaica did put her in mind of cotton candy. But she liked this almost-fuchsia one too.

"It's giving great cleavage," she said.

"Don't gloat. I swear I hate you big-titty girlies," Jamaica said.

"Aw, don't be salty—there's plenty of room in the pool for you B-cupsters," she joked.

"Ha ha. That's why you've got a permanent houseguest now, and just when you finally started getting some in-house dick."

"You're not funny," she replied. "That's not even the worst part—plus, Granny always uses the bigger guest room, which has a bathroom and is the farthest away from mine. But the worst part is, I stepped in Frito-poop this morning."

Jamaica's frown would've been hysterical if not for the memory of that nasty mess on her bare feet at seven thirty this morning when she'd made her way downstairs to start a pot of coffee. "Granny says he gets nervous poops and forgets to go out to handle his business. I'm like, really? That dog has been to my house a million times, and now he's nervous."

"No, he's nervous because his owner just ran his little ass through the front window of that house," Jamaica added.

Looking at her through the mirror, Vanna nodded. "You got a point there."

"So, what's the verdict? 'Cause you can't possibly be buying all of these. The pool party is only four hours long. You gonna be making outfit changes like you're hosting an award show?"

Vanna ran a hand down her very smoothed-out stomach one more time. "Definitely this one and the other one with all the strings on the side. And no, I'm thinking one change. I'll wear the first one as my party outfit, then put this one on when I'm ready to get in the water."

"That's a plan. And that's definitely the one you get wet . . . you know, before Aden gets you even wetter," Jamaica said with a wiggle of her eyebrows.

Vanna couldn't help but recall Jamaica's parting remark when she walked into the conference room later and saw Aden sitting next to Jovani. The call from Jovani's assistant telling her about this evening meeting at the Metro Police Department had come just as she was leaving the mall with Jamaica. So instead of going home to check on Granny and Frito, she'd driven there. She hadn't known what to expect from this meeting, but she knew she hadn't expected to see Aden here.

She hadn't spoken to him since he'd checked in via text earlier this afternoon. After waiting at her house for the construction guys who had worked on the renovations for his gym to show up, he'd had to get to work himself. That hadn't been a problem for her; he'd already helped so much throughout the night, with getting Granny and Frito settled, talking to the police who showed up at the house because one of her neighbors had called them, and then talking Vanna down from the ledge she was ready to toss herself over after all that had happened.

She'd just made it to her office when his text came in, so nobody had been able to see the way his words made her smile.

Right now, she wasn't smiling, though, as she moved farther into the room. Aden stood and walked toward her. He touched a hand to her elbow and leaned in to kiss her on the cheek before leading her to a seat between him and Jovani.

"You doing okay?" Jovani asked when she was settled into the chair. "How's your grandmother?"

So, Aden had told Jovani everything. Last night before the walls had literally come crashing in, he'd said "they" would call Jovani this morning, but while she'd talked to the contractors, he'd taken care of the call.

"Yeah," she said with a wave of her hand. "It's been a long day, but I'm as good as I'm gonna get. And I called Granny before I came into the building; she's holding up too."

Honestly, Granny had probably spent the afternoon cleaning Vanna's house from top to bottom. She always cleaned when she was upset. Even though she'd insisted she wasn't upset when Vanna had left the house.

"I'm sorry all this is happening," Jovani said. "But I'm going to try to get to the bottom of some of this mess tonight."

"Good," she replied with a nod, and clutched her purse that was sitting in her lap. "It's kind of late for a meeting, right?"

"The detectives were on the evening shift," Jovani told her. "I thought about asking for their lieutenant but figured I wouldn't go over their heads just yet."

Vanna was about to ask another question when a second door on the other side of the room opened. Detectives Parish and Beaumont sauntered in. Beaumont carried a notepad and a file folder, while Parish was empty-handed. They both took seats across the table from Vanna and what felt like her two-man team.

"Mrs. Carlson," Beaumont said. "Nice to see you again so soon."

Jovani cleared his throat. "Thank you for meeting with us this evening, Detectives," he said. "Mrs. Carlson would like to report an incident which took place at her home yesterday morning."

Parish's brow went up. "Yesterday morning, you say? We got word that a report was taken from her home address late last night. Something about a car crashing into your house—but you didn't want to press charges because you knew the person."

In her lap, her hands gripped her purse again, but she sat with her shoulders straight, her gaze leveled at Parish. "My grandmother had an accident. She doesn't see well at night." And was slightly buzzed and not wearing her glasses, but they didn't need to know that part.

Beaumont chuckled. "Oh my. Well, I'm sure that's a mess. But I don't know how that relates to this case."

"Because that's not the incident we're here to report," Jovani said. "Yesterday morning, there was a strange car with two men inside parked across the street from Mrs. Carlson's house."

Parish shrugged. "And?"

"*And* we want to file an official report giving the description of the car and the occupants in case it's connected to this case you've decided to include my client in," Jovani said.

Beaumont flipped open the file folder, which he'd set on the table. "You mean, the case your client is knee-deep in."

"I am not knee-deep in anything," Vanna said, and felt Aden's hand on her arm at the same time that Jovani made a motion with his hand for her to remain silent.

But she didn't want to keep quiet; she wanted to scream to the rafters that this was some BS! These detectives were still looking at her like she was guilty, disregarding all that Jovani had said and preferring to joke about her grandmother's incident instead.

"Oh, but you are," Beaumont continued. "You see, since the last time we met, we've uncovered a few more interesting facts."

"What facts?" Jovani asked. "Because so far, all you have is circumstantial evidence against her."

"You might consider this more circumstantial evidence, Counselor," Parish said. "But the more we dig, the more dirt we find."

Vanna clenched her teeth and narrowed her gaze at him. She didn't know which one she despised more. Probably Beaumont, because even though she was sitting there between two men, he still had come right in letting his gaze shamelessly drop to her breasts, just as he had before.

"Do you know Elliot Joble?" Beaumont asked.

Vanna glanced over at Jovani, and when he nodded, she replied, "No."

Parish had sat back in his chair, but his arm was stretched onto the table, where he now drummed his fingers. "You sure? Because he seems to have known you."

"What does that mean, Detective?" Jovani asked. "She said she didn't know him."

"Then how do you explain someone you don't know having your business card?" Beaumont asked.

"Anyone can pick up a business card in an office; that doesn't mean they know the person whose name is on the cards," Jovani replied. "Not to mention, this isn't what we're here for."

He seemed really calm as he stared at the detectives. He hadn't even glanced down at the file Beaumont had, while Vanna had tried to sneak a peek at it several times now. She knew that amused Beaumont by the way he hadn't tried to hide any of the papers inside.

"Well, it's a coincidence that you requested this meeting tonight, because we were going to schedule another, more formal interview with you," Beaumont said. "You see, on Tuesday night, Elliot Joble was involved in a motorcycle accident. Witnesses say a black SUV drove him off the road until he and his bike crashed into a tree. You drive a black SUV, right, Mrs. Carlson?"

No, she didn't. Well, not normally. Her Camry was blue. But the Explorer she was renting because her car was in the shop was black.

"Don't answer that," Jovani directed.

"It rained pretty hard on Tuesday night, so witnesses couldn't get a good look at a license tag, but they were adamant that it was a black SUV that was speeding down the road behind Elliot on the motorcycle," Beaumont continued, his gaze locked on Vanna.

"We're sorry to hear of his passing, but that has nothing to do with my client," Jovani said. "Now, I've prepared an official statement from my client on what took place at her home yesterday." She hadn't seen the leather briefcase on the empty chair beside Jovani, but now he reached into it and pulled out a file folder of his own.

He set it on the table and used the tips of his fingers to push it in the direction of the detectives. "While you're looking for your SUV, keep an eye out for this vehicle as well."

Beaumont didn't even glance at the folder, but Parish picked it up.

"Elliot Joble worked as a cage cashier with your husband," Beaumont continued. "Perhaps that's how he came to be in possession of your business card. Maybe you were referring him to one of the lawyers you work with, had your husband give him your card to set up a meeting. Or maybe . . ." Beaumont leaned in, an annoying grin sliding across his face. "Maybe he needed your card so he could get in touch with you about the money from their last heist before the botched one. Seems every member from the team hadn't received their payment for that job. Do you have their money, Mrs. Carlson?"

Jovani chuckled. "This fishing expedition is over, Detectives." He grabbed his briefcase and stood.

Aden stood as well, and reached out a hand to help Vanna from her seat.

"If you get any leads on that car, please let us know," Jovani said. "In the meantime, if my client sees it again, she's calling 911, so make sure your guys know someone is stalking her. I'd hate to file a complaint against the department for ignoring my client's concerns."

Jovani moved from behind the table first and headed for the door. Vanna followed him, noting that neither of the detectives stood. When

Aden abruptly released her hand, she looked back to see him lean over the table to get into Beaumont's face.

"And next time, I'd advise you to keep your eyes on her face," Aden said, his voice tight with irritation, "or sexual harassment will be another complaint filed against you."

Beaumont had the good sense to look momentarily flustered before Parish grumbled and stood. "Don't leave town, Mrs. Carlson. This investigation isn't over."

Vanna didn't acknowledge his words with a response, but let Aden take her hand in his again as they walked out of the room.

The front door was still intact, but the large picture window and a portion of the wall going toward the opposite side of the house was now covered with plywood. There was a huge dumpster on the grass in front of the house and supplies stacked in her driveway when she pulled up at almost 8:00 p.m.

For a few minutes, Vanna could only stare through the windshield at the mess. Then she whispered a prayer of thanks that it hadn't been worse. Granny had refused to go to the ER, even when the uniformed officers had arrived and asked her several times. So Vanna had cleaned and put a bandage on the cut—which actually hadn't been that deep—on her forehead. And the car had been towed a couple hours after the impact. But the fact that this could've been so much worse hadn't escaped her.

Her grandmother could've been killed in an accident like this. The house could've had much more extensive damage that Vanna would have to figure out how to pay for. As it stood now, she didn't want to put in a claim with her homeowner's insurance for fear they would want to sue Granny and recoup any funds they paid out from Granny's car insurance. Which was actually Vanna's insurance as well, as Vanna had added her grandmother to her policy the moment

Granny had retired. Either way she was going to end up paying for the damages, so leaving the homeowner's policy out of the equation made even more sense.

But now, after all the grace that had seemingly been offered in that instance, a black SUV had run down some guy who Caleb used to work with. Lowering her forehead to the steering wheel, she wondered how she'd managed to draw the short straw when life's journeys were being given out. Who the hell had she pissed off so badly that all this awful karma was coming back on her? Sighing, she almost chuckled at those thoughts. But she couldn't laugh, couldn't cry—hell, she was even tired of feeling at this point. She knew for certain she was tired of worrying every damn day. And that nagging feeling that there was more drama just waiting around a corner for its chance in line to wreak havoc in her life was turning into a burning rage.

When her forehead started to hurt, she lifted her head from the steering wheel and reached over to the passenger seat to grab her purse and phone. She hadn't bothered to pack a lunch today since she'd gone into the office so late. The loud growl her stomach gave the moment she stepped out of the truck signaled that was a problem. Stepping over a bag of what looked like cement or sand, she made her way up the front steps and to the door. She could hear the music blasting from inside, and a smile ghosted her face.

Granny was safe, and Frito too. That's all that mattered right now.

Vanna found her in the kitchen, barefoot and dressed in a white nightgown that stopped just above her ankles. Frito was sprawled on his stomach in front of the sink.

"Hey, Vannie," Granny said when she turned to see Vanna enter. "I was just putting this plate in the microwave for you. Didn't know how much longer you were gonna be, but I wanted you to have some dinner."

"Thanks, Granny," Vanna said, going closer and leaning in to kiss her grandmother's cheek.

Granny wrapped her arms around Vanna when she was close and held on tight. "I'm sorry, baby," she whispered. "So sorry to bring all this mess to your doorstep. I don't know what came over me last night."

Vanna hugged her grandmother back and kissed the top of her head. "Oh, probably that Long Island iced tea and that Mabeline temper."

Granny chuckled as she pulled out of the embrace. "Yeah, well, I might be getting too old for them both."

At the mention of that word, Vanna looked at Granny a little more closely. She did look older tonight. Something around her eyes and her mouth seemed tired, and her shoulders sagged just a little bit more. "What did you cook?" she asked, because thinking about her grand-mother getting old and that brush with death last night was about to make her collapse into tears.

"I made a meat loaf. Some mashed potatoes and corn. I know you love to mix those two together," Granny said, and reached into the microwave to take out the plate. She set it on the counter and was about to remove the foil she'd wrapped it in, but Vanna stopped her.

"Yesss, and thank you so much. I'm starving. But I want to get a shower first, so I'll warm it up when I get done."

"Oh yeah, that makes sense," Granny said. "Well, okay. Guess I'll go on up and lay down."

"You sure? You can keep my company while I eat," Vanna said.

"No. No. I'm not gonna be in your way while I'm here, Vannie. I know you've got yourself a little boyfriend now, and I don't want to intrude on y'all's time."

"First," Vanna said with a shake of her head, "Aden's a forty-two-year-old, six-feet-one-inch-tall man, so there's nothing 'little' about him. And he's not my boyfriend. We're just . . . ah . . . we're just . . ."

"You're just fuckin'."

"Granny!" Vanna scolded.

"What? I know what you're doing. Hell, I've been doing it more than half my life," Granny said. "And doing it is what almost had me catching a charge last night."

Vanna didn't know what to say to that, so she just laughed. There was no one like her Granny. Nobody she loved more than this woman, who didn't know what to say out of her mouth most of the time but had a heart of gold.

Chapter 15

The pool party had been a great success, the fuchsia bathing suit as enticing as Jamaica had predicted. And the time spent with Aden after the party . . . well, that had been quite memorable as well.

So memorable, she was at her desk after lunch on Monday with her body still tingling as she recalled the highlight of the evening.

To be fair, having twenty-six people gathered to celebrate her and frolic around at a hotel pool was a fantastic time. In addition to renting the pool and a room close to it at one of DC's premier hotels, Vanna had also hired a DJ and a caterer. Light fare had been on the menu—shrimp tostadas, deviled eggs, creamy chicken salad bites, pepperoni pizza bites, and charcuterie cups. Drinks other than punch and water needed to be purchased at the hotel bar near the lobby, but nobody seemed to mind. The highlight of this event was definitely the hotel's inside pool, since the day had been a sizzling ninety-eight degrees and 85 percent humidity.

"You look amazing," Aden said when he'd sat on the lounge chair next to hers.

They'd been situated there, facing the top end of the pool, since the start of the party. On her other side were four more lounge chairs where Jamaica, Davon, Ronni, and Croy sat. Granny couldn't swim and detested the idea of taking off most of her clothes to sit by a pool she had no intention of getting in. That, from the woman who just last week had lifted her dress, pulled down her panties, and shown her bare ass to two elderly persons and a middle-aged married man with three kids.

"Thank you," Vanna replied, trying not to blush.

When the first two hours of the party passed, she'd stood and announced she was going for a wardrobe change. Aden had stood as well and offered to get them more food.

"I might have to get you to plan my next birthday," he said, picking up a chicken salad bite—which was salad and a cucumber slice on top of a Ritz Cracker—and bringing it to his mouth.

She reached over to the plate he'd set on the small table between their chairs and chose a deviled egg. She'd pretty much eaten those and the pizza bites the entire time. Dessert was fruit cups and mini cupcakes from the same baker she was using the entire month. She couldn't wait for those to come out.

"When's your birthday?" she asked, before taking a bite of the egg.

"January seventh," he said.

"Ooohhh, winter activities. Lots of possibilities, but we'd have to do a little travel. A ski trip would be great!" Her mind was already soaring with ideas, and as she talked, he chuckled. "You laughing at me, Mr. Granger?"

"Nah, I'm laughing *with* you, Ms. Savannah. I like hearing you get excited. And I like seeing you smile."

"Well, she's been smiling at you a whole lot today," Jamaica said as she got up to start walking toward the pool. "And now, since you've changed into your 'wet approved' outfit, let's get in this water."

Vanna ignored the wink Jamaica gave at the words *wet approved*, recalling her remarks from their swimsuit-shopping trip. "I guess you're right," she said. "About the time to get in the pool part. I mean, it is a pool party."

And because it was, she'd sat for eight hours after work yesterday to get her hair braided. By the time she'd gotten home, she'd been exhausted and her scalp was on fire, the knotless braids were so tight. Today, they were still tight, but cute as hell as they cascaded down to stop at the small of her back.

By the time the party was over and the last guest had been hugged, thanked for coming, and seen out the door, Vanna was still smiling, and Aden—just as Jamaica had predicted—hadn't been able to keep his hands off of her.

"One last swim," he suggested when he stepped close enough to put his hands on her waist.

"It's almost eleven," she said. "Somebody from the hotel is bound to come in here soon and tell us it's time to get out."

He shook his head. "We've got sixteen minutes," he said. "I checked."

She chuckled. "You want another swim that bad?"

They'd played in the water for over an hour during the last half of the party. Somebody introduced a volleyball, and the competition had begun. Not only was it the three guys against the three girls, as it had been during the bowling outing, but now other guys had joined the team led by a very competitive Davon, and their partners had joined an equally-as-competitive team led by Jamaica. It had been a super-fun time, but now, Aden was suggesting a solo swim.

He eased into the pool first, reaching his hands up for her like he really expected her to jump into them. With a shake of her head, she knelt down and put one leg at a time into the pool, just as she'd done before. His hands were at her waist again the moment she was submerged up to her breasts.

"I had a great time at your pool party, Savannah," he said, then lowered his face to nuzzle her neck.

She closed her eyes, loving the feel of being in his arms, combined with the buoyancy of being in the water. It really seemed as if she were floating, even though her feet touched the bottom—at least, they had until he lowered his arms and cupped his hand beneath her thighs. He lifted her legs and wrapped them around his waist.

A tiny yelp of surprise escaped her, and she asked, "Why do you call me that? Nobody calls me by my full name."

"You answered your own question," he said, walking them to the farthest edge of the pool, where he pressed her back against the wall. "I like being the only one who calls you that. Makes me feel special."

His touch was making her feel more than *special* at this moment. "Oh, so you want to be special in my life?"

He traced a slow, heated line down her neck with his tongue. "Absolutely," he whispered. "The same way you're special in mine."

"I am?" she asked with genuine question in her tone.

He must've picked up on that too, because he lifted his head and stared into her eyes. "You don't believe me?"

In his eyes, she definitely saw sincerity and lust and something else she wasn't quite sure she could decipher. But in her heart, she felt trepidation. She wanted to be all in with this new thing, which was checking a lot of boxes on that nonexistent list, but her mind was too weary of the try-and-try again motto. "I want to believe you," she admitted quietly.

Because she really did. She wanted to believe and to take one day at a time, to follow the budding feelings of happiness brought on by being with him.

"Then believe, Savannah," he said, bringing his lips close to hers. "Let go of all that other bullshit clouding your mind, and believe." The kiss that followed his words was every bit as deep and delicious as the quick strokes he eventually gave her before they both found release.

Now, sitting in her office alone, Vanna shivered at the thought. It felt like the same pleasure she'd experienced in the pool at that moment on Saturday night was still present in her body on Monday afternoon.

"Damn," she muttered. What the hell was this man doing to her?

The loud shrill of the phone on her desk had her jumping in her chair like she'd been caught doing something illicit—if recalling a great orgasm could be considered that. With a frown at the interruption, she reached for the phone and answered, "Hey, Neshawn," because she could see that it was an interoffice call.

"Hey, your grandmother is on line four, and she's yelling and screaming. I can barely understand what she's saying," Neshawn told her.

"Okay. I'll grab it now," Vanna said, and pressed the button to end the call with Neshawn. Then she pressed the blinking number 4 button. "Granny?"

"Vannie, baby! You gotta come quick! Come right now, baby! The police are here tearing up your house!"

When Vanna turned onto her block, she saw the flashing lights from the police cruisers. Her heart had been thumping on overtime the moment she'd hung up the phone and shot up from her desk. Her call to Jovani had gone to his assistant because he was in court, but she promised she would get the message to him as soon as he was out. Her next calls had actually been text messages to her J&R thread: OMG! They're searching my house! And to Aden: I can't believe they're searching my house!

Her phone had been buzzing as she drove, but she'd only looked at it when she was at a stoplight. Jamaica and Ronni were both shocked. Aden hadn't responded yet. She couldn't even think about why that was—not now, when she saw an officer run up the steps to her front door with huge brown paper bags in his gloved hands.

She had barely brought her vehicle to a stop before she opened the door and jumped out. About three steps away, she remembered her purse and phone and ran back to grab them off the passenger seat. Then she headed for the house again. The second she walked inside, she heard the commotion. Frito barking, Granny fussing, and the project manager, Jack, trying to calm her down.

"They just need to get out; my granddaughter is innocent," Granny was saying as Vanna walked into the living room.

"I understand, ma'am, but it'll be over soon. And it's better if you and I just stay out of their way." Jack was probably in his late fifties, a handsome man with curly salt-and-pepper hair and gold-rimmed glasses.

"Thanks, Jack," Vanna said, moving closer and taking Granny's hand. "I'm so sorry this is happening while you're here trying to work."

Jack shook his head. "No, don't you apologize. I'm glad me and my crew were here with your grandmother when they arrived."

She sighed heavily. "How long have they been here?"

"Just about an hour now," Jack said. "Haven't found anything yet, as far as I can tell. But one of 'em just ran out of here to grab an evidence bag, so . . ." He let his words trail off, and then he looked away, as if wanting to give Vanna the space to be even more embarrassed without an audience.

"That's not possible," she said, shaking her head. "What could they possibly have found?"

She heard dry laughter and turned her attention back to the stairs by the door. As her house was a split-level, the front-door entryway led to a choice of either coming up the stairs to the living/dining room/ kitchen space or going down the stairs to the basement area, which consisted of a room Vanna used for storage, a larger room that was set up like a second living room, a bathroom, and a laundry room.

Detective Parish cleared the top step, one of those brown paper bags she'd seen the other officer carrying in his hands. "You sure you want to stick by your statement that you had nothing to do with the robberies?" he asked.

Beaumont, with his lecherous glare, came up right behind Parish. He carried one of those brown paper bags as well.

"No, I don't, because it's the truth," Vanna shot back.

"Oh, the lies we tell," Beaumont said, and reached into the bag he was carrying to pull out another bag.

"What is that?" Vanna asked.

"Oh, this?" Beaumont feigned surprise as he looked down at the second bag he was holding by its handle. "It's what they call a money bag—and what do we have here?" He looked up at her with arched brows as he turned the bag around so that the front of it was facing her. "Is that the logo for the Lennox Casino?"

Oooooh shit!

Vanna wanted to shout that it wasn't hers. She wanted to yell that they'd planted that in her basement, but she knew enough to keep her mouth shut at this moment. Granny, on the other hand . . .

"You dirty bastards!" she yelled, and stepped out from behind where Vanna and Jack still stood. "You know good and damn well you brought that in here with you, and now you're acting like it was here all along. You've been in here all afternoon, and you just found that! Bullshit!"

They were the words right out of Vanna's mind, but she reached out and put a hand on Granny's arm. "It's okay," she said in a tight voice. "It's okay. Just let them do their job."

Even if their job seemed to be to frame her for the crime that Caleb had committed, because Caleb's wretched behind went and drowned himself. Or had somebody drowned him the way somebody had driven that guy Elliot Joble off the road? She hadn't asked for an autopsy because she'd accepted when the ME told her he'd drowned, yet the police had requested one. Only she hadn't seen the results.

"Are you finished now?" she asked them, beyond ready for them to leave.

"Yeah, I think we've got what we came for," Parish said with another chuckle. "You might want to call your attorney now, see if he can set up another meeting. This time with the AUSA to talk about making a plea deal. You're gonna need one."

Vanna didn't speak another word, just stood there and watched the detectives and all the other officers who had been in her house leave.

"I'm gonna have my crew walk around and put things back in order," Jack said once they were gone. "They didn't mess it up that much. I've seen them do much worse."

Vanna couldn't find the words to ask how or why he would've seen such a thing; she'd simply muttered a "Thank you," then took the stairs up to her bedroom.

Granny and Frito followed behind her. She didn't want any more strangers in this part of her personal space, so she'd come up here to put things in order herself. Jack had been right: there wasn't that much damage. They'd closed her dresser drawers, but when she opened them, she could tell her things had been riffled through. Same for her nightstand drawers. Her closet door was open, some shoeboxes knocked over; a couple of jackets had fallen on the floor, probably when they'd brushed through her clothes.

"If that boy wasn't already dead, I swear I'd kill him," Granny grumbled from where she sat on the edge of Vanna's bed.

"You have no idea how many times I've said that same thing," Vanna said as she put a pair of multicolored wedges into the appropriate box.

At the sound of hurried footsteps on the stairs, Frito jumped down off the bed, where he knew he didn't belong in the first place, and headed toward the door.

"Get out of my way, goofy dog," Jamaica complained as she came in and had to skirt around Frito, who thought he was standing guard.

Ronni was right behind her, but she knelt down to try to calm Frito. The dog was such a traitor, because the moment she rubbed his head and started speaking in that weird baby voice she used with Jonah, he was putty in her hands.

"Girl, what the hell?" Jamaica said, wrapping Vanna into a hug as soon as she was close enough.

Vanna accepted the hug and threatened her tears not to fall. She would not break. Not now.

"I don't even know, J. I don't even know," she said, and shook her head when her friend released her.

"Did you call your attorney?" Ronni, who was now carrying Frito's spoiled ass, asked.

"Yeah," Vanna replied. "I called as soon as I got in the truck. Then I shot you two a text."

"Did you call Aden?" Granny asked.

Vanna had moved out of the closet and was heading toward her bathroom now. "Yes. I sent him a text."

"A text?" Ronni asked. "Why didn't you call him? How often does he check his texts?"

"The more important question is, Did they find anything?" Jamaica asked.

Aden normally responded to her texts throughout the day fairly quickly—unless he was in a meeting or had a client, which he had gotten into the habit of telling her about. She never asked about his schedule or requested explanations for his time spent away from her, because she didn't think he owed her any of those things. They talked when they talked, saw each other when they did, and she was fine with that. Or at least, that was what she had been telling herself, because Ronni's question did have her wondering why she hadn't heard from him yet.

However, Jamaica's question trumped Ronni's. So Vanna stopped picking up the trash can the police had knocked over. Then she stuck her head out the door to look back into the bedroom where Jamaica was standing. "Why the hell do you think they would find something?"

Jamaica held up her hands in surrender. "It's just a question, Vanna. You know I know you didn't do this, but you also know I'm down with what law enforcement does to make a case."

That was true. Jamaica had gone through training and started working at the jail right after they'd graduated from college. She was now a lead correctional officer, and advised staff as well as mentored lower-level officers. If any of them in this room were more versed in the legal field than Vanna, it was Jamaica. And in the criminal law field especially, Jamaica definitely surpassed her.

"Them bastards planted a couple of those casino money bags," Granny said.

"What?" Jamaica asked. "This is crazy. It's bad and it's crazy."

"But she's innocent," Ronni said.

"We know that, which is why it's crazy. But for some reason, they're hell-bent on making it look like you're guilty," Jamaica said.

Vanna had gone back into the bathroom, but she could still hear them talking. And she agreed with every word being said—this *was* crazy. She was innocent. And they were determined to pin this on her. But why? Who had she pissed off to earn this?

In the back of her mind, thoughts of how life was always coming at her with not just curveballs, but fuckin' hardballs that smacked at her with painful persistence, surfaced. But she couldn't lean into those thoughts. Couldn't spiral down that black hole, where the possibility existed that perhaps she somehow deserved all the strife that plagued her. At the same time, she couldn't quite come up with a positive vibe, a word of encouragement, or any of that therapeutic shit at the moment.

Jamaica appeared in the doorway of the bathroom. "Has Aden hit you back?"

For whatever reason, the cops had yanked everything out of the bottom cabinets of the vanity, so Vanna had knelt down to pick them up and put them all back. She looked over her shoulder to see Jamaica. "What?"

Her friend leaned against the doorjamb, her arms folded over her chest. "Aden. Has he texted or called you back after you told him what was going on?"

"No. Not yet. At least, I don't think so." She looked around and then sighed. "I left my phone downstairs with my purse, so he could've called while I've been up here."

"But he's not here," Jamaica said. "We got here before him."

There was a hint of something in Jamaica's tone, something that took the place of what she hadn't actually said. And one of her excellently drawn eyebrows was raised in question, which made Vanna oddly uncomfortable. She sat back on her heels and sighed. "You were off today, J. Your house is barely twenty minutes from here—twelve—when you're speeding, which I'm positive you were. And the school Ronni works at is just down the road. That's why the two of you got here so quickly."

When Jamaica didn't respond, Vanna sighed again. She leaned forward and planted her hands on the floor so she could push herself up to a standing position. Then, because she knew her friend well, she turned to face Jamaica. "Say what you want to say."

"I don't think you're gonna like it," Jamaica replied.

"That's never stopped you before."

"True." Jamaica pushed off from her leaning position and held her hands out in front of her. "Just hear me out. I'm only going on what we know definitely. You know, just the facts."

Vanna leaned a hip against the vanity. "Okay."

"The first time you saw Aden after fifteen years was at the cemetery where you'd just buried your husband. Right?" Jamaica didn't wait for Vanna's reply. "Then you're arrested at the cemetery. Aden has a lawyer he can call to get you out. You see a strange car up the street. Aden calls Jovani, and they set up a meeting with the detectives. Your house gets raided; they find money bags that had to be planted, and Aden has been spending a lot of nights here, so . . ."

"Stop!" Vanna said. Her temples were throbbing, and she suddenly felt a little sick. "You're right, I don't like where you're going with this."

"You ever heard of hero syndrome?" Jamaica asked.

"I told you to stop." Vanna moved to turn on the faucet. She leaned forward and cupped her hands to toss cool water onto her face.

Jamaica—true to her obstinate personality—continued anyway. "It's when somebody creates a situation where they can then swoop in and act like the savior."

Vanna could hear her step farther into the bathroom until she stopped right beside her.

"He's been coming to your rescue since this whole thing started. You don't think that's kind of weird?"

Grabbing a towel that had miraculously remained in place on the rack during the search, Vanna dried her face and turned off the water. Her fingers had begun to shake, but she tried to breathe her way past the irritation currently swirling through her. "He didn't get here in time to save me from the humiliation of watching strangers go through all of my personal belongings. And he's not here right now. Not saving me at this moment."

Jamaica tilted her head. "And that's even more weird. Where is he? Why hasn't he called or returned your text?"

Turning around to lean against the vanity once more, Vanna wrapped her arms around herself. "Why are you doing this? I thought you liked Aden. He answered all of your questions that night we went bowling, so I figured he'd passed your test. You even hugged him good night when you left the pool party." Vanna didn't understand what was going on, and this was the absolute last thing she needed going through her mind right now. Her priority for the moment should be staying the hell out of jail. Not second-guessing the man who—despite how many times she told him she didn't need it—had been showing up for her in a way no man ever had before.

"I like him as long as he's good to you and good *for* you. But if he's here to fuck with you, to pick up where Caleb left off in destroying your life, then he's public enemy number one to me. And you know that," Jamaica said seriously.

Vanna did know that, mostly because she felt the same way about Jamaica and Ronni. They were super close, ride-or-dies, 110 percent devoted to each other. So there was no way Jamaica would say something that she knew would hurt Vanna's feelings unless she wholeheartedly believed it could be true. Which was the only reason Vanna let everything Jamaica had just said settle into her mind without completely dismissing them.

"I don't believe he would do that," Vanna said with a shake of her head. "Why would he do that?"

"He met you first," Jamaica said with a shrug. "Didn't you say he told you that?"

"It's true, J," she said, growing more annoyed with this conversation. "He didn't have to say it; I was there, remember? And so were you. I told you after I bumped into him and you were with me the night I saw him again at the step show."

"But what if this is get-back?" Jamaica asked. "What if setting you up is a way to get back at you for choosing Caleb?"

"You really believe that?" Vanna asked. "It doesn't even make sense that he would be that tore up over me all this time. We didn't hold hands, kiss—nothing but bump into each other. And before you say it, I know there are guys that act stupid over less, but Aden's not like that."

Jamaica raised that brow again. "You sure? Because you thought Caleb—"

Vanna held up a hand then, because she knew exactly where Jamaica was going with that sentence. And she couldn't take it. Not at this moment, not after all that had happened today—hell, this month. She just couldn't take it. "I can't do this again, J," she said quietly.

Ronni stepped into the doorway. "Do what?"

Jamaica sighed heavily. "I told her what I just told you I was thinking about Aden."

Vanna must have missed that part of the conversation going on in her bedroom while she was picking up toiletries off the bathroom floor. But Granny had heard it, and now Vanna wondered what she thought about Jamaica's assumptions too. Probably that her granddaughter just couldn't seem to get this right. Because that's exactly how Vanna was feeling right now.

"Ooooh," Ronni said, a sad look covering her face.

"Guess you believe it too," Vanna said. She let her head fall back and stared up at the ceiling, praying the tears that formed wouldn't fall. "Well, I can't believe it."

"V, listen to me," Jamaica started again. "I don't want Aden to be a bad guy either. I want you to have every ounce of happiness you deserve. But I also want you to be smart about this. Just let the facts marinate for a minute."

"No," Vanna said, bringing her gaze back to the two closest friends she'd ever had. "I can't. Because if I let those facts marinate, if I believe what you're saying, if I admit that a small part of me has already grabbed hold of those words and is ready to run to the police with every one of them, I'll have to admit I've failed yet again."

"What?" Ronni asked.

Vanna closed her eyes, opened them, and felt the warmth of the tears streaming down her cheeks. "I can't do this," she said. "I can't do this relationship shit. It's just not for me. Love and happy endings. Through good times and bad. I'm not built for it, so I should just give it up."

"What are you talking about?" Jamaica asked, coming in closer to wrap an arm around Vanna's shoulders.

Ronni stepped farther into the bathroom as well, stopping to stand just in front of Vanna.

Vanna gave a wry chuckle and reached a hand up to knuckle a tear away. "You're right about one part of this. The part you started to say about Caleb. You would think I'd learned my lesson, but obviously not. If what you're suggesting about Aden is true, then I'm just not meant to be loved and treated right, I guess. But damn, I wanted it. You know? I wanted it. After all I've been through, all I put up with during my years with Caleb, I figured I fuckin' deserved it!" She huffed. "Joke's on me, huh?"

"No," Ronni said, taking Vanna's hands and holding them tightly in her own. "The joke is definitely not on you. Because you do deserve love and happiness, Van. If ever I knew anyone who did, it's you."

"And you'll have it," Jamaica added. "You will have all the things you've ever wanted, because you're strong enough and bold enough to go out there and get them. Don't let this bullshit deter you. You're better than that, V."

She *was* better than that. She knew that. She was stronger and smarter. Hell! Vanna had told herself all these same things over and over again. She'd read those stupid cards on her dresser multiple times, until some of them had grown worn with use. Just last week, she'd thought she needed to go online and find herself a new box of them. But what the hell for? Why was she plucking a card out of a box each day just to tell her how to feel on that day, when every time she allowed herself to breathe freely around a guy, some wild and deceitful shit popped off?

Why was life always delivering these swift—hell no, these debilitating—kicks her way? Why was she the one who was supposed to bear all the bad breaks and figure out how to keep standing after each one?

"This is not how my celebratory month is supposed to be going," she said on a half laugh, half sob. More tears poured down her face, and she eased a hand away from Ronni's to swipe at them.

"Then don't let it go that way," Jamaica said.

"And besides, this is just a thought. J doesn't have any real proof about any of this. She was just spouting off things like she usually does," Ronni said.

"Okay, shade," Jamaica said as she looked over to Ronni.

"You know what I mean," Ronni replied. "And you know Jamaica is always suspicious. Hell, we all can be suspicious when it comes to these trifling-ass men out here. But if *you* believe there's something to what she's saying, then just ask him. If you want to trust him, trust what's happening between the two of you, then do that. Just because a thing looks bad doesn't mean it is."

"Is that like 'a rose is still a rose even if it smells different'?" Jamaica asked.

Both Vanna and Ronni looked at Jamaica now.

"You mean 'A rose by any other name would smell as sweet'?" Vanna asked, her brow furrowed.

Jamaica waved a hand and pursed her lips. "Look, you're the one into all those quotes and nonsense. I just keep it real. I like Aden. But I'm not blind, and neither are you. So just ask him and see what he says."

Ronni nodded.

Vanna thought it was worth an ask too, and that was the problem. If she believed any of this could be true, then she didn't trust Aden. Didn't believe he genuinely wanted to be with her and that they had a future together, as he'd asked her to do at the party on Saturday. But Vanna didn't know if that was something she could ever believe in again.

Chapter 16

Vanna's legs were crossed at the ankle and swaying from side to side as she sat on her couch at seven thirty Monday night. Aden had finally called her about a half hour after Jamaica and Ronni had left. Jack and his crew left a little while after that, and after Granny had taken Frito for his evening walk, she'd gone to her room with a glass of Sprite and two of the mini cupcakes that were left over from the pool party.

"Hey," he'd said when she answered on the fourth ring. From the moment Jamaica had planted the seeds of doubt, an internal battle inside her had been brewing. "Sorry, I'm just seeing your text. Cell service was spotty in Crystal City. Guess our meeting location was too close to some space the Pentagon had marked as restricted. I'm just getting on the road now and finally got some bars, so I hurried to call you back. Are you okay? What happened? Have you talked to Jovani?"

Again, Aden didn't owe her an explanation as to why he hadn't immediately responded to her text. They weren't boyfriend and girlfriend, and they definitely weren't husband and wife. Those were the only scenarios where she felt she had a right to explanations or commitments of any type. They were . . . They were just lovers, and with that came zero strings.

Just as she acknowledged earlier, this was how she carried all her interactions with men post-separation. What she hadn't wanted to accept was that deep down, she really did want it to be more with Aden. No, she hadn't told him—or her girls—that, because protecting herself from hurt and scrutiny had become second nature. But for the third time—because she considered wanting and losing her mother in almost the same category—it was clear that she wasn't meant to get what she wanted.

It was that train of thought that had been festering in her mind since her girls had left.

"It's fine," she said dryly. "And I'm fine."

He did that thing where he grew silent, and this time it irked the hell out of her. Truthfully, it added to the mountain of things that were pissing her off. All the things that were beyond her control to stop and, therefore, she had to suffer through. "Is that all you called to say?" The question was terse, and while a small part of her said she was being unfair, the bigger part of her screamed *Fuck him and everybody else who was causing drama in my life!*

"No. I asked you some questions," he replied. "Do you want to answer them over the phone or when I get there?"

"I didn't invite you over," she snapped.

"True," was his simple response.

More silence.

"Can I come over to see if you're all right, Savannah?"

No. Tell him no! Tell him to take his smoothies and workouts and go straight to his own home. And stay there. Forever. Or at least for the next fifteen years. Because try as she might, she couldn't take this. She didn't have one ounce of strength to power through this time.

She sighed, knowing that was the coward's way out. And she wasn't a coward. Never had been, and wasn't about to let this man take her there.

"Yes," she said.

"I'll be there in forty-five minutes."

He disconnected the call before she could say another word.

So she'd put on sweatpants, a T-shirt, and a pair of fuzzy socks; left her bedroom, which, for whatever reason, still felt like the least invaded space in her house now; and plopped her behind on the couch to wait.

When the doorbell rang, her head jerked toward the plywood wall, and she sighed. For what felt like the billionth time in the last few hours, she considered just walking away from all this. Cutting her losses and moving the hell on. Aden had only been back in her life a couple weeks; surely she wouldn't be heartbroken if he was no longer in it. Especially since it was causing her so much doubt. The fact that there'd been good with him in these weeks as well didn't go unnoticed. It was just harder to hold on to that positive in the midst of this current storm.

Another fact that didn't go unnoticed was that she didn't want Granny disturbed any more than she had already been today. So she stood and went to answer the door. When she opened it, Aden gave her a tentative smile that she didn't have the energy to return. She turned and walked back up the stairs and resumed her position on the couch.

She heard him closing and locking the door behind him—something he always did when he came over—then walk slowly up the stairs. When he entered the living room, he was loosening his tie. With one hand he slid the tie from around his neck and stuffed it into the back pocket of his slacks. He'd probably left his suit jacket in the car. He removed his sunglasses next, setting them on the TV stand as he passed it. Crossing the remaining space between them, he came to a stop a few cushions away from her on the sectional and adjusted his pants before taking a seat.

"What happened?" he asked as he leaned forward and rested his elbows on his knees.

He looked so cool, so debonair, and so damn smug that she wanted to toss one of the pillows on the chair at his handsome face. How dare he waltz back into her life only to destroy it! If that was what he'd come back to do. Hell, she didn't know. She'd gone over everything that Jamaica had said numerous times. And there was still a part of her that just couldn't believe any of it. The problem was, Vanna didn't know if she could trust that part of herself. It had led her wrong before.

"Why did you come back to DC?" she asked, because beating around the bush wasn't an option. She was sick of the volleying back and forth that had been going through her mind.

After staring at her for a few seconds, he gave a slow nod and replied, "My time at Thomas Karn was up. I missed my family. I was ready to come home."

"Why did you come to the funeral? I mean, why did you make a point of coming to say something to me after it was all over?"

"Because once upon a time, we were friends," he said. "I don't like to see my friends hurt. I wanted to make sure you were all right then, just like I do now."

"The answer is no!" she yelled back, not caring if she ruffled his ridiculous calm. There were so many emotions churning inside her that she didn't know what to do with. "No, I'm not all right, Aden. And I haven't been all right since I found out Caleb was dead."

"Okay," he said, clasping his fingers together in front of him. "That's fair. How can I help?"

"See, that's the thing," she said, giving a nervous laugh. "You've been helping every step of the way. Getting me an attorney, coming by for wellness checks, taking me out for workouts, getting someone to fix my house. Every time something bad happens, you try to fix it. Like you're my savior. Well, I don't need a man to swoop in and save the day for me, Aden!"

"Okay," he repeated. "Anything else you want to get off your chest?"

"Yes, as a matter of fact, there is." She leaned forward until she could plant her elbows on her knees the same way he was and glared at him. "Are you doing this? Are you framing me? If you are, just tell me. I'm not gonna whack you over the head, because I've had my share of jail to last a lifetime, and I promise I'll hold Granny back if she comes at you, but I just need to know, Aden. "

For a long moment he didn't say a word. She was used to these silent stretches, which she presumed came along whenever she said something he didn't like. From the way he was staring at her, she could tell he was thinking about what he wanted to say. Would it be a lie? She'd googled *hero syndrome* and found that it was a real thing. Not that she'd thought Aden could have a condition like this, but among other shows she watched, *Criminal Minds* was in her rotation, so she knew you couldn't always tell who or what a person really was just by looking at them. Or sleeping with them, in this case.

"Are you serious right now?" he asked her finally.

"I'm dead serious, Aden. Because you know what? My life is on the line here. Those police officers found money bags from the casino in my basement. How did they get here? You said before that you'd been in touch with Caleb when you first came back to the city three years ago, but not with me. You reached out to him and you knew we were separated, but you never reached out to me. Is that what this is about? Are you still pissed because, as you said, you saw me first?"

He grinned then, but it wasn't that sexy-as-hell grin he had whenever he was ready to laugh or joke about something with her. No, this was an incredulous look, and when he stood up slowly, she knew this was about to go badly. He slid his hands into the front pockets of his slacks and walked away, stopping when he got near the steps. Then he turned slowly and walked toward her again.

"I'm gonna address your questions because I don't want there to be any more ambiguity between us," he said, his voice tight. "But you make this the very last time you insult me like this, Savannah. The. Very. Last. Time."

If she hadn't realized how serious this situation was before now, it rang loud and clear through the tension, which seemed to be bouncing off his toned shoulders, the firm set of his mouth, and the furrow of his brow. She'd never seen Aden angry, and this was definitely angry Aden.

"You wanna know why I didn't come to you when I came back to the city? Because I couldn't trust myself with you just yet. I never stopped wanting you, never stopped hating the fact that you were with Caleb. So when I came back to the city and found out the two of you were separated, of course the first thing I wanted to do was come and shoot my shot. But then Caleb tells me he's still in love with you, that he's trying to get you back. That he's *gonna* get you back. What was I supposed to do with that?

"I'm not a college kid anymore, and I'm definitely not about to get in the middle of a married couple's squabbles. Not even for you. But when I found out he'd died and I saw you again . . ." He stopped and shook his head. "I couldn't stay away.

"As for whether I'm doing this to you—doing what, exactly? You think I put those money bags in your basement? You really think I'm framing you?" He laughed now, a sickly type of laugh that echoed throughout the room. "How dare you immediately think the worst of me when you allowed Caleb to gaslight and play you for over fifteen years!"

Immediately stung by those last words, Vanna stood, fists clenched at her sides. "Don't you stand there and tell me about my relationship with Caleb. You don't know a damn thing about what went on between us!"

Another wry chuckle erupted from his throat, and this time, Aden moved a hand from his pocket and ran it down the back of his head. "Are you serious right now? I mean, yeah, I guess you are." He shrugged. "If anybody knows how he treated you, it's me!" He slapped that same hand against his chest. "I was there, Savannah. You remember that? *I* was there."

"No," she shot back. "Not for fifteen years, you weren't. You were off becoming a big-time financial adviser and forgetting those you called friends." *Forgetting about me.* She wisely clamped her mouth shut before those words could tumble free. Never, not until this very moment, had she admitted that on some level, she had wanted Aden to be her savior back then. To save her from Caleb.

"I never forgot you," he said, his tone only moderately softer now. "I never forgot you, Savannah. And I always knew exactly who Caleb was. You were the one who couldn't see it. Who couldn't accept what you so willingly walked into."

She gasped, brought her fingers up to rub her temples, then dropped her arms again in exasperation. "What are you talking about?"

Aden went silent again. His gaze pinned her where she stood. "You really want to know?" he asked.

"Yes, dammit! Don't you think I should know? At least now, amidst all that's going on, don't you think I should finally have some answers?"

"I always wanted you to have answers," he said. "It just wasn't my place to give them to you. And that was a choice you made, and I had no other recourse but to respect."

He wasn't wrong, at least not about that. She had chosen Caleb over him, had decided that Caleb would be her future, and she'd never looked back at Aden.

With a heavy sigh, Aden scrubbed his hands down his face. He walked back to the stairs again as if he couldn't decide if he should leave or stay. But when he came back this time, it was to lean his back against the wall near the TV, only one hand going into his pocket this time. The other was in a fist at his side. He looked like he was posing for the cover of a magazine—the brooding businessman.

"He was a low-level drug dealer when we were in school," he began. "Used to sell small bags of weed to the underclassmen at first, then the guys on the basketball and football teams. Once he became a brother, he supplied every party until he started messing up the money and got his ass kicked by his supplier. Me and a few other brothers, since we were supposed to act as his mentors, picked his ass up in an alley downtown one night after getting a call with him wheezing into the phone."

He paused, looked toward the plywood wall, then back to her. "We sat at the ER with him that night, then took him back to the house. The next morning, we gave his ass a hard talk, told him to get it together or get out."

"Kind of hypocritical if he was supplying your parties, don't you think?" she countered with a smirk.

"Excellence," he said. "That's what we strive for. That's what we represent. Excellence in all things. So no, it wasn't really our thing to condone drug dealers—but hell, if you were gonna do it, then do that shit right. Caleb was a mess."

His head fell back and he waited a beat. "I got closer to him than some of the other brothers. They were ready to kick him out after that first incident, but I saw something familiar in him, so I tried harder. Caleb was always trying to impress everybody, even himself. It was like he needed to prove a point, that he was somebody, that he was doing great things. And even when he was getting better grades and looking toward a future somewhere in the tech field, he didn't believe in himself enough to see it through. It was like he was fighting against himself all the time. Do the right thing, but then you gotta turn around and do the wrong thing for counterbalance. He straddled that fence all the time, and nothing I said or did could sway him.

"Did you know his father used to beat him? I mean, from stitches in his head to broken bones. He was a cruel bastard, and Caleb took the brunt of his every mood swing. And his mother, hell, she wasn't much better, talking to him like he was dirt. Hating him for what his no-good father refused to be." Aden dropped his head, then slammed his fist into the wall behind him.

Vanna jumped.

"That's why I didn't want him with you," he said when he brought his gaze back up to meet hers. "Yeah, I wanted you the first moment I saw you, but then he introduced you and said he was gonna make you his girl. I wanted to come to you so bad and tell you to stay away from him, but how was that gonna look? And for a while, I told myself, *Maybe she'll make him better. She's smart and she's pretty; she's going to have a bright future, and maybe she'll rub off on him.* But I knew," he said, bringing his fist up to rub the center of his chest this time. "I knew in here that things would only get worse. That Caleb would never change."

Tears stung her eyes now, and she wanted desperately to keep them from falling, but it was too much. Everything he'd just told her, all that she'd lived through with Caleb—it all fit like finding the perfect puzzle pieces. Some things about his past she had known, but others—the selling-drugs part, the cruelty from his mother, because she'd never seen that, and Caleb always respected Gail—she just had no clue.

"I offered to pay for counseling for him," Aden continued. "During our senior year. He didn't have any health insurance, and the therapist was going to cost $125 per visit. I was going to use some of the leftover financial aid money I had to pay for him to go for a month or two, just to get some positivity poured into him. But he refused, said he wasn't relying on no stranger to fix him, because he wasn't broken. So many Black men take that same stance against any type of mental illness, or any trauma they need to work through." He sighed. "I wanted Caleb to get better, Savannah. Not just for himself, but so that he could be better for you too. By then I knew you were in love with him, knew you would do everything you could to keep him happy. And by the time I graduated, I was so damn jealous of Caleb's broken ass for having you in his corner."

"I don't know what to say," she replied. "You're giving me all this information now when it's too late for me to do anything about it." She interrupted him the moment she saw him open his mouth to speak: "And I get it. I know why you didn't say anything, couldn't do anything more than you did. But it doesn't change what happened, and it doesn't change what's going on now."

He pushed himself off the wall then, walked directly toward her, and stopped a couple steps away. She could smell his cologne, could see the muscle clench in his jaw as he stared at her. "I didn't plant those bags in the basement. I'm not framing you."

She blinked, and the first tear fell. Hurriedly, she swatted it away and swallowed.

"On some level, I guess I can understand your fear and unwilling-ness to trust again, because I knew Caleb, and so I can imagine what you endured all these years with him," he said.

Another pesky tear fell, and this time, he reached out to thumb it away before she had the chance.

"But I'm not him, Savannah," he said, quietly this time. "I never will be. And if you don't see that, *won't* see that, then there's nothing else I can say."

She dropped her head then, because she knew more tears were going to come, and she just didn't want him to see them, didn't want him to wipe them away, didn't want to feel this weak and defeated. The same way she'd felt when Diane had left her at that bus station. And every time Caleb had let her down.

A few moments later, she heard him walking away. Then she heard the door open and close.

Then she dropped back down onto the sectional and cried.

Chapter 17

There was sand in her eyes, and they were possibly sewn shut. That's how Vanna felt when she tried to wake up to her blaring alarm on Tuesday morning. If she thought the struggle to open her eyes was real, rolling over and extending her arm to fumble around the nightstand until she finally found her phone was a herculean effort.

She was able to snap the phone free of the charger without seeing it, but to shut off the alarm that now had her ears ringing, she had to apply all her strength to opening first one eyelid, then, very reluctantly, the other. She punched in her password and swiped to kill the alarm, then dropped the phone on her chest and let her eyes close again.

How badly did she need a sick day? In the worst possible way. But if she took today off, she'd have to go in the Tuesday after Labor Day. With her birthday falling on a Saturday this year, that gave her a long weekend to celebrate. Taking that Tuesday after the holiday off was going to be icing on the cake—a mini vacation, of sorts—which she absolutely deserved. Staying right here in this bed for the rest of the day also held massive appeal.

Yesterday had been as trying a day as so many others she'd experienced this month, and there were still two more weeks to get through. How had her birthday month—the time she'd planned for all year long, the thirty days that would signify her launch into a new phase of her life—ended up being two of the worst weeks she'd ever experienced? A part of her was afraid for the remaining days in this month, scared that whatever bad mojo was circling over her head had only just begun to make her life a living hell. Her breath hitched as a sob struggled to break free. But she clamped down on that emotion, pressed her eyes closed even tighter—causing even more pain, by the way—and forced back those feelings of pity and despair. She couldn't afford them. Couldn't sit here and feel sorry for herself or wonder *Why me?* any longer. It wasn't going to get her anywhere, and it would make her feel like a failure.

Pushing herself up to a sitting position and grappling to catch the forgotten phone as it started to slide from her chest, she took a deep breath. Then another and another, until she felt like she could at least get out of bed and make it to the shower. She needed the water as hot as her skin could take it, and used her eucalyptus and spearmint body wash to create a soothing lather all over.

Twenty minutes later, she emerged from the bathroom and went straight to her dresser to reach into her card box. Whether out of habit or some other reason she was too tired to contemplate, she hadn't tossed it out the window, despite her thoughts of doing so last night. Once a week, she would remove all the cards and shuffle them, hoping that with each random selection, she would come up with exactly what she needed to hear on that given day. Today she needed a damn miracle of words.

"'You are allowed to walk away from anything that gives you bad vibes,'" she read from the card she now held.

Moments ticked by as she stood there staring down at those words until she finally asked herself, "How do I walk away from criminal charges?" Or from a man who, in just a couple of weeks, had awakened feelings she hadn't experienced in far too long?

In the shower, lathered in the body wash that was supposed to relieve her stress, she'd sobbed like a baby. Like she had for most of last night, and she hated it. Now she stuffed that card back into the box and opened the top drawer to grab her underwear.

By the time she'd put on a pastel ombre maxi dress and natural-colored wedges, she'd felt a little more like herself. Most of her get-ready time had been dedicated to her makeup since she'd had to cover the bags and attempt to minimize the puffiness in her eyes. Just another reason she hated to cry. It wasn't until she'd gotten downstairs and heard Granny arguing with Frito about being afraid of a little rain that it occurred to her to check the weather. Normally, as soon as she woke up, she would turn the TV in her room on to the local news channel so she could hear the day's weather. This morning she'd basked—or rather, suffered—in silence.

She avoided the kitchen, and instead walked straight down the stairs and into the coat closet. Finding her denim jacket, she slipped her arms into it and glanced down at the basket, which held extra umbrellas. She didn't need to grab one since there was a travel one in her purse and a bigger one in her car that worked much better on those windy and rainy days. That reminded her, she needed to call the body shop today to get a better ETA on her vehicle. The sooner she got rid of this rental, the sooner it could stop reminding her of the SUV that had apparently run down Elliot Joble.

And who the hell was Elliot Joble, anyway? She'd never met the man, yet his death was now on her conscience too.

"I'll see you later, Granny!" she yelled.

"Oh. Okay! Be safe!" her grandmother yelled back.

It was a little after nine when Vanna finally walked into the office. During her commute, she'd called Neshawn to say she was running a little late. As with more than a few days this month, this time of morning was actually very late for her since she usually arrived in the office before eight each morning and before anyone else. But today, they were just lucky she'd decided to come in at all.

"The senior wants to see you ASAP," Neshawn said as soon as she approached her desk.

Vanna groaned. "Do you know what it's about?"

Neshawn shook her head. "Nope. Just that he's been out here twice since he came in twenty minutes ago, asking if you were in yet. I told him you were running late, and he said for you to come directly to his office when you arrived."

She rolled her eyes. "Then I haven't arrived yet. I'm gonna go to my office first; then I'll go see him."

Her stomach growled as she walked to her office. Skipping breakfast was never a good idea—for her, anyway. But she hadn't wanted to open her refrigerator and see the containers that held the makings for the daily smoothie she'd started having. And she certainly didn't want to stand in that kitchen and listen to Granny ask what she was having for lunch, what she wanted her to cook for dinner, and what the hell had happened between her and Aden last night. She had no doubt her grandmother knew he'd come over and also that he hadn't stayed.

Pushing all that out of her mind, she dropped her purse into her desk drawer but grabbed her phone and slipped it into the pocket of her dress—she loved a maxi dress with pockets. After mumbling a quick prayer for strength and peace, she left her office and made her way down the hall that would lead to HC Sr.'s corner office.

She knocked on the partially open door, then pushed it the rest of the way. "Good morning, you wanted to see me?"

HC Sr., with his wiry silver beard and beady brown eyes, looked up from his desk. He lifted a hand to wave her in. "Shut the door."

So, no *Good morning*—that was odd. HC Sr. was a lot of things, but he wasn't normally rude. In fact, he was quite the gentleman around the office, something that obviously hadn't rubbed off on his son.

Doing as he said, she made her way farther into the office and took a seat in the guest chair across from his desk.

"Is something wrong?" she asked. "Do we need to talk about the settlement conference coming up later this week?"

"No, no. Junior has that all under control. And you already know to have all the paperwork ready for when we send you the numbers," he said, sitting back in his chair.

"I do," she replied with a nod. She wanted to ask again what this was about but decided to just wait.

"Two detectives came to see me yesterday," he said without further preamble.

Damn. All that work she'd done this morning to get her mind in a decent enough place to come to work and function with at least 75 percent clarity today had just flown right out the window.

"They had a lot of questions about your job duties and how I perceived your performance. Or if I ever suspected you of stealing." He folded his hands in his lap, his thin lips moving at what seemed like a slightly slower pace than his words were actually being spoken.

She knew that wasn't possible, or perhaps it was just because her mind had started operating at less efficacy because she was damn tired of expending so much of its energy on things that just shouldn't involve her.

"What did you tell them?" she asked, praying her voice sounded confident and unbothered. She couldn't tell over the loud beating of her heart.

"I told them the truth," he said. "That you've been a good employee for the last eight years. That you handle our money with efficiency and integrity as if it were your own, and that I've never, not for one second, suspected you of doing anything dishonorable where our accounts are concerned."

Well, that was a relief—not that she thought his answer should've been any different. It's just that with all that was going on, she couldn't predict a damn thing right now. And she didn't really know who she could trust.

"Thank you," she said, because it felt like the right response.

"Don't thank me," he said, then raised a brow that was as bushy and silver as his beard. "Tell me what the hell is going on."

She didn't want to tell him. Hadn't wanted any of this to get back to her place of employment, but here they were.

"It's a horrible misunderstanding," she began, then gave him a very condensed version of Caleb's death and everything concerning the charges against her.

He surprised her for the second time today by letting loose a low whistle and using a finger to stroke one of those weird-looking brows of his. "That's a lot," he said.

"It sure is," she agreed. "But listen, it will not affect my work. I come in here and it's actually a relief to put my mind on other things."

"Do you have an attorney?" HC Sr. asked. "You know I can make some calls."

"I do," she said. "But thanks. I'm sure this will all be going away soon." She prayed it would. Prayed with every ounce of faith she possessed.

"Well, if I can be of any assistance, you just let me know," he said. "I'm not going to say anything to Junior about this. Doesn't matter right now, since we know you'll prevail." He cleared his throat. "But I have to put you on notice that if this doesn't go away soon, if there has to be a trial and any type of media coverage, I'll have to rethink things."

What he actually meant to say was that he'd have to fire her. With all the dignity she could muster, when she really felt like giving in to the despair that had begun to spread throughout her chest like a bad rash, she squared her shoulders and held his gaze. "I understand," she lied. "And I'll get back to work now."

Pride wouldn't let her jump up and run the hell out of that office, so her steps remained measured, her motions average speed as she acquiesced to his final request and closed his door behind her. She also ignored Neshawn's questioning gaze as she made her way back to her office. And she stayed there until the end of the day, doing the firm's work to keep her mind occupied and resisting the urge to text or call Granny or any of her friends. They couldn't help her right now, couldn't make this worry and irritation go away. She had to manage that herself, as she did so many other times in the past.

What was that saying, *When it rains . . . ?* Well, big fat raindrops were coming down at a vicious pace as she pulled into her driveway at a little after six that evening. Granny's car wasn't there, and she pushed back the questions of where she might be in this storm when she recalled Granny's text at five, saying she was going to the market to get some spices for the chicken-and-rice soup she planned to make for them tonight.

Grabbing her stuff from the passenger seat, she leaned down to the floor and scooped up the umbrella. Then she got out and made a dash for the front porch. There, she skidded to a halt, eyes wide, mouth falling open at the person she saw standing there.

She wasn't actually standing but leaning against one of the thick wooden makeshift columns that Jack and his crew had installed to keep the roof of the porch upright while they worked on the wall. Her clothes—jean capris and a dark-green T-shirt that hung off her body like a rag—and black leather flip-flops were soaked. Her hair—or what was left of it, was cut close like a man's—what used to be her caramel-hued face was now darker and drawn, another sign that she wasn't eating well.

"Mama," Vanna whispered, the word a rasp in the back of her throat.

"Hey, Vannie," Diane said, lifting her bony arm to give a slow wave.

Only two people called her Vannie: her grandmother and her mother.

"I told Mama I was coming by today, but she wasn't here when I got here." Diane wrapped her arms tightly around herself. She was obviously chilly, yet Vanna made no attempt to let her inside her house.

"She didn't tell me you would be stopping by," Vanna said.

"I was supposed to come earlier. While you were at work."

Oh. So she wasn't supposed to know that her mother was coming to her house. Because why would the woman who'd given birth to her come to her house just to visit, say hello, check on her only child? She bit back those words.

"She texted me a little while ago and said she needed to go to the market." Granny had probably waited all day for Diane. Vanna had wondered why she was going to the market to get started on dinner so late in the day. It wasn't like she'd told Granny she had to cook every night or clean the house, for that matter. Her grandmother could stay with her for as long as she liked without doing anything except taking care of her spoiled dog, as far as Vanna was concerned. But Granny would always do whatever she could to help take care of Vanna. Unlike Diane.

"Okay, well, I'll just wait right here until she gets back," Diane said.

"It's raining and you're cold," Vanna replied. With a huff she went to her door and unlocked it. "Come inside and wait."

Try as she might, she could never be as cold and distant with Diane as the woman had always been with her.

"No. I'll stay out here," Diane insisted. "I don't want to drip water all on your floors. I know it's probably nice in there."

That's right, her mother had never been to her house before. Not in all the years Vanna had lived here. She hadn't been at Vanna's college graduation, her wedding, the reception in Granny's backyard after, or at the hospital when Vanna had her gall bladder removed seven years ago.

"It doesn't make sense for you to stand out here in the rain any longer than you need to," Vanna told her, and pushed the door open. "Just come inside. You can stand right here by the door and wait for Granny if that's what you want to do."

She didn't wait for Diane to decide, was going to go in the house and put her stuff down regardless. Her patience with this woman was thinner than thread, but she had been raised to be respectful.

Vanna had just dropped her closed umbrella onto a rug near the coat closet that Granny had probably put out because of the rain. There was always one just inside the doorway for feet to be wiped on, so she did that and continued moving toward the steps.

"It is nice in here," Diane said from behind her.

She'd come inside and now stood right on that rug by the door, as if she didn't dare move.

"Oh, let me close the door." Diane turned and placed her thin fingers on the knob, pushing the door closed behind her. "Yeah," she said as she turned back to Vanna and looked around the foyer space where she stood. "It's real nice." She leaned over slightly and peeped down the stairs toward the basement, then brought her gaze back to Vanna.

"Are you going to just stand there?" Vanna asked.

Diane nodded.

"Why?" That was a loaded question where Diane was concerned. There were so many *whys* that had gone unanswered that despite her big ole age of thirty-nine, Vanna still wanted to ask.

"Told you, I don't wanna mess up your place," Diane replied with a slow shrug.

All her movements were slow, her eyes wide and bloodshot. As usual. For as long as Vanna had memory of this woman, she'd been drunk. In the morning when Vanna was in preschool, she'd awaken in the tiny apartment they lived in to Diane's slurred words and the scent of what Vanna would later learn was alcohol clinging to her skin. She'd also learned that Diane's preferred drink was Jack and Coke. Probably why Vanna stuck with light liquor.

"How would you mess up my place, Mama? All you have to do is walk up these stairs. I can get you some towels, maybe try to find you something dry to put on, and you can sit in the living room and wait for Granny." Vanna sighed. "I won't even talk to you." Because it seemed to pain her mother so much. Anytime Vanna was near her or tried to have even a basic conversation with her, Diane always acted like it would literally kill her to participate.

"I'm just gonna stay here, Vannie. That's all."

"Fine," Vanna snapped, and turned to leave her there. But then she stopped, one foot on the first step, the other still on the floor. She turned back to face Diane. "No, it's not fine. The way you treat me like

I'm the worst mistake of your life is not fine. It wasn't when I was a child, and unfortunately it's still not now."

Diane looked away, focusing her gaze on the mirror positioned on the wall above that table where Vanna normally put her purse. Today, for whatever reason, Vanna's purse was still on her shoulder.

"I don't push you," Vanna continued. "I never pushed you. I just accepted that this was who you were, how you wanted to treat me. And I still accept that." She breathed out slowly. "I know I can't change you, but I am going to get this off my chest. You might have come here today for one reason, but I'm going to take advantage of the fact that I'm even seeing you to tell you how much you've hurt me."

There was the smallest shake of Diane's head, but she still didn't turn back to look at Vanna.

"You abandoned me. Just walked away and never looked back. I don't know why or how you could even do such a thing to your child, but I guess it's not for me to understand. But I want you to know that everything you did, and even more so what you didn't do for me, has scarred me, probably for life. I won't blame all of my mistakes on you, but there's a part of me that still carries that trauma that you inflicted. So if I never get the opportunity to speak to you again, Mama, I just want to say, thank you."

For what felt like the billionth time since last night, tears stung Vanna's eyes. "Thank you for the resilience and the strength being the child that you didn't want has provided me."

She stopped speaking then and waited.

But Diane had nothing. Not even another glance Vanna's way.

So Vanna left her there. For her own self-preservation, she didn't say another word, didn't allow herself to expect anything more from the woman who'd only ever given her life.

It was an hour and a half later when a soft knock sounded on Vanna's bedroom door. She knew who it was.

"Come in," she said.

The door opened and Granny stepped inside. "Dinner's ready," she said.

"Thanks," Vanna replied from the spot where she lay across her bed. She'd been watching one of her *I Love Lucy* DVDs, desperately searching for more nostalgia to cocoon her than the harsh realities she'd been forced to live with. "I'll come down and get it in a little bit."

Granny wasn't so easily dismissed. She came farther into the room and sat on the edge of the bed by Vanna's feet.

"She's sick, Vannie." Those words settled in the air. "End-stage liver disease."

Vanna continued to stare at the TV.

"After I picked you up from the bus station that day, I found her ass and told her not to come back until she was sober and ready to be a mother. Told her she better find everything she needed in that bottle 'cause I had absolutely nothing for her if she couldn't do right by you," Granny continued. "She stayed away for a long time. I actually thought I'd never see her again. Then one day, when you were at school, I got a call from the hospital, so I went. She was there. Somebody had found her passed out on the street and brought her in. They did a bunch of tests, and she was diagnosed with cirrhosis of the liver. They talked about treatments, told her she definitely needed to stop drinking and smoking to be able to live with the disease, 'cause it wasn't going away. But she didn't do a damn thing."

Granny sighed heavily, and Vanna wanted to reach out and hug her. To tell her that she didn't need to say any more, but as always, she knew it was best just to let her get it all out when it came to Diane.

"I didn't give her money for anything for years, figured she was finding her own way, even if it was to another bottle. I'd done my job in raising her, I couldn't do anything for the adult who didn't wanna help herself," Granny said.

Vanna felt her grandmother's hand on her leg as she started to rub like Vanna was the one who needed soothing.

"Last year she came by the senior home. I don't even know how she knew that's where I was living. I hadn't seen her in a long while. But she walked into the rec room, moving all slow, her eyes filled with tears. She told me then she was gonna die, and we sat in that rec room not saying another word to each other for, oh, I guess another hour. Then she got up to leave, and I got up, put twenty dollars in her hand."

Tears spilled from Vanna's eyes.

"She's still my baby, Vannie. I know she hurt you. I know that she could never find it in herself to be a mother. It took me a while to accept that I couldn't do a damn thing about that. But she's still my baby, and now—" She sighed wearily. "Now I just want her to be at peace. However that looks for her for the time she has left on this earth, I want her to be at peace." Granny choked back a sob, and Vanna moved until she was able to sit on the side of the bed and fold her grandmother into her arms.

They sat that way for Vanna didn't know how long. Crying and rocking and crying some more.

Chapter 18

Frito was barking like crazy.

Vanna could hear him through her closed bedroom door and Granny's. Just hysterical barking. Then she heard a thump that had her sitting up straight in her bed. Granny had to be up by now, with all this noise going on. Still, Vanna swung her legs over the side of the bed and stood. She pushed her feet into her slippers, then left her room, just in time to hear glass shattering downstairs.

Granny swung her door open, and Frito bolted down the hallway and the steps, barking like he'd caught a scent and wouldn't rest until he found it. There was somebody downstairs. Vanna was about to head down the stairs when Granny came up beside her.

"Why don't you wait up here," she said, then stopped when Granny brandished the hand holding a narrow can with a spray nozzle.

Okay, Granny was coming with her.

They eased down the first few stairs, Vanna having no clue what they might be walking into. But then Frito's barking turned into a growl, and a man's voice shouted, "Shoot that mutt!"

"Oh, hell no!" Granny pushed past Vanna and took the last few steps.

Vanna hurried down behind her, both of them coming to a halt the moment they saw two men in the dining room. They were standing near a window, a pile of glass on the floor. Frito had one hemmed up in the corner as the dog stood in front of the man, snarling like he was ready to pounce and sink his teeth into him at any minute. That was the man holding the gun. The other guy, presumably the one who'd yelled for Frito to be shot, was closer to the opening of the kitchen, a ski mask on his face as he turned to see them.

What the hell was going on?

Granny didn't wait for an answer to the question Vanna hadn't even asked. She went straight at the man with the gun with a guttural cry. She aimed that can of pepper spray and started a steady stream of the liquid.

"Fuck! I'm gettin' outta here!" Ski Mask Guy turned to run toward the window Vanna now realized was pushed halfway up.

Her Mace was in her purse, which was too far away to get at this moment, but there was the pretty coral-colored vase she'd bought from HomeGoods on the table right next to where she stood. Grabbing it, she threw it with as much strength as she could muster. It smacked Ski Mask Guy in the back, and he fell to the floor.

The guy with the gun howled in pain as Frito finally sank his teeth into his shin, and Granny stood right up on him, spraying him directly in the face. The gun was still in his now-limp hand even though his eyes were shut and he'd lifted his free arm to shield his face from Granny's onslaught. But Vanna wasn't gonna feel better until the gun was out of his hand completely, so she ran toward him and picked up one of her dining room chairs. She slammed the chair down on his arm, and the gun skittered across the floor.

"Stupid bitch!" Ski Mask Guy yelled as he came up behind her and wrapped his arm around her neck. But before he could get her in the choke hold he was aiming for, Vanna elbowed him in the gut as hard as she could. As he tried to catch his breath, she turned and pressed a thumb deep into his eye until he jerked back so hard that he fell, this time going straight through her glass-top dining room table.

"Call 911!" she yelled to Granny, who was turning from one of the intruders to the other, her pepper spray aimed and ready to fire again. "Go into the kitchen and get the cordless phone, Granny!"

"You do it!" Granny shot back. "I'm the one with the weapon here."

Vanna looked back at Ski Mask Guy, who had rolled over onto his side, moaning in pain as blood dripped from down the back of his neck. Granny was right: she was the only one of them who had a weapon, so Vanna looked in the other direction, where she recalled the other guy's gun had slid across the floor.

"Get this mutt off of me!" the man who had backed into a corner—his hands still pressed to his eyes, Frito still holding on to his leg—cried.

"Fuck! I told you to shoot them all, man!" Ski Mask Guy yelled from the floor.

Vanna hurriedly took the few steps until she picked up the gun; then she aimed it at Ski Mask Guy. "Don't move," she said. "I'll shoot you right there, and you'll bleed a hell of a lot more."

"Yo! What's wrong with you people?" he yelled again, this time because he tried to roll over onto his hands and knees, but both pressed into the shards of glass on the floor.

Now he was on his back again, screaming in agony, and Vanna wondered who the hell these two were and why it seemed like they didn't have a lick of sense.

She eased her way farther into the kitchen, still keeping her gun aimed in Ski Mask Guy's direction. She found the only landline phone in the house—a cordless that sat on the island—and picked it up. Her fingers couldn't press 911 fast enough.

Sixteen minutes later, she and Granny were still in their same positions. Frito had finally let that guy's leg go, but he stayed right in front of him, giving him a glare that said he'd take another chunk out of him if he dared to move. When her front door flew open, five to six officers filed into the house, guns drawn.

"Get down on the floor!"

"Drop the gun!"

"Get down!"

They all yelled, and when Vanna and Granny didn't move at first, they did when the officers grew closer, putting the guns in their face. Granny dropped the pepper spray, and Frito turned to bark at the next person he thought was endangering his owner. Vanna dropped the gun she was holding.

"This isn't my gun!" she shouted. "It was theirs, but he dropped it, so I picked it up."

The officer closest to her shouted again, "Get your hands up!"

Frito went full on hysterical—or beyond that, because Vanna would swear the dog had barked more in this last half hour than he had his entire life. She moved quickly and picked him up. The last thing she wanted was for these cops to shoot her grandmother's dog. Because one thing she knew for sure about some police officers: if they had no qualms shooting an unarmed man, they wouldn't think twice about shooting a feisty dog.

"Hands up!" the officer yelled again, and this time, Vanna held up her free hand.

"My attorney is Jovani Kincaid. I'd like to call him right now before this goes any further!" she shouted back.

"That won't be necessary," a familiar male voice said, and she looked around the goofy officer who was standing in front of her to see Detective Beaumont.

The next few minutes were a flurry of activity. So many things were going on at once. Both intruders had been cuffed and were now sitting on the floor in her dining room. Paramedics had arrived and were looking at the wound on Ski Mask Guy's head. They removed the ski mask, and Vanna gasped.

"That's the guy that was in the car," she said, and Beaumont turned his attention away from Granny, who was giving her account of what happened.

"What did you just say?" Beaumont asked.

He'd made her and Granny move from the dining room to sit on the sectional in the living room. And had watched her walk every step of the way from where, at that point, he'd stood behind her. She wore tiny boy shorts and a tank top, which was her nightwear and not an outfit for general consumption. But this was beyond her control, something she also knew Beaumont was loving.

"That guy over there is the same one I told you was sitting in that ugly brown car up the street last week," she said.

Beaumont's response was a curse, and she frowned. "You know who he is, don't you?"

"Mrs. Carlson, I'm trying to get your grandmother's statement," he told her. "I'll talk to you in just a moment."

"You'll talk to me now!" Vanna yelled, not giving a damn who heard her. "They broke into my house tonight, Detective. They had a gun, and now they're both sitting in my dining room, being seen by paramedics like Granny and I were wrong for defending ourselves and our home."

"I didn't say you were wrong," Beaumont told her. "I just want to get all your details while they're still fresh."

"The detail I need you to pay attention to is that the guy over there with that big gash in the back of his head was sitting in a car at the corner of my street just last week. He stared at me and I stared right back at him. But it was like he knew me, knew who I was, and now where I lived. And I think you know who he is." She'd bet money on that.

Detective Parish entered the room with a grim look on his face. "He's William Baylor, the cage shift supervisor at Lennox Casino," he said, his tone edged with something like fury. "He worked with your husband."

She sucked in a breath and blew it out in release. "So this is about that damn armored-truck robbery again. I swear, I can't catch a break."

"If you'd just calm down," Beaumont said. "I'm going to get your statements, and then we'll move on."

"Don't tell me to calm down!" Vanna shouted. "You're not the one who just faced two intruders—one with a gun—in the middle of the night."

"Mrs. Carlson—" Beaumont began, frowning at her.

Parish rolled his eyes and said, "Will just gave a full confession about him and his cousin, Cordell, breaking in here to look for the rest of the money from that robbery back in June."

Beaumont's gaze returned to hers. "And why would they think it was here?" he asked. "Because they had knowledge of those bags being in your basement, wanted to see if their money was in them."

Vanna wanted to know if there'd been any money found in those bags. Both Beaumont and Parish had made a big show of making sure she knew they'd found them in her basement, but that's all they told her about it. Had there been money in them? And again, how the hell did those bags get there?

"You wanna tell us where you hid the money, Vanna?" Beaumont asked. "Or do you want to wait to see if either of these dumbasses will make bail. Because they're not finished with this. The missing money is a huge incentive to go all the way in order to find it."

Vanna doubted *go all the way* meant what the detective was trying to imply where these guys—Will and Cordell—were concerned. If they really thought the money was in her house, why not just break in to get it after they'd seen her leave the house? How much sense did it make to wait until the middle of the night to break in when they knew people were in there? And why hadn't that goofball Cordell shot Frito when Will directed him to? One thing she knew for certain was that if you pulled a gun out, you'd better be prepared to use it. Cordell, apparently, was not.

"Don't try to scare me," she said, even though fear had definitely become part of her daily diet these days. "I know my rights, and I know how this scene will play out. Now that you have a few more players in this game, you'll learn the truth, and you can get out of my life."

"Don't get ahead of yourself," Parish said. "For all we know, this could've been the result of them asking for the money and you refusing to give it to them."

"Or you can get your head out of your ass," Granny snapped.

"Shhh," Vanna told her. The last thing she needed was for either of them to get the bright idea to arrest her grandmother. That would be the moment Vanna really did something worth getting arrested for. "We're not saying another word until our attorney gets here."

When they'd been moved into the living room, she'd asked for her phone to call Jovani, and while she suspected that was the last thing Beaumont wanted her to do, there were too many other cops present for him to ignore her request a second time. With a frown, Parish turned and walked away from them. He went to join the other officers who had gone out onto her deck, checking the dining room window that was open because they probably suspected the same as she had—that it was the way the intruders had entered her house.

Beaumont gave her one last long, lingering look before he walked away as well. Granny leaned in and whispered, "I ain't got no attorney."

"You do if I do," Vanna said.

"Yeah, but Aden only paid for you."

"Then I'll pay for you if need be." Vanna sighed heavily, wishing none of this was needed. Wishing she'd never married Caleb. Wishing that Granny hadn't mentioned Aden's name.

"You sure you don't want to stay at a hotel tonight, Vanna?" Jovani asked two hours later, when the police and those two men had finally left her house.

"I'm not leaving my home because of this nonsense. I shouldn't even be involved in any of this." It wasn't the first time she'd said this tonight, or that she'd thought it in the last couple of weeks. But her words seemed to fall on deaf ears.

"I know how you're feeling, and I promise you we'll get to the bottom of this. William Baylor and Cordell Smith were the last two in the robbery scheme that the cops were looking for. With them in custody now, they should be able to get a better picture of this case. A picture that doesn't involve you," he said.

"But what about those moncy bags?" Granny asked. She was still sitting on the sectional, this time with Frito asleep in her lap.

"They didn't find your fingerprints on those bags. And they received street-camera footage from the area where Elliot Joble died. The license plate on that black SUV doesn't match the one on your rental car. I just found that out late this afternoon and was going to call you with the developments tomorrow."

"I'm so sorry I had to call you at this time of night. I hope I didn't disturb your wife," she said. "But this news is definitely a relief."

"My wife's at home eating pistachio ice cream with iced oatmeal cookies crunched up inside of it. If my baby is anything like her, she's laid back, enjoying the midnight snack." He chuckled, and for the first time tonight, Vanna cracked a smile.

"Still, I'm sorry," she said.

"Don't be. You did nothing wrong, and we're going to prove that," he said. "Now, I want you and Granny to lock up tight and get some rest."

She stood and walked him to the door. "We will. And thanks again."

"Stop thanking me and stop apologizing to me; I'm doing my job, Vanna," he said. Then he tilted his head as he continued to stare at her. "I'm also looking out for a woman one of my really good friends cares about deeply."

Oh no, she was not going there with him. Aden was not a topic of discussion she wished to have tonight. Not with Jovani or anyone else.

"That's not fair, you already told me I can't thank you again," she said, and gave Jovani another smile.

He chuckled. "That's right. You catch on quick. Lock these doors and those windows. And tomorrow see about getting an alarm system installed. Aden probably has someone you can call since he just had one installed at the gym and the storefront for the shop."

"I think I'll be able to find someone. Google is my friend," she joked.

He grinned. "Good night, Vanna."

"Good night, Jovani."

Later, when Vanna finally climbed into her bed, the clock on her nightstand read 3:47 a.m. After Jovani left, she and Granny walked around the entire house, making sure every window was locked. The dining room was in shambles, and those cops from the crime lab had made a mess too, with their fingerprint dust and other nonsense. But the cleanup would have to wait.

She, Granny, and Frito went upstairs at the same time. Vanna said she was going to take a shower. Granny said she wanted one too. When Vanna emerged from her bathroom, it was to find Granny dressed in a clean nightgown in her bed and Frito lying beside her.

"You two look way too comfortable," she said as she trekked across the floor and went to her side of the bed to climb in.

"Your bed is bigger than the one in that other room," Granny said.

"My room is bigger than that other one," Vanna replied. "But if you want, we can get you a new bed. That's only a full size in there. I think a queen will fit."

"That might be nice," Granny said, and turned over on her side to snuggle under the blankets. Frito followed suit, tucking his body right up against her back.

Since when did she say this dog could sleep with her? She didn't mind Granny so much. There'd been way too many occasions to count when she'd climbed into her grandmother's bed, which included times in her late teens. There was nothing like the comfort of sleeping with Granny, and tonight she needed that—just as Granny did, apparently.

But it was when the lights were out and she lay in the dark, listening to Granny's soft breathing and Frito's congested snore, that thoughts of Aden returned. They always came to her at night, when her defenses were down and there was nothing else happening to keep her mind off him. It had only been two days since their argument on Monday night. Two days since he'd texted or called her. Two days that she hadn't texted or called him.

She didn't know what to say to him or how to say it. Should she apologize for even considering that he could be framing her? Probably. Would he want to hear it? She wasn't sure, and truthfully, she just didn't feel like dealing with that right now. Because while Aden might not be the one framing her, somebody certainly had been, and she still didn't know why.

Aden brought a lot with him, just as she knew she brought a lot to the table as well. Maybe their past was just too much to overcome. Maybe Caleb and what he was to both of them would always be an obstacle, even after Caleb's death. And maybe it was just too soon to be thinking this seriously about any of this. It wasn't like she and Aden were in a deep relationship, like they were in love or something. Two weeks of really good sex, good conversation, shared memories, common goals and interests—that's all. She could get over that.

But something Jovani had said before he left rang true in her mind: Aden probably did know someone who could install a security system. And if they were on speaking terms right now, he would've probably already called that person to handle it for her. It didn't occur to her until this very moment how good it had felt to have someone—other than Granny—taking care of her for a change.

Chapter 19

"Bingo!"

That one word was music to Vanna's ears. Having the forethought to add the Pretty in Pink Girls' Club's annual Bingo and Brunch fundraiser to her roster of birthday celebrations may have been the smartest thing she had ever done. Who knew how much she'd need this time with these young women dedicated to rising above their circumstances and to making a difference in this world?

For six years, she'd been volunteering with the organization, enjoying every moment she spent with girls ages thirteen to eighteen. How many times had those girls ended up refilling her well, instead of the other way around, the way it was supposed to be. Something about seeing that hopeful gleam in their eyes, listening to the plans they were making for their future, the optimism that rang through their voices, was so overwhelmingly invigorating. They met once a month, usually at the community center, but sometimes, like today, funding was available for them to rent a larger space and open their event up to the community.

Bingo and Brunch was a major part of their yearly budget, something Vanna knew because she was on the finance committee for the organization. A belated thought hit her then, and she had to grit her teeth to push it out of her mind. What if this embezzlement investigation reached as far as this organization's books being audited? Parish and Beaumont had already shown up at her job asking ridiculous questions and putting her livelihood on the line. Jovani immediately filed a complaint with their superiors when she told him about it, but the damage was already done. Well, not exactly. HC Sr. knew damn well Vanna hadn't been taking money from the firm. He kept his eyes on the firm's bank account as keenly as he did his personal accounts. So the only thing the detectives had been successful at accomplishing was embarrassing the hell out of her . . . again.

The break-in at her house a few days ago, however, had ended with egg on the detectives' faces instead of on hers. Will and Cordell had both made statements, and nowhere in them did they say that she was ever mentioned during the planning or execution of the robberies. Jovani had called her yesterday morning with the news. Both men were aiming for plea deals that would keep them from serving a full prison sentence and paying a hefty fine to the casino. Jovani hadn't been optimistic that they would get everything they wanted in a deal, but he was only concerned with whatever they were saying as far as it linked to her. Which wasn't much at all. Neither of them knew about the credit union account in her and Caleb's names—the sole reason the detectives assumed she was connected in the first place. And although that was the account that held the money they'd accused her of embezzling, the detectives had indicated to Jovani that there was more money missing. But without another account with Vanna's name on it with a chunk of money that had been deposited in the last three to six months, they still had very little evidence against her. Will and Cordell couldn't corroborate their theory that she was in on Caleb's plan. Nothing connected her to Elliot Joble's murder, and nobody she knew—meaning her employer—had given any indication that she'd embezzled money before.

"I'm filing a motion to dismiss first thing Monday morning," Jovani had said when she spoke to him yesterday afternoon.

So she awoke with a smile on her face Saturday morning. And one big reason for that smile was the girls she saw walking around the room they'd rented at this hall. They were dressed in pink polo shirts and black shorts, or some of them wore black leggings. Vanna, along with the other adult staff present, wore the colors as well. Jamaica used to joke that the only reason Vanna had signed on to work with this organization was because of their shared affinity for the color pink. Vanna had only half denied that.

In fact, she'd found more gratification in watching some of these teenagers grow into beautiful young ladies. She'd been to more than one high school graduation and, as of earlier this year, the college graduation of two of her Pinks—that's what they called the girls in the club, a fact Vanna adored.

"I can't win if Granny's over there scooping up every round," Ronni complained from where she sat across the table from Vanna and Granny.

Jamaica was sitting beside Ronni. They all had a board to play and a dot marker to use to mark their cards. All except Granny, who played three boards, had a marker in her hand, and two more on standby in case she ran out of ink during the round. She'd won four times in the hour and a half they'd been here.

"Do we have to take her to the movies with us when we leave?" Ronni continued to whine.

"You're a sore loser," Granny quipped. "I sure hope you're teaching your kids better. Plus, if you stop running your mouth and pay attention, you might win a round or two."

"How? You're playing all the boards, Granny," Ronni argued.

"Girl, I ain't even got all the boards. There are six tables of people playing here. And three or four tables of people just running their mouths and eating all the food. Maybe you should go over there and join them," Granny told her.

"All right, you two," Vanna interjected. "It's just a game."

Jamaica laughed. "I can't tell. This seems to be getting serious."

"Too serious," Vanna said, and chuckled.

"Oh, you mean like things between you and Aden were before the smart detective over here suggested he wasn't trustworthy," Ronni snapped.

"Oooooohhhh, shots fired!" Jamaica said, putting a fist up to her mouth to stifle another burst of laughter. Then, as if just hearing everything, frowned at Ronni. "Hold up."

But before Jamaica could continue to go at Ronni, Vanna added, "Wow. Did I deserve that?"

She had, of course, told them about her conversation with Aden. And while they'd both been as relieved as Vanna that he wasn't involved, only Ronni had immediately blamed Jamaica for causing the discord that Vanna and Aden were currently experiencing.

Ronni sat back in her chair and pouted. "Well, you're defending Granny, and you know she's winning all the time."

"You're legit sitting there whining about not winning at bingo. Do you really want a heated blanket or the full season of *Rizzoli & Isles* on DVD?" Vanna asked. To be fair, she would've liked to win the DVDs herself, but she could also just buy them. "Besides, we're here for the charity—you remember that, don't you? We bought tickets, sold a few, and bid on the silent auction, all so that the club can raise money."

Ronni looked at Jamaica, and Jamaica rolled her eyes. "Well, that's true. And maybe that was a cheap shot. So I apologize. But you still dodged the Aden topic."

"Hmph," Granny said. "She sure did."

"Wait a minute," Vanna said, and looked at Granny. "Whose side are you on?"

"Nobody's, I'm playing bingo," Granny said, and kept her gaze focused on her boards. They hadn't even started a new round after that last winner, so Vanna wasn't buying that act.

"For your information, there is no Aden topic," Vanna told them. "We had fun while it lasted, and now we're going on about our business."

219

"Translation: y'all got busy for a minute, had a fight, and now you're walking away," Ronni said.

"Oh wow, you're on a roll today," Vanna quipped.

"I know," Jamaica added with a chuckle. "And I'm kinda over here living in the moment."

Vanna narrowed her gaze at both of them. "You're not funny," she told Jamaica. "And neither are you," she said, turning her gaze to Ronni.

"I'm just saying we had fun with him at bowling and the pool party; then everything went haywire, and you've been tight-lipped about him ever since," Ronni said.

"Not true," Vanna replied. "I told you how the conversation went down and that I felt like there was just too much going on to deal with any of this now. So that's it. Whatever it was ran its course. End of story."

"That's weak and you know it," Jamaica said.

"It's the facts," Vanna replied. "And I don't need any more of your comments on the subject, thank you very much."

Now Jamaica looked concerned. "Okay, so I accept the charge of telling you he might be framing you. But I certainly didn't say break up with him if he wasn't."

"Really, though?" Ronni asked Jamaica. "What did you think was gonna happen?"

"Exactly!" Vanna said. "Which is why I don't even know why you brought it up." She sent Ronni a pointed glare.

Both of them were getting on her nerves in this moment, and she wanted them to shut up so they could get back to having a good time.

"Hmph, hmph, hmph," Granny mumbled.

"I just pointed out some things, that's all. And you needed answers," Jamaica said.

"And I got them," she said, hating even more that they were having this conversation while four other people they didn't know sat at the other end of their table.

Today had been going so well. And now it wasn't.

"Look, it doesn't matter," she continued "I asked the questions I needed to ask. He answered them. And now, here we are." She shrugged.

"And where is that, exactly?" Granny asked, pinning her with a wide-eyed stare.

"It's . . . it's . . . wherever we are," she replied, feeling flustered. "And why are we even talking about this right now? They're starting another game."

"Ms. Vanna?" A soft voice entered their conversation, and Vanna turned to see one of the middle-school Pinks standing beside her.

"Hey, Cashae," she said, adding a smile that she really didn't feel at the moment. "What's up?"

"Ms. Gloria needs you at the ticket counter," Cashae told her.

Great. A reason for her to get up from this table and get away from all these unwanted questions and accusations.

"Oh, sure. No problem," she said, and got up without saying another word.

As she walked away, she knew the three she'd left behind were talking about her. Nothing negative, but definitely a discussion on what may or may not be going on between her and Aden right now. A discussion that Vanna was definitely happy to not be having. She'd had it in her head too many times to count this week, and she hadn't liked it at all.

A group of five had purchased tickets from a woman who wasn't at the event, and they didn't have the actual tickets with them, so the debate over whether to let them in on their word or insist they pay the at-the-door price had ensued the moment Vanna made it to the ticket booth. The suggestion for someone to call the woman who'd sold them the tickets seemed like a no-brainer, and Vanna was annoyed that none of the other grown, professional women who were on the finance committee with her had thought of it. After the call was made, the women were shown to seats in the back of the space, which sparked another argument. But again, that resolution was obvious as well. They could either sit or leave, because who showed up to an event an hour and a half late and expected to get great seats?

Vanna was just about to get something to drink and maybe another one of those delicious maple-and-brown-sugar-infused waffle wedges before heading back to her table when her phone buzzed in her back pocket. She pulled it out while walking toward the glass doors that would take her into the hallway, because the bingo caller was pretty loud.

The second she was in the much quieter hallway and glanced down at her phone, she paused. It was Aden.

How had he known she was going for the second helping of waffles instead of another one of those fruit-parfait cups? With a slight grin, she shook her head because she knew damn well he couldn't know that. Her conscience had obviously decided to step on the scene.

"Hello," she answered when she realized the phone had been ringing a few times and would soon go to voicemail.

"Hey, Savannah," he said, and her body instantly reacted to the sound of his deep voice. And by *reacting*, she meant she felt warm all over, the same way she recalled feeling whenever he'd wrapped his arms around her.

Rolling her eyes, she inwardly berated the helpless romantic that she rarely brought out to play. And for good reason, considering her track record with men.

"Hey, Aden," she replied, and hoped she didn't sound too chipper, given the way they'd left things five days ago.

And yes, she'd been counting the days.

"I wanted to check in with you to see if you were able to find a security company," he said.

She was just about to ask how he knew she was looking for one when he continued, "I spoke to Jovani earlier this week, and he told me about the break-in."

"I'm fine," she said out of habit.

"I know," he replied. "Jovani told me that you and Granny were amazing, considering all that had happened. But then, I already knew that."

She didn't smile at the comment, although her traitorous stomach did a whimsical flip-flop anyway. "I did find a company that was in my price range," she said. "They're coming out on Tuesday."

"Tuesday?" he asked. "As in a few more days away? You couldn't get someone to come sooner? I was thinking you and Granny were secure in the house by now."

"It's the earliest appointment I could get," she replied.

"I'd feel better—hell, I'd be able to get some sleep at night if I knew you had a system in place today," he replied.

That comment, as well as this call, warmed Vanna in an unexpected way. A way that highlighted what she'd really been feeling this past week when she hadn't reached out to him was fear. Everything she'd done and said to Aden that day had come from that place. And him leaving the way he did and not contacting her provided the safe haven she'd needed to retreat into.

It took a very concerted effort to resist the urge to do a deep dive into how she really needed to stop letting negativity overwhelm her.

"I appreciate your concern," she said. "But I've taken care of the issue."

"Okay," he said after a moment's hesitation. "It's just that I care about you, Savannah. And I want to be sure you and Granny are safe."

She let out a slow, shaky breath that she hadn't been aware she was holding. "Thank you," she said, and then cleared her throat. "Thank you for your concern. I know I might not always act like it, but I do appreciate it."

"You've got a funny way of showing your appreciation," he said. The slight chuckle that followed suggested he might be joking. But another part of her guessed he was serious.

"You're right," she replied with a sigh.

"Wait a minute . . . Who is this on the phone, and what have you done with Savannah?" Now he was really laughing, and she couldn't help but grin along with him.

"All right, don't go overboard," she said.

"I mean, I'm just shocked. Usually, I would have gotten more of an argument from you."

"Well, I'm not at home, and I need to get back to the bingo game."

"Yeah, I saw that was on your schedule for today. But I just wanted to call to make sure you were okay," he said in a much softer tone. "I've wanted to call you every day this week."

And now her heart swelled in that way that had her even more afraid than she'd been before. Because this was a definite sign that no matter how much she'd tried to convince herself that she couldn't deal with this right now, that she could just walk away from him, she was already in too deep with this man. "Why didn't you?"

"Because I didn't want to argue with you again."

"Then why did you call today?"

"Because I missed arguing with you," he said, and she smiled.

"Oh. Well, I thought you called because you somehow knew I was going for a second helping of maple-and-brown-sugar waffles instead of fruit."

He chuckled. "No. But I'm glad you're getting used to holding yourself accountable."

"Whatever, Aden," she said, smothering her urge to smile. "I really do have to go."

"Okay, that's fine. Go and finish your bingo game. Can I call you later? You know, without having an excuse?"

Now she was smiling so hard her cheeks hurt. "I mean, I guess, if that's what you want to do."

"Yeah," he said, and she could hear that he was smiling too. "That's definitely what I want to do."

Chapter 20

Don't feed what you don't want to grow.

Vanna sat on the side of her bed, holding the card in her hand. She had read it four times now, from the moment she'd taken it out of the box on her dresser until she'd walked back across the room to take a seat. The feeling that she needed to sit with those words, especially today, was overwhelming. It seemed as if she'd come to the edge of a cliff and some tough decisions needed to be made before she took another step. And surrounding those tough decisions was a vicious combination of negative thoughts that had been prickling against every positive affirmation or motivational quote she'd read this month.

Counterproductive. That's how she felt she'd been moving. Like for every two steps forward, she would take three steps back. And while most of that was due to events that had taken place in her life, she knew it was her reaction that she was responsible for.

Whatever Caleb was and whatever he'd done in the last year of his life ultimately had nothing to do with her. They were his decisions, his actions. Now, it was a fact that she'd been caught in those decisions and actions, but she didn't have to act defeated because of that. Just as throughout the marriage she hadn't needed to be the victim. At any point during that time, and what she'd actually finally done five years ago, she could've decided to remove herself from the situation.

To believe in herself more than she wanted to create the illusion of a happy union.

As for the charges that were—as of yesterday—still pending against her, she had to put that in God's hands. When Jovani called her just before she'd left her office Friday afternoon, she'd been expecting to hear that the motion he'd filed had been successful and that she no longer had a criminal case dangling over her head. She'd thought that would be the perfect birthday present. But that wasn't what he'd said. A hearing on the motion was scheduled for Tuesday morning, which meant the resolution was further delayed. Still, she had decided to believe that all things would work out for her good.

And this morning, her fortieth-birthday morning, she'd felt like that was even more true. It was a combination of the beautiful sunrise she'd witnessed when she'd first climbed out of bed at six thirty and the *I Love Lucy* theme music that had been playing when she turned the television on because she'd apparently forgotten to turn off the DVD player when she fell asleep last night. Thankfully, her TV had auto-power off, or that would've played all night.

There'd been a definite pep in her step as she headed into the bathroom to take a shower and then came out to select her card of the day. Now she read those words again: *Don't feed what you don't want to grow.*

It was more than fitting, she thought just as her phone buzzed from the nightstand. She set the card down on the bed beside her and reached for the phone.

Aden: Happy 40th birthday, beautiful.

The smile that covered her face was probably brighter than the sunshine slicing through the open blinds in her bedroom. Her fingers moved quickly to type out a reply:

Vanna: Thank you!

They'd been back to texting every day since the Bingo and Brunch last Saturday, settling into an informal rotation of him doing the *Good morning* text one day, and her following up on the next. Daily check-ins throughout the day of funny memes, inspiring words, or random questions were now the norm. And in the evening, they'd settled into talking on the phone an hour or so, or putting each other to bed, as Aden had called it. That part had reminded Vanna of her teenage years of sneaking to stay on the phone all night with some boy. Only now, the boy was a full-grown, fine-as-hell, successful and mature man who seemed to like her a lot. Despite her moods and all the baggage she still carried.

Jamaica: Happy birthday V!! My bestie!! 🖤

Vanna grinned at the next text to come through.

Vanna: Thanks boo!

Ronni: Yay! You're up. Didn't want to wake you, but happy birthday!

You ready to turn up tonight?

Vanna: You know it! Granny scheduled our mani/pedis for ten this morning,

but I'm about to get dressed now and go find me some breakfast.

Jamaica: You and your addiction to breakfast. LOL Be ready at five.

Vanna: Again, you know it!

Ronni and Jamaica had rented a party bus for just the three of them to travel to the party. It would be the culmination of their special time with Vanna before the big celebration. She loved them so much for sticking with her through everything and for knowing exactly what she would like to kick off tonight's festivities. They would already be on the bus when it arrived at her house at five; then they would head directly to the venue for a mini–photo shoot before the party started. Vanna was especially looking forward to that because the only photos she had of them together were the ones they used their phones to capture. This was going to be a phenomenal way to memorialize this moment of two of the most important people in her life enjoying this day with her for all time.

Aden: I pray today will be everything you hoped and more.

This man and his buttery words. Could she be filled with more happiness than she was at this very moment? That was it—this feeling, this smile on her face, this energy to get started with her day, this joy was exactly what the words on that card meant. This was the feeling she wanted to grow, this was what she needed to feed, right here.

Vanna: I think it will. Thank you for getting it off to a great start. 🐾

Granny called up the stairs then, announcing that breakfast was ready. She'd thought she smelled bacon while she was texting but had chalked it up to wishful thinking since she'd mentioned breakfast in her text. But Granny's words were confirmation, and Vanna wasn't wasting another second. She pulled on her robe and pushed her feet into her slippers. Replaced the card in the box and went back to the nightstand to grab her phone and slip it into the pocket of her robe. Then she opened the door to find Frito standing there with an expectant look on his face.

"Were you sent up here to get me?" she asked as she stared down into his oddly cute face.

His response was one of those ridiculous growl-mumbles that she wished she could really decipher instead of guessing what they meant. "Did you just wish me a happy birthday?" She smiled down at him this time and could've sworn his panting response was him smiling right back.

Vanna followed him down the stairs like she needed an escort and walked into the kitchen to see all her breakfast favorites: french toast, bacon, cheesy scrambled eggs, orange juice, and a bowl of watermelon and green grapes.

"Happy birthday, Vannie," Granny said as she came over to hug her.

And Vanna hugged her right back. "Thanks, Granny. I love you so much."

"I love you too, baby."

Tonight was the pinnacle of Vanna's FFSF celebration. Dinner at Simplicity, a new chic restaurant owned by Domonique Sampson, a friend of hers and Jamaica's from college. Domonique had gone on to culinary school after college, then returned to DC starting out with a food truck, then moving up to a pop-up, and now, for the last three months, her first restaurant. Vanna had been eager to support her old friend, and Domonique had been ecstatic to make tonight a very special night for Vanna.

The decor was top tier, not that she'd expected anything less. Simplicity had an art deco design, with warm cream-and-teal walls, and gold-and-cream accents in the table linens and at the host stand. Sleek, dark cement floors and a combo of low- and highboy tables in the main dining room. White wrought iron furniture occupied the patio area. That's where Vanna's party was being held—thank the Lord for the fantastic weather, not too muggy on this late summer's evening, and no rain in sight.

The smaller square tables on the patio had been put together to create three nine-foot-long tables, draped in white linen cloths. Pink satin bows were tied around the backs of the white chairs. Small vases overflowing with dark- and light-pink roses created a runner down the center of each table. Gold candelabras held long blush-pink candles at measured intervals, and clear chargers rimmed in gold marked each place setting. There was a bar at the far end of the patio, with Vanna's signature birthday drink—the pink vodka-lemonade—at the top of the drink menu. In another corner was a picture backdrop of pink, gold, and white balloons. The last part of the photo shoot with her, Jamaica, and Ronni had been taken there, with the bulk of the pictures at different locales around the city that the party bus had stopped at for that purpose specifically.

"Like a bunch of cotton candy, just like I said," Jamaica said, coming up to stand behind Vanna.

They'd been at the venue for half an hour now. The party was set to start at eight, and people had begun to arrive. But Vanna was staring at the picture backdrop and thinking of how blessed she was to be here in this moment.

"It's pretty," she said, not bothering to toss Jamaica a nasty look. It didn't matter what her friend thought of the decor tonight because this night was all about Vanna. Jamaica knew that and respected it, but that didn't mean she wasn't going to joke about what she also called "little-girl colors" along the way.

"I was coming to tell you that Croy and Davon just arrived, so you know that means the party is going to get started whether you want it to or not," Jamaica said.

"Oh no," Vanna began with a shake of her head. "The DJ already knows to play light jazz until we bless the food. Then we're going to eat, I'll say my thank-you's, and *then* the party can begin."

Jamaica raised a brow. "Oookay, well, I'll go over and try to explain the order of the service to them, but they've already stopped at the bar."

And by *they*, Vanna knew she really meant Davon, because he always drank more than Croy.

"Y'all better get y'all's men. I'm not in the mood for no foolishness tonight," she said, but her tone was light and easy.

Just like her mood.

Which, about fifteen minutes later, was lifted even higher when she saw Aden walk out onto the patio. It was the first time she'd seen him in person since the night of their argument two weeks ago. He wore black slacks and a white shirt, a black vest and a tie that matched the dusty-rose color of her dress. He walked toward her in that signature confident way he had, and her heart almost thumped right out of her chest.

She shifted her weight from one foot to the other, clasping her hands behind her back. She'd tried to look away from him, to appear unbothered by his appearance, but failed dismally. The good thing was that, as transfixed as she seemed to be on him, he was equally as focused on her even as he moved through the crowd. He never broke eye contact with her and didn't bump into anyone in the process. It was almost like they all knew to get out of his way, to let him through to his desired destination. To her.

The DJ was playing some smooth-jazz rendition of a Luther Vandross song, and Vanna thought it couldn't be more appropriate . . . if she and Aden were having this second reunion alone at her place or his. Beneath the evening stars and surrounded by fifty guests, including her grandmother, she couldn't run and jump into his arms, wrap her legs around him, and whisper her nastiest thoughts into his ear. But damn, if that wasn't exactly what she wanted to do.

"Hey," he said when he was close enough to reach out and pull both her hands into his.

"Hey," she whispered just as he brought her hands to his lips for a soft kiss to each one. The smile that spread across her face couldn't be contained, not that she even tried. "Why didn't you tell me you still planned to come tonight?"

Throughout all their communication this week, Vanna had been careful not to invite him anywhere, and he hadn't invited himself anywhere. Of course, he already knew the schedule of plans for her FFSF weekend, and by the time they'd begun speaking again, tonight's celebration was the only thing left. Still, she hadn't wanted to bring it up, hadn't wanted to give the impression that she needed him here with her tonight. But she was damn glad he was here.

"Why would you think I wasn't going to show up?" he asked, the corner of his mouth lifting into that teasing grin she hated to love. "It's your birthday, Savannah. I wanted to spend it with you—I mean, along with all your other family and friends."

She nodded and glanced quickly away to see those family and friends either sitting down or standing in small groups, socializing. When she returned her gaze back to him, she admitted, "I'm glad you're here."

Now Aden's smile was broad, laughter twinkling in his dark-brown eyes. "That didn't hurt too much, did it?" he asked.

Vanna rolled her eyes. "Whatever, Aden," she said playfully, and attempted to pull her hands from his grip. "You know I'm not used to this."

"Nah, you know I'm just kidding. But it's good to hear I finally did something to please you."

"You've done a lot of things that pleased me," she said.

"Ah, man," he groaned. "Don't talk like that when we've got all these people around us. You look good as hell, so I'd hate to rip this dress off of you."

If she hadn't already thought she looked sexy in the off-the-shoulder rose-colored dress that molded against her every curve and stopped at her knees with a small split on the left side, she felt like a whole snack after his words and the way he was gazing at her.

"Oookaay, come through with the matching prom look, Aden," Jamaica said as she walked up to them.

"Glad you're here, man," Davon, who was right beside Jamaica, said. He extended his hand to Aden, and Aden released Vanna's hands so he could shake it. "Your lady's got a whole program before we can cut loose. I need you to try to talk her out of that."

Aden laughed. "Nah, man. This is her night. I'm just here to be whatever she needs."

"Oooohhh, that sounds nasty," Jamaica said, and Vanna swatted her arm.

Moments later, Domonique came out to grab Vanna and go over a few things scheduled for the night. Ronni blessed the food, and they ate while soft music continued to play. The candles were alight on each table and, combined with the twinkle lights that covered the few bushes surrounding the patio, they created a casual-chic atmosphere that Vanna adored.

Jamaica tapped a fork to her glass and looked expectantly at Vanna a few minutes after the meal had been completed. Vanna frowned at her friend and said, "This is not a wedding girl, stop it."

Laughing, she picked up the glass of champagne that one of the servers had just filled for her and stood. Right on cue, servers were now moving around the patio, filling every guest's glass with champagne.

"I want to take this moment to thank each of you for coming out tonight," Vanna said. "You have no idea how much it means to me that you thought enough of me to spend some of your time celebrating my special day. How much it means to be able to stand here today and focus on the significance of joy around a birthday celebration in light of our ancestors who were brutally stripped of age, life, and milestones."

A round of applause sounded, and Vanna paused, glanced around once again at all her friends. Granny, who sat on one side of the table to the right of Vanna's head of table seat. And Aden, who sat on the left side. To Jamaica, Davon, Ronni, and Croy, her closest crew, who held their glasses ready to toast her.

"I'm blessed beyond measure," she continued. "And while I sometimes forget that, I always feel you with me. Your support and your positive energy is appreciated. Your—"

Clap. Clap. Clap.

The singular clapping sounded through the quiet, and everyone looked in the direction from which it had come.

"Bravo," Gail said in a slurred voice as she made her way from the far end of the patio. "Bravo. What a great performance." She clapped again, this time so hard that the glass she was holding slipped out of her hand and crashed to the floor, splashing its contents onto the bottom of Gail's white slacks.

Vanna slowly lowered her glass, not sure of what exactly was happening but acknowledging the rise of a sickening heat in her stomach.

"You been standing up and showing out since the day I met your ass," Gail said as she came closer to the head table where Vanna stood. "Always talking, always stealing my boy's shine. Acting like you were better than him. Better than e'rebody else around you."

"Gail," Vanna said when she could finally find her voice again, "you weren't invited."

Gail let out a nauseating laugh. "See what I mean? That's it right there. Your ass always acted like you were the big boss. I mean, you're big—always have been. Told Caleb he needed to put you on a rabbit diet." That laugh sounded again, and she stopped beside the chair where Croy sat.

Aden stood then. "I'll take care of this," he said, but Vanna shook her head.

"No," she said, and stepped from around the table. "She obviously has something she wants to get off her chest. I'm game for giving her the stage to show everyone here what a trash mother she was to her child and how disrespectful she still is to me after all I did to keep him upright in this world."

There was a part of her that wanted to assure Aden that she wasn't refusing his help because of her *Don't need a man to save me* routine, as he liked to call it. This was based solely on the fact that she was tired of Gail Carlson. Tired of her slick comments, her rude behavior, and, like she'd just said, the blatant disrespect she'd continually dished out to her.

"Oh, you always did think you were tough," Gail said, and shook her head. "You don't know the meaning of the word, with your bougie ass!"

"You're interrupting my party, Gail. Say what you have to say so we can get on with our night," Vanna spat.

By now, Jamaica and Ronni had both gotten up from their seats and were standing to Vanna's right. Croy stood, but moved so that he was a few steps behind Gail.

"Don't rush me, girl! If you knew what was comin', you'd sit your ass back down and shut up," Gail said. "But no, you too good for that. Good and damn foolish. But I swear you've got a little bit of luck on your side. How else do you keep escaping everything I put in place for your downfall?"

That last part had Vanna raising a brow and Aden stepping up closer to flank her left side. She felt his hand on the small of her back and knew that he would intervene the second she gave him the word.

"What are you talking about?" Vanna asked, that sickening feeling swirling in her stomach now.

Gail's eyes were bloodshot just like Diane's had been the last time she'd seen her. Vanna had witnessed Gail drunk before, but never like this. She practically reeked of alcohol like she'd been drinking nonstop for weeks. Her steps had been wobbly, and now she was barely able to stand still without swaying from one side to the other. But none of that stopped her.

"You know what I'm talkin' 'bout." More slurred words, this time added to a wave of her arm that almost sent her sprawling across the floor.

Croy had held out his arms, indicating he was ready to catch her whenever she finally toppled over.

"I tipped those cops off to that bank account!" Gail yelled. "When they came to my house to talk about my Caleb, ask if he had any enemies that might want to see him dead. Or if maybe he jumped in that water himself. I told 'em, you! You were the enemy! And I made sure they knew that's where Caleb put his money. I knew because the statements came to my house along with all his other mail after you put him out."

"What?" Vanna asked, her voice a raspy whisper.

"Caleb's lovesick ass told me a while ago about that account. Said he wanted to make sure he had all the money he would need to take care of you right this time. All that boy talked about was getting your trifling ass back. Made me sick!"

"Wait a minute," Vanna said. "You knew my name was still on that account."

"Caleb didn't never take it off. Tossed those papers you signed right in the trash one night. Said he wasn't letting go of the last thing he had of your life together. I told him he was a fool right then and there. Told him he was a sorry excuse for a man, letting a woman dominate him the way you did."

At her words, Vanna thought about all that Aden had told her about Caleb's relationship with his mother. Vanna had never heard Gail talk to or about Caleb like this. She'd only ever doted on him and berated Vanna for not doing enough to take care of him. How the hell had she even formed those words when it was obvious now how badly she'd spoken to her own child?

"And I knew he had all that money, so I told the cops that's where it was, and that's how they knew to arrest your ass," Gail said. "But then you got out of jail, and I knew I had to do more, to fix it so you'd stay behind bars until you died just like my son. So I put those bags in your house."

"How the hell did your drunk ass get into her house?" Jamaica asked.

Gail's head turned to Jamaica and frowned again. "You, the cop bitch," Gail said with a shake of her head. "You should know better than to hang around criminals." Gail laughed again before returning her gaze to Vanna.

Then she started to dig into the deep pocket of the white three-quarter-length jacket she wore. She pulled out keys and jingled them in the air. "I told you, you was dumb. You never changed the locks on the house. Caleb still had his key, so I used it and I was so ready to see you fry when I checked in with the detective and learned that they'd searched the house."

"You vindictive—" Vanna moved toward Gail, ready to put hands on her, when Gail pulled a gun out of that same pocket and aimed it directly at her.

"Get back!" she told Vanna. "You stand back until I'm ready to end this for you."

Aden had inched an arm around Vanna's waist, pulled her back, and tucked her behind him. "I think it's time for you to go," he said in a voice that was far too calm for the rage Vanna felt jumping off him as she placed a hand on his arm.

The guests were immediately up and out of their seats, all rushing toward the opening where the patio led back into the restaurant.

"I ain't goin' nowhere," Gail continued. "Not until I'm finished with her. If you'd just gone down with the cops, then I wouldn't have to do this, but it's probably better this way."

At this moment, Vanna wished she hadn't taken Granny's gun from her after that night when she'd pulled it on Aden. Not that it had any bullets, anyway.

"Nah, you're leaving," Aden said. "Going out the door with the cops you love talking to so much." He nodded just beyond Gail's shoulder, and Vanna's eyes widened as she saw two uniformed cops coming through the opening to the patio.

She hadn't heard them before, but now the sound of sirens in the distance broke through the air. Somebody at the party must've called the police, thankfully, or this situation could've ended much worse.

"You killed my son, and all he did was love you!" Gail cried out as one of the officers came up behind her and demanded she drop the gun.

Another officer came around until Gail could see him. "Drop the gun!" he yelled "Drop it now!"

"No!" Gail yelled back. "She killed my son!"

Davon had gotten up and had moved Granny to the other side of the DJ stand, out of the line of fire, and Vanna whispered a silent thank-you to him as she glimpsed them out of her peripheral. Aden never moved from in front of her, and Jamaica and Ronni still stood beside her.

"Ma'am, we're only gonna ask you one more time," the officer who stood in front of Gail said now.

Behind her, the other officer yelled, "Drop the gun! Drop it!"

Gail didn't drop the gun; instead, she started to turn the gun so it would be aimed at herself, but the officer who had been in front of her fired, shooting her in the leg. She dropped like a ton of bricks; the gun she'd been holding skittering across the ground.

Aden backed them up as more officers came from everywhere, one picking up Gail's gun, another turning her over onto her stomach so he could pull her hands behind her back. Vanna watched in shock as the woman she'd once wanted to like and accept her was cuffed, blood gushing from her leg, as she continued to yell and rail at Vanna. This time when tears stung Vanna's eyes, she let them fall freely. Instead of pushing back on the anger, the hurt, the confusion she'd been grappling with for weeks, she let it all loose until gut-wrenching sobs escaped and her legs gave out beneath her.

Chapter 21

A dam had broken, and Vanna let it surge. The tears, the screams, the defeat she felt in the moments after Gail had been shot and arrested, powered through her like a bulldozer, until the entire world spun around her.

Strong arms kept her from falling to the floor and possibly hurting herself. Aden had gone to his knees too, continuing to keep his grip on her even as she needed to let go of the weight that had been holding her upright for so long. It had pulsed through every fiber of her, daily struggles mingled with the remnants of the new storm that had come to ravage her life. Every day of this month, she'd been cognizant of all that she was carrying, but she continued to move on, to press through, because that's what she'd been so used to doing. It was what so many women felt they had to do. But all of a sudden, it all became too heavy. Too much to remain standing and hold on to, so she let it go.

"What . . . what did I ever do to her?" she choked out the words. "What did I do to deserve any of this?"

Vanna usually hated a *Why me?* cry, but she couldn't help the words, couldn't keep them contained any longer.

"Nothing, baby," Aden said, keeping one hand at her back to steady her while his other hand rubbed up and down her arm. "This was never about you."

"But it was!" she screamed. "Didn't you hear her? It was always about me. She hated me because I took her son away from her and then

I didn't treat him the way she thought I should. Then he dies and that's my fault too." She shuddered at those words.

"No, ma'am," Jamaica said as she knelt down on the other side of Vanna. "You are not going to sit here and blame yourself for that whacko woman or her trash-ass son. They were a mess before you even met him."

"She's right," Aden said. "You know that, Vanna."

She knew what they were saying, had heard and digested the words, but she didn't want the excuse. No, in this moment, she wanted to take the blame, to hold it near and dear for every day that she'd used all her energy to push those thoughts away. If she embraced it now, maybe it would be over sooner. Maybe this hurt and anger would leave her the hell alone. "I can't do this!" she screamed this time, and started to push herself up off the floor.

Aden moved with her, giving her permission to lean on him as much as she needed to. "Let's go over here and sit down."

"No," she said in an eerily soft voice. "I don't want to sit at the table that was so prettily decorated for my birthday party." Another sob broke free. "It's my birthday, dammit!"

"Oh, Vanna," Ronni said, tears filling her eyes. "Honey, I'm so sorry it turned out this way."

"I should've known," she said. "Shouldn't have expected—" She let those words trail off because they didn't feel right against her tongue. None of this felt right, and she couldn't figure out how to fix it. Vanna always fixed things, especially for herself. Whatever went wrong, she figured it out and did what was required to get through it. That was her thing—it was her superpower. But not this time.

"I don't want to be here," she said. "I want to go home."

"Okay, I'll take you home," Aden said.

"We'll follow you," Jamaica said. "We'll take the celebration back to your house. And it'll be just us."

Vanna looked at them, each of them—her best friends and their plus-ones, and Granny. They were her support system, the people she could lean on for everything, and yet she knew she hadn't leaned on them enough. Hadn't shared all her thoughts and fears in these past weeks. And Aden, the man who'd come along and pushed himself into a space she was perfectly fine with being empty. Why did she need a hero when she could be one for herself?

But what was she supposed to do in moments like now, when she couldn't do it? Couldn't immediately pick up the pieces and do the things she needed to do to move on?

"Yeah," she said with a slow nod. "I'd like it to be just us." And she reached out to take Aden's hand. "Take me home."

Home had turned out to be Aden's place, as sometime during the ride, Vanna decided she didn't want to go back to the house where she'd once lived with Caleb. Not at that moment. So Aden had suggested his place, and a quick text to the group had them all rerouting and landing at the door of Aden's cozy town house. They'd had a couple of drinks, two more toasts to the birthday girl, and then they'd all headed home.

Jamaica and Davon offered to take Granny back to the house, while Vanna had accepted Aden's invitation to spend the night there. He'd extended that invite to Granny as well, but Vanna had heard her grandmother tell him, "No. She needs you tonight. And I trust you to take care of her."

That's how she'd ended up sleeping in Aden's arms all night. Now, as sun poured through the window through the half-raised shade early the next morning, she pulled the charcoal-gray-and-white sheets up over her shoulder and rolled onto her side.

Memories of last night filtered through her mind as she blinked slowly to remove the sleep from her eyes. Aden's bedroom was as neat as the other parts of his house she'd seen last night. The living room, with its brown-and-beige decor, and the kitchen, with the huge table he'd told Granny was bought at his mother's insistence because she expected him to help his sister in hosting some of their family holiday dinners. Something he hadn't done yet because he'd been so busy opening the gym and now the supplement storefront.

His bedroom was large and airy, as he only had the bed and two dressers in it. A huge TV was mounted on the wall across from the bed, and she'd glimpsed a walk-in closet last night before she'd taken over his bathroom for a long, hot shower. He'd let her take the shower alone and had one of his T-shirts and the sheets already turned down for her when she emerged. Exhausted from last night and the prior month's events, she'd been asleep by the time Aden joined her in the bed.

Sometime during the night, she'd awakened enough to recall she wasn't in her own bed but that a wonderful man had her tucked safely in his arms. So she'd drifted back to sleep until this moment, when she'd awakened to thoughts that threatened to suffocate her.

There was no box of cards on Aden's dresser that she could flip through and find some semblance of strength and encouragement for the day. No, today she would have to figure this shit out on her own. She would have to decide what her mood was going to be and how much of what had happened last night she was going to carry.

None of it, was the quick answer. Not one tiny bit of it. Because none of it was her fault or her burden to share. Gail's issues, which Vanna didn't even have a clue where to begin with, were her own. The woman was definitely going through something, had been through something, and would probably continue to let that something haunt and torment her. But Vanna didn't have to do the same.

She didn't have to, nor did she want to. Seeing what Gail had turned into after years of probably being bitter and resentful had been proof that Vanna's desire to breathe positivity into her life on a daily basis through her cards was a smart one. Now she just had to figure out how to keep that positivity going beyond the words. She had to implement them into a new lifestyle.

And to do that, she had to let go of this old life once and for all. That's what this month was supposed to have been about anyway, but this morning, Vanna realized that she hadn't been fully prepared to close the door on some things. Sure, she'd told herself, and she'd even shared with Aden, her plan to start the divorce proceedings in September. But truthfully, she didn't have a lawyer in mind to handle it for her, and so there was no appointment in her planner to start that process. Which was odd because she knew a handful of divorce attorneys, most of whom had offices in the same building where she worked. So how easy would it have been to make that appointment ahead of time, just as she'd so meticulously planned out her FFSF weekends? She wasn't going to spiral so far to start asking how easily she could've done that long before now, because she was over having regrets. And now divorce wasn't an issue she had to address at all.

But letting go of the chapter of her life that had included Caleb was. It was long past time to close that book, put it on the shelf, and never look back on it again. Well, no, not exactly. There was something to be said about burying the past but keeping the lessons. A phrase from one of her cards. Even now that she had a better understanding of who Caleb was, none of it excused how he'd treated her. And it finally occurred to her that's what she'd been looking for all this time. A reason for why things had turned out the way they had. Someone to blame. An apology. Absolution. None of which would be coming. A fact she would now accept.

Bad things happened, and she dealt with them—that was the type of woman she was. The type of woman she'd had to be. Right or wrong. Fair or unjust. It just was. But she didn't have to wear that anger and resentment as a shield. She didn't have to remain in a holding pattern of despair and uncertainty. She could just be who and what she was and be happy at the same time. She *wanted* to be who and what she was and be happy at the same time.

"You think too much." Aden's deep voice rumbled against her neck as he rolled over to spoon her and dropped his arm over her waist.

He pulled her back tightly against him, similar to the way he'd held her most of the night. And she snuggled back against him, loving the feeling of warmth and safety he provided.

Safe. That's how she felt with Aden. It had taken her a while to move past the fear and distrust, but when she had in this past week, she'd understood the foreign feeling that had really been plaguing her about him was safety. Something she'd only felt with a few people in this world. Granny, Jamaica, and Ronni. They'd been her rocks for so long, had loved her even when she'd thought she was unlovable, and she hated that she hadn't really seen that until they'd all stood with her last night.

"But they're good thoughts, though," she said on a heavy sigh. "I'm allowed to have good thoughts."

"You are," he replied. "You wanna share any of those good thoughts?"

Instinct had her wanting to retreat, to keep her private thoughts and feelings to herself because if she dared speak them aloud, they might be laughed at or dispelled. But with a slow shake of her head, she took a deep breath and said, "Sure."

Aden rolled over onto his back then, pulling her with him as he moved. Until they were settled into a new position, with his arm still holding her tightly against him, but with her partially on top of him so she could look up at him. He looked amazing even first thing in the morning. His chest was bare, eyes focused on her, lips still kissable despite the possibility of morning breath.

"I owe you an apology," she said.

"No, you don't," he countered.

"But I do," she insisted, and then tapped a finger to his lips. "Just let me get this out."

When he nodded, she pulled her hand back from his face, but not all the way. Her fingers moved through his beard and over to cup his jaw as she continued. "I didn't expect you. I didn't want to want you at first. And then, after I'd had you, I didn't want to need you."

She took another breath and swallowed, pushing back the uneasiness that threatened to bubble up. There was no fear here, she reminded herself. This could be—*he* could be a safe space if she opened herself up to it. And today, the first day of her new beginning, she was determined to do this.

"I thought if I let myself dream about another happy ever after that I would be just setting myself up for failure again," she said. "And I couldn't fail, Aden. Not at love, not again. My heart, my sanity, wouldn't have survived it. So I thought if I just kept that door closed—you know, the way I did with the other guys I'd been with since my marriage—that was the smart move. To not want too much, not expect the impossible."

Tears filled her eyes, and she swore this must have been the month of crying, because she had done way too much of it. But probably not really enough. What if she hadn't spent so much time bottling up her emotions, putting on the strong face all the time? How much sooner would she have reached this place in her life? How much sooner would she have been able to claim this peace that she'd been searching for so very long?

"But I should have expectations," she said, her voice stronger than she'd heard in a very long time. "In addition to loving myself, I should expect love when I'm willing to give it. Even if I may not get it, I should still have that expectation. And I should endeavor to find it instead of convincing myself that I was never worthy of love in the first place."

Now he lifted his other hand to cup her face. "Why?" The question came in a hoarse whisper. His brow furrowed as he continued to stare at her. "Why would you have ever thought you weren't worthy of love?"

Vanna leaned into his touch and closed her eyes. There was so much this man didn't know about her, and yet he had shown up to take care of her, to offer her all of himself, time and time again. She felt like such a fool for trying to push him away—but again, no more regrets. Lifting her gaze to his, she smiled.

"My mother left me at a bus station when I was seven," she said, then had to clear her throat of the emotion that stuck there with those words. "Before then, she used to oversleep—or rather, be passed out from a hangover—so I'd miss the school bus and, subsequently, school. I learned how to push the chair over to the counter, then climb up so I could get the box of cereal and a bowl out of the cabinet when I was five. Spilled my share of milk and got my share of beatings for doing so, but eventually I figured out how to feed myself. Because Mama couldn't always do it."

"Baby," Aden whispered, and rubbed his other hand up and down her back.

"No, don't feel sorry for me," she said. "Granny came and got me from the police station the day of the bus-station incident, and I never went back to live with my mother. She has a drinking problem. She had it before she had me, so I know now that it's not because of something I did or didn't do. Still, her problem became my trauma, and I let that shape my life."

Another deep, shuddering breath came, and those tears fell slowly until Aden caught them with his thumb to both sides of her face.

"She's dying now," Vanna said for the first time since Granny had given her the news. "And I don't really know how I feel about that. What I do know is that I'm sick of being in this holding pattern. Of waiting for the other shoe to drop on whatever type of relationship I'm in. My marriage was a mess, but that's been over for quite some time. It should've been in my heart as well as my mind, but I think the bigger lesson was in going through all the emotions and finally finding myself."

"Is that where you are now?" he asked, still cupping her face and rubbing his hand over her back.

"Yeah," she said with a nod. "I believe I am. And I have you to thank for that, partially. I mean, I've been working my way to this point. Had already decided this was my time for a new beginning. But then you came along and put the proverbial cherry on top."

His grin spread, and the sight of it warmed her heart. She could make him smile. Just her. Wearing no makeup, without a shower or brushing her teeth, she made this amazing man smile.

"So, while I wouldn't change our first meet-cute or our reunion meet-cute at all, I'm hoping for more good times with you, Aden Granger. More getting to know each other, more exploring new feelings and expectations. I'm just looking forward to more."

He maneuvered them until she was fully on top of him now, her legs straddling his hips, her breasts smushed against his chest while one of his arms remained tightly around her waist. The other moved up her back until his hand cupped the back of her head. She was thankful for the braids because the impromptu overnight stay had left her without her bonnet, and her hair out in curls would've surely been a mess by now.

"You can have as much as you want, Savannah. The world is yours, baby. *I* am yours; take everything that makes your heart soar."

It was him, she thought as she lowered her face to his. In this moment, it was *he* who made her heart soar. And she poured all those thoughts and emotions into the sweet and sultry kiss they fell into.

Chapter 22

They met in Jovani's office instead of at the courthouse, since the motion-to-dismiss hearing had been canceled. The AUSA filed a voluntary dismissal after receiving a copy of Gail's recorded statement from Saturday. The detectives had delivered it to his office an hour before the hearing in the judge's chambers was scheduled to begin. But Jovani had asked her to meet in his office anyway.

"I just wanted to go over everything that I know now to assure you that this is in the past," he said from where he was seated behind his desk.

Aden and Granny had both come to the meeting with her. To be honest, neither of them had let her out of their sight since Saturday night. In fact, they'd conspired to come up with a schedule where when he'd dropped her off at her house on Sunday afternoon, Granny was on duty until he'd returned late Sunday night. On Monday, they'd had a small impromptu cookout in Vanna's backyard. Just her, Aden, and her crew, Frito included.

This morning, Aden and Granny had decided to tag-team her, but Vanna wasn't upset. She was adjusting to letting both of them in, in a way she hadn't before. Last night, she and Granny had had a long talk about Diane and about how they would work together now to make sure her mother had what she needed for whatever time she had left.

She'd also let Aden call his guy for the security system. He was at the house now while Jack and his crew were there working.

"All the charges were dropped, though, right?" Granny asked from the guest chair she sat in to Vanna's left.

Jovani nodded. "Yes, all of the charges against her are dropped."

"What happened?" Aden asked.

"Yes," she said. "I want to know how this happened. What did Caleb do to bring me into this?" It would be her final time allowing thoughts of this man to have priority in her mind, but at least she would finally have some of the answers she deserved.

"That's the thing," Jovani said. "I don't think he intended to involve you in any way. At least, not from what the detectives have pieced together from all the statements they have now."

Jovani opened a file and cleared his throat. "Caleb worked for the Lennox Casino as a cage cashier. Will Baylor was his shift supervisor, and El, or Elliot Joble, was another cashier they worked with. Together, the three of them concocted the scheme to embezzle money from the casino."

Beside her, Aden shook his head. Vanna knew he was thinking that this sounded just like something Caleb would do. Something he wasn't actually smart enough to do and have it done right.

"Six—or rather, seven—months ago now," Jovani continued, "Caleb and El were responsible for balancing cash drawers and reconciling daily summaries of transactions at the casino. They manipulated the records so that a portion of the money from each shift was undocumented. The amount of that undocumented money was reported to Will, and he made sure that the undocumented money was put into casino money bags and tagged specifically before they were loaded onto the armored trucks for bank deposits.

"Will's cousin Cordell—the guy still threatening to sue Granny for the twenty stitches he had to get thanks to Frito taking a bite out of him—was a driver for the armored-truck company contracted by the casino. El knew a couple of guys from around the way named Nino and Sarge. They paid Nino and Sarge to rob the truck in one of the dead spots en route throughout the city. All Nino and Sarge took off the trucks were the tagged bags."

"What?" Aden asked. "So what, did they report back to the casino if the money was undocumented?"

Jovani shrugged. "Apparently, the casino money wasn't the only pickup on the truck's route. But here's the thing: nowhere in any of the statements from the actual players in this scheme was Vanna's name mentioned. The guys only knew about her because Caleb talked about her during their downtime, but never in the details of planning the robberies. So there was no conspiracy for them to link her to."

"Only the conspiracy between Caleb and his cohorts," she said, feeling overwhelmed at hearing these details. "How had they thought they were going to get away with this?"

"They did get away with it," Jovani said. "For a good while—six robberies, to be exact. But then, on this last one, three months ago, things quickly fell apart. Cordell failed a random drug test and wasn't able to drive that day. So when Nino and Sarge pulled up to the truck, the new driver got spooked and started shooting. Nino was killed, and Sarge was wounded, but he got away. During the detectives' investigation of the robbery, they noticed tagged bags weren't logged in on the armored-truck log. That's when they started to dig into Nino's background and financials and connected him to a few other robberies where Sarge was his codefendant.

"They bust Sarge, and he cooperates to get a plea deal. He tells them that Cordell was in on the robberies, but by now Cordell is on the run."

"So, wait, why didn't Cordell just tell his cousin he wasn't going to be on the truck that day?" Vanna asked.

"Will said he did, but by the time he got the text, it was too late to stop Sarge and Nino. But Caleb and El already had another few bags tagged for the next pickup, so Will told them to get the money out of the casino. That's where their tech guy—Flynn, who was also the one to line up the dead spots for the truck heist—killed the feed within the casino so they could get the money out," Jovani said. Then he flipped over a few papers. "These statements are wild as hell. They get the money out of the casino, and Caleb takes control of it all, told them he had an account he could hide it in."

"That damn credit union account," Vanna whispered. "So did they kill Caleb—or was his death an accident?"

Jovani shrugged. "Medical examiner ruled it an accidental drowning because they had no indications that it was anything else. And Will and the rest of his crew are smart about one thing: none of them are voluntarily copping to a murder."

"He was such a simple bastard," Granny said with a shake of her head.

"So it was solely Gail's doing to pull Vanna into this," Aden said, residual anger adding a slight buzz to his tone.

Jovani nodded. "Yep. And she gave a more coherent statement once they had her leg stitched up and she sobered up a bit. She was pretty pissed at you."

"She was delusional, just like her son," Vanna snapped.

Granny chuckled. "You ain't lyin' about that. But what's going to happen to her now?"

"She's facing a few charges, the handgun and interfering with an investigation," Jovani said.

"A whole hot, stinkin' mess," Granny said, and stood from her chair. "Frito needs to pee." And with that announcement, she walked out of the office.

"But it's over now," Jovani said after they all watched her go with barely masked confusion. "I'm even going to have the arrest expunged, since this was all a horrible setup from the start."

"Good," Aden said.

"Very good," Vanna replied. "Now I can finally get on with this next phase of my life."

Epilogue

February 14

Just after dawn on a Friday morning, Vanna stood on the back deck of their new house. She'd signed all the paperwork and received the keys the week before Christmas. They'd buried Diane at a cemetery just fifteen minutes away the day after New Year's. Vanna had wanted her close so that Granny could visit her on her own as often as she liked.

Jack and his crew had come into the new house three days later, transforming the basement into an apartment for Granny and Frito. There was a small sitting room, kitchen nook, a full bathroom, and bedroom. They'd even added a door so Granny could easily let Frito out into the large fenced-in backyard to run around and *do his business*, as Granny said.

The main level and upper level of the new four-bedroom, three-bathroom house was all Vanna's. Each room newly designed and furnished, her kitchen a cheerful tangerine color she'd debated with Jamaica and Ronni would look amazing. And it did. She'd wanted everything new, another fresh start to add to her life. All the memories, the trauma, the past mistakes, were left at the old house. The fluffy snowflakes—the season's first snow—that began to fall confirmed her feelings of regeneration and recalibration. Today was the beginning.

Even though she'd started on this track back in September after ending the legal ordeal and agreeing to be in a relationship with Aden.

Later that month, she'd asked Granny to live with her permanently and, with her agreement, had started the hunt for a new house. Vanna had known without a doubt that a true new start was going to take more cleansing than she'd originally planned. Today, she felt totally free from her past and was more than ready to keep pressing forward.

"You're gonna freeze out here," Aden said, stepping up behind her to wrap the thick sherpa blanket he'd taken off the couch around her shoulders.

She was only wearing her slippers and a pink-flannel pajama set Granny had given her for Christmas, so the blanket was welcome. And so was the man.

"Thanks," she said, and settled back against him as his arms also wrapped around her.

Aden had also been a new beginning. After her horrific but eye-opening birthday celebration, they'd had their first official date. From that fabulous candlelight dinner on the water to movie dates, another bowling competition led by Team Davon and Team Jamaica, and dressing up as Tiana and Naveen to attend the Pretty in Pink's Halloween party, she'd agreed that they could date exclusively.

They weren't living together. Aden still had his house, where she now had half his closet space and a cabinet for her makeup and toiletries in his bathroom. But they were a couple, and she was comfortable with that. She was comfortable with this man, who insisted on treating her the way she deserved to be treated. And while that was all good—fantastic, actually—Vanna had decided to treat herself better.

That month last year, her fortieth-birthday month, which had been planned to be a phenomenal celebration to usher her into this new chapter, had almost drowned her. And despite all the people she had around, all those who loved and supported her, she'd had to find her way to the surface on her own. The only way to do that was to shed all that deadweight she'd shackled herself with throughout the years—the guilt, disappointment, heartache, disillusionment—every single link in a chain that was destined to strangle her. She'd had to let it all go just to breathe. Just to find herself and give herself permission to be.

"This place is going to make a great rental property someday," Aden said from behind her.

"Huh?" she asked, thinking she must've missed something while her mind was wandering.

"Yeah," he continued, as if she hadn't made that quizzical sound. "The resell value would be good. You wouldn't have that much equity in it, but Jack's renovations will help. And this is a great family community. A starter home for a young couple working in the city, but renting first for those who might not be in a position to buy just yet. My place will have good equity in another six months, so that resale shouldn't be a problem. We can look to relocate to Alexandria. You love it when we go over there for the day and dinners."

"Wait. What are you talking about?" she asked, because he'd just said a lot, none of which she was fully digesting. "I'm not moving again, I just got here."

"Did I tell you Jovani's opening a second office in Alexandria?" he asked, again ignoring her.

She was about to turn around, to look him in the eye and ask what the hell was going on, but he held her tighter.

"Yeah, now that they have Jasmine, Megan wants out of the city. And he doesn't want that long commute every day, so he's going to open another office, leave his top associates in DC to handle the bulk of the Superior Court cases and get into more defense litigation at the new place. It's a solid family-oriented career move."

"I agree," she replied, speaking slowly. "But, Aden, I still don't know how that factors into me and my new house." Or him selling his home, but she wanted to tackle this one confusing brick at a time.

Instead of a verbal answer, one of his hands that had been tangled in the blanket he'd wrapped around her turned so that his palm was upright. And in that palm sat a black box. Snowflakes falling and melting on top of it.

Her heart was in her throat, and try as she might, swallowing was difficult, breathing wasn't proving any easier.

"What . . . what is that?" she asked, afraid to blink or attempt to move.

"It's the future I've always envisioned for us, and before you tell me for the billionth time that you don't need me to save you," he said, this time maneuvering her so she could face him and the blanket remained wrapped around her, "think of this as a second birthday celebration. A gift of the life you've always wanted for yourself."

Because her insides had suddenly turned to mush as she stared up into his face and listened to his words, a bubble of laughter escaped. "And you're the gift that I always wanted. Wow, Aden, that's corny as hell."

He chuckled. "Corny? I thought it was more buttery. You know, like something smooth Denzel or Morris would say."

Now she laughed louder. "You're not even Denzel or Morris," she replied, and then sobered as she eased her arms out of the blanket to wrap around his waist. "You're better because you're right here. You've been right here for me in these past months, and I cannot begin to tell you how grateful I am to you for that."

A snowflake fell onto her nose, and he leaned in to kiss the moisture away.

"You can tell me that on your forty-first birthday, you'll become my wife," he whispered, and dropped a soft kiss onto her lips.

"Let me see it first," she said, and grinned what she knew had to be the goofiest sight in the universe.

He eased back and opened the black box so that the beautiful and big-ass princess-cut diamond set in a platinum band glittered brightly amid the snow.

"Did I do good?" he asked when she must have been silent for too long.

She looked up at him then and nodded. "You did really good."

"Soooo, what do you say?" he asked with his brows going up in expectancy.

"I say we've got lots of plans to make. My forty-first birthday/wedding is going to be the biggest and bestest celebration ever!"

ABOUT THE AUTHOR

Photo © 2023 Sean Evans Photography

A.C. Arthur is the multiple-award-winning author of more than eighty novels, including those under her *USA Today* bestselling pen name, Lacey Baker. She has worked as a paralegal in every field of law since high school, but her first love is and will always be writing. After years of hosting reader appreciation events, A.C. created the One Love Reunion, an event designed to bring together readers, authors, and other members of the literary industry to celebrate their love of books. A.C. resides with her family in Maryland, where she's currently working on her next book, or watching *Criminal Minds*. For more information, please visit www.acarthur.com.